DON'T LOOK BACK

A FENTON HOUSE NOVEL

BEN CHEETHAM

Visit the author's website at www.bencheetham.com

Printed in the United Kingdom

First Printing: December 2018

ISBN-13 978-1-7907602-9-9

CHAPTER 1

The words were finally flowing. Only a hundred or so more and Adam would hit his daily target. From beyond the study door came raised voices. Adam registered no reaction. When he was in the zone, the only voices he heard belonged to his characters. Feet thundered across the landing. The door flew open and two young boys charged into the room. That the boys were twins was obvious from their sandy curls, chestnut eyes, freckles and other matching features. People who didn't know them had difficulty telling them apart, but to Adam the differences were as glaring as the similarities. Jacob's hair was a shade lighter and his cheeks a fraction fuller than Henry's. He was a pound or two heavier and a centimetre taller too. The greatest difference, though, was in their expressions. As usual, Jacob had a sparkle of mischief in his eyes and a cheeky grin on his lips. In contrast, Henry's eyes were pulled together by a frown and his mouth was set in a serious line.

"You're not allowed," said Henry, dragging at his brother's arm.

Jacob pushed him off. "Yes I am."

Adam raised his hands for quiet. "What have I told you boys about coming in here when I'm working?"

Henry shot Jacob a *See I told you* look.

"It's six o'clock," protested Jacob. "You said you'd be finished by six o'clock."

"No, I said I'd try to be finished by six," corrected Adam. "Look, I've got..." he checked the word count, "eighty more words to write and then–"

"Then you'll play with us," Jacob broke in.

Smiling at his son's puppyish eagerness, Adam nodded. He made a wafting motion. "Now go."

Jacob gave Henry a playful jab in the ribs and darted from the room.

"You're dead meat," shouted Henry, chasing after him.

Jacob laughed at the threat. He almost always came out on top in fights. Not just because he was bigger, but because Henry lost his temper easily. And the more he lost it, the more provokingly calm Jacob would become.

Adam refocussed on the computer screen. His fingers moved over the keyboard, gathering speed as the exterior world once again became a far off place... *The blade slid between her ribs. She fell onto the bed with a soft thump, blood spreading over her blouse like...* Like what? Spilled wine? No. Too obvious. "Like... Like..." he murmured to himself. The door opened again. He turned sharply. "Right, I'm starting to get annoyed with you–" He broke off at the sight of his wife.

Ella was wearing a knee-length black dress that hugged her hourglass curves. Her light brown hair was piled on her head, with a few tendrils framing her face and neck. Dark mascara outlined her large almond eyes. Her lips glistened with pink gloss. "How do I look?"

"Gorgeous." *More than gorgeous*, Adam realised. *Beautiful.* He'd always been attracted to Ella, but way back when they met at university he'd described her to his housemates as *cute, a girl next door type.* Sometime in the intervening years, he couldn't pin down quite when, she'd graduated from cute to beautiful. It wasn't simply that she'd shed her puppy fat or that her eyes had mellowed to a soft, almost caramel brown. The way he looked at her had changed. He no longer noticed the fine lines beneath her eyes or the slight crookedness of her teeth. She was like a painting he'd always enjoyed looking at, but whose true beauty had only become apparent once he learned to see past the imperfections. He smiled.

"What's so amusing?"

"I spend half my life trying to avoid clichés, but I think I'm turning into one."

Ella smiled back. "It's called getting old."

"Hey, I'm still young. Or at least youngish."

Ella fiddled with her dress's plunging neckline. "You don't think it's too low-cut?"

"I think I wholly disapprove of you looking so fantastic for a night out without me."

"Is it too much? I can change into–"

Ella broke off as Adam rose and put his hands on her hips. She shuddered as he kissed her neck. "You smell good," he murmured, running his hands down her thighs. He closed the door with his foot.

"What are you doing?"

"What do you think?" Adam began to slide her dress up to her waist.

"The boys will hear."

"I'll be quiet."

"But what if–"

Adam silenced Ella with another kiss. He dropped back onto his chair, pulling her to straddle him. She chuckled. "You're bad."

"Then you'd better punish me."

A car horn sounded. Ella peered over Adam's shoulder out of the window. "It's my taxi."

"Oh for fu–"

Ella pressed a finger against his lips. "I'll just have to punish you later." She smoothed down her dress and hurried to check her lipstick in their bedroom mirror.

"What time will you be back?"

"I'm not sure. I shouldn't be too late." She grabbed a handbag, slipped her feet into high heels and tottered downstairs.

Adam followed Ella to the hallway. Jacob and Henry came sprinting out of the living room and flung their arms around her legs. "Don't go out, Mum," said Henry. "We don't like it when you go out."

"Yeah, Dad's always grumpy when you go out," Jacob added with an impish glance at Adam.

Adam laughed. "Is there any wonder when I don't get a moment's peace?"

Ella stooped to kiss her sons. Henry offered up a cheek. Jacob reeled away, wrinkling his nose. "Yuck! I hate that pink lipstick. It's sticky."

Ella planted a kiss on Henry. With a flash of jealousy in his eyes, Jacob pulled his brother away from her lips.

"Let go," exclaimed Henry, trying to twist free. The twins staggered into the living room and fell onto the rug.

"Play nicely, boys. I don't want any tears while I'm gone," Ella warned them. She looked at Adam with the same twinkle in her eyes that Jacob had inherited. "Have a good night."

Adam smiled at the gentle taunt. "You too."

"Will you wrestle with us, Dad?" the twins called out in unison.

"I'm working."

Ella raised an eyebrow as if to say, *You could have fooled me*. "You know what, Adam, they're eleven-years-old. In another year or two they won't want to play with you. You should enjoy it while it lasts."

"You're not the one getting beaten up on a daily basis." Adam rubbed his lower back. "I'm still aching from yesterday's wrestling match."

Ella puckered her lips in mock sympathy. "Aww, I think I was right. Daddy's getting old."

Laughing, the twins crowed, "Daddy's getting old, Daddy's getting old."

The taxi beeped again. Ella gave Adam a quick peck. She opened a full-length frosted glass door that led to a small porch. She put on a long coat, buttoning it up against the chilly November evening as she stepped outside.

"Don't get too drunk," said Adam.

Ella flashed him a cheeky grin. "Would I?"

She ducked into a black cab and waved. Adam waved back and turned to the twins who were rolling around in a red-faced tangle of limbs. He watched them uncertainly for a moment, then he returned to his study, telling himself, *I'll just finish the sentence I'm on.* He read out loud, "Blood spreading over her blouse like... like an ink stain." He shook his head. That wasn't quite right either. He chewed thoughtfully on a fingernail, picturing the blood, its colour, the shapes it made as it pooled between the woman's breasts. He flinched as a noise from downstairs burst into his consciousness – the slam of a door. It was followed an instant later by the crash of shattering glass. He jumped up and hurried onto the landing. "What's going on down there? Are you boys alright?"

"Dad."

The voice was so faint and tremulous that Adam couldn't be sure which of the twins it belonged to. Peering worriedly over the bannister, he saw a gaping hole where the glass door had been. Broken glass was heaped inside the porch. A pair of bare feet was splayed out amongst the jagged shards. His heart pounding in his throat, Adam bounded downstairs. His eyes swelled in horror at the sight that confronted him. Henry was standing with his back against the front door, pale and rigid, his left hand pressed to his neck. Blood was seeping between his fingers, running down his wrist and dripping from his elbow onto the back of Jacob's head. Jacob was facedown on the tiled floor, arms outstretched to either side with blood pooling around his wrists. One pool was small and glossily dark. The other was large and startlingly bright red. There was a faintly metallic butcher's shop smell in the air.

"Jacob!" cried Adam, dropping to his knees, heedless of the glass crunching beneath them. He scooped his son into his arms. Jacob's eyes were closed. His head lolled like a broken doll's. Blood oozed from a razor thin cut that stretched from his palm two or three centimetres up his left wrist. It spurted spasmodically from a cut twice as long on his right wrist. "Oh shit! Oh shit!" gasped Adam, his panicked eyes darting around for something to stem the bleeding. He snatched one of Ella's satin scarves off a peg and wrapped it tightly around Jacob's right wrist. Blood instantly soaked through it. He used another scarf on the other wrist. "Get a coat or something and press it to your neck," he instructed Henry.

Adam struggled to his feet, hugging Jacob to him. He grabbed a bunch of keys from a hook and fumbled one into the front door. Without closing the door behind himself, he ran the few paces between the house and where the car was parked in the street. Quickly and gently, he put Jacob into the front passenger seat. Henry clambered into the back. Adam stabbed the key into the ignition and started the engine. The car lurched forwards. There was a crunch as it clipped the rear bumper of the car parked in front. Jacob slumped forwards from the impact.

"Shit," Adam exclaimed again. He straightened Jacob up and tried to hold him in place while speeding along narrow streets of terraced houses.

Jacob breathed a tiny moan and his eyelids flickered.

"Hold on, son. We're on our way to hospital. You're going to be alright." As if to convince himself, Adam repeated, "You're going to be alright."

"I feel really dizzy," Henry slurred.

Looking in the rearview mirror, Adam saw that Henry's eyes were drifting shut. "Keep your eyes open!"

With what seemed a great effort, Henry parted his eyelids.

Hammering the horn, Adam screeched onto a busy main road. A chorus of beeps sounded as he careered around a roundabout, passing a sign with a red square on it marked 'H. A & E'. There had been plenty of times when the day-and-night blare of ambulance sirens had made Ella and him regret buying a house so close to a hospital, but at that moment it seemed like the best decision they'd ever made.

Narrowly avoiding an oncoming bus, Adam swerved onto a road flanked by 'Whipps Cross University Hospital' signs. He raced towards a three-storey, redbrick Victorian building with tall arched windows. Squealing to a stop outside a modern glass-fronted extension, he sprang out and ran around to the passenger side. He lifted Jacob's sickeningly limp body into his arms again. With Henry trailing behind, he dashed through automatic doors into the 'Emergency + Urgent Care Centre'. A queue led to a bank of reception desks in the busy waiting area.

"I need help!" shouted Adam. "My son's bleeding to death."

A nurse emerged from a double door. She took one look at Jacob's injuries and motioned for Adam to follow her. Beyond the door was a large room of blue-curtained cubicles. Adam laid Jacob on a trolley-bed.

"I want to stay with my dad," whimpered Henry as another nurse guided him to an adjoining cubicle.

"I'm right here, Henry," called out Adam.

Adam reluctantly retreated from the bedside as, from out of nowhere, a dizzying array of medical staff clustered around Jacob. Working fast and calmly, they placed an oxygen mask over Jacob's waxy face, hooked him up to a heart monitor and replaced the makeshift bandages with thick gauze pads.

"Where are you taking him?" Adam asked as the bed was manoeuvred out of the cubicle.

"Your son needs immediate surgery," a nurse informed him.

"Can I go with him?"

"Yes, but first I need some information from you."

As Adam watched Jacob being swiftly wheeled away, the feeling that he was seeing his son for the last time struck him like a sledgehammer. In a daze, he answered the nurse's rapid-fire questions about Jacob's medical history.

"Dad, Dad."

He turned towards Henry's tremulous voice. A doctor was emptying a hypodermic into Henry's neck close to a freshly swabbed small but deep looking cut. Adam hurried to his son's side.

"You need a couple of stitches," the doctor told Henry. "And I need you to stay very still. Can you do that for me?"

"Yes."

Adam took his son's hand. "Don't look at the needle, Henry. Look at me."

Henry grimaced but held still as the doctor sutured the wound.

"Good boy. Almost finished," said the doctor, cutting the thread and applying a bandage. To Adam, he added, "He's been extremely lucky. A millimetre to the left and his jugular would have been perforated."

"Where's Jacob?" asked Henry.

"The doctors had to take him away to..." Anxiety clogged Adam's voice.

A pleading look filled Henry's eyes. "I didn't mean to hurt him, Dad."

"What happened?"

"He hit me so I hit him back and made his lip bleed and he got really angry. I was scared so I ran into the porch and shut the door to keep him out but he ran into the glass." Tears streamed down Henry's cheeks. "It was an accident, Dad. Honest."

"Mr Piper."

Something about the voice made Adam's stomach squeeze with dread. He turned to a grave-faced female doctor. "Yes?"

"Could you come with me please?"

"Why?"

"It would be best if we speak in private."

Adam suddenly felt ice cold. Henry made a distressed sound as his dad moved away. "I'll only be a minute," Adam reassured him, looking to the doctor for confirmation of his words. The doctor gave him none.

His legs trembling as if he'd run a marathon, Adam followed the doctor to a room where chairs were arranged around a coffee-table with a box of tissues on it. The doctor gestured for him to sit. Adam shook his head. "Just tell me."

"I'm very sorry to have to inform you, Mr Piper, that your son passed away before we could perform surgery."

Adam's voice scraped out. "Are you sure?" He knew the question was needless. The doctor would hardly have said such a thing if she wasn't sure.

"I'm afraid so."

A storm of conflicting voices battered Adam's mind. *Is this really happening? Yes, Jacob's gone. He's never coming back. How can that be? Half-an-hour ago he was fine. It can be and it is. He's dead. Dead. Dead...*

Adam stared at his bloodstained hands. They seemed to be getting smaller, as if they were floating away from him on an outgoing tide. The noises of his mind and the hospital were receding too, until all that remained was a silence like an ocean.

CHAPTER 2

Nine months later...

Adam reread the unfinished sentence for what must have been the hundredth time that day. *She fell onto the bed with a soft thump, blood spreading over her blouse like...* He tried to picture the woman, but all he could see was Jacob sprawled amongst glass and blood. The image was like an impregnable wall. Day after day he hurled himself against it until he collapsed in a heap of frustration.

He silenced the music blaring from his computer. He'd used to cherish the times when he had the house to himself and could work in peace and quiet. Since Jacob's death he couldn't bear to sit at the computer without music on loud enough to cover the absence of feet thundering around and voices arguing and laughing. He left his study, pausing on the landing to listen at a closed door. After a moment of frowning silence, he opened the door.

Henry was staring blankly at the ceiling from the single bed that had replaced the bunk beds he'd shared with Jacob. He sat up as Adam entered. Suppressing an impulse to look away from the sadness in his son's eyes, Adam asked, "What are you doing?"

Henry shrugged.

"Do you want to watch a film?"

"No thanks."

"Are you sure? We can watch whatever you want."

"There's nothing I want to watch."

Adam hid his own sadness with a pitiful attempt at a smile. Henry and Jacob had liked nothing better than to slob out in front of a movie with him. "I'll be downstairs if you change your mind." He left quickly. The bedroom made him uncomfortable. It wasn't the things he saw in there that hurt him the most. It was the things he didn't see – the blank wall spaces that had been occupied by Jacob's Star Wars posters, the empty drawers that had been filled with Jacob's clothes.

The bottom of the stairs was doused in gloom. The glass door had been replaced by a solid wooden one. The workman who fitted it had warned that the hallway would be like the black hole of Calcutta if they put in a windowless door, but Adam would rather have had no door at all than one with even a square inch of glass in it.

Ella was chopping vegetables in the cramped dining kitchen at the rear of the house. She looked at Adam as he entered. His expression prompted her to pick up a glass and swallow the last of the wine in it. "Do you want a glass?" she asked, pouring herself another.

Adam nodded. He sipped his drink, staring out of the window at a little walled yard that had lost all but a tiny triangle of early evening sun. "I'm starting to wonder if I'll ever be able to write another word."

"Of course you will. You just need to–"

"To what?" interrupted Adam. "To stop thinking about what happened? That's all I ever think about. Every second of every day it's the same question – what if I hadn't gone back upstairs? Would Jacob still–"

Ella's voice sharpened with weariness. "Stop it, Adam. Just stop it." A chasm of silence opened up between them. Eventually she sighed and said, "What if the accident had happened while we were fooling around in the study? What if I hadn't gone out? What if we'd replaced that fucking door years ago? We can carry on asking ourselves questions forever, but we'll never find the answers because there's no one to blame. It was just something that happened."

"Just something that happened," Adam echoed. He shook his head as if he couldn't accept that.

Ella laid a hand on his back, but he moved away from her into the living room. He slumped into an armchair and mindlessly channel-surfed. After a while, Ella called him and Henry into the kitchen to eat. They sat around the table, not looking at each other or the empty chair where Jacob had always sat.

"I was thinking we could go to the Natural History Museum tomorrow," said Ella. "There's a new dinosaur exhibition."

Adam and Henry were silent. The Natural History Museum had been one of Jacob's favourite places.

"I really think it would be good for us," persisted Ella.

"I've got homework," said Henry.

Ella looked at him sceptically. "It's the summer holidays."

He avoided her gaze. "Can I leave the table, please?"

"No you–"

"Yes," broke in Adam.

Henry pushed back his chair and headed for the stairs. Ella frowned at Adam, her expression more upset than angry.

"He's not ready," said Adam. "Neither am I."

He returned to the living room and blanked his mind with the TV again. Ella stretched out on the sofa. She stared at Adam as if trying to make her mind up about something. Sighing softly, she picked up a newspaper.

After skimming over the headlines, she said, "Hey, listen to this. Haunted house seeks new occupants. Fenton House is a stunning Gothic mansion on the Cornish Lizard Peninsula. It stands in several acres of gardens commanding breath-taking views of The English Channel. Nestling in a nearby valley is the fishing village of Treworder which barely appears to have changed since the days of pirates and smugglers. Think this sounds like a romantic idyll beyond the reach of all but the rich and famous? Well think again because it can all be yours for the princely sum of absolutely nothing! The house's owner, Rozen Trehearne, 79, has placed an advertisement in a national newspaper inviting potential tenants to apply through an online questionnaire. A shortlist will be drawn up, from which one lucky applicant will be chosen to live rent-free in Fenton House. Sounds too good to be true, right? Well it is! According to Miss Trehearne the winner will have to share Fenton House with some otherworldly residents. The identities of these residents are unknown, but the tragic history of Fenton House has long been a source of spooky stories. In 1920 the house's original owner, reclusive industrialist Walter Lewarne, hanged himself from its highest turret. His body dangled there for days until villagers spotted crows and gulls feasting on it. In 1996, the house's then inhabitants, George Trehearne, his wife Sofia and their young daughter Heloise disappeared without a trace. The mystery was a national sensation. There were months of speculation in the newspapers about what happened to the family, but the mystery remains unsolved to this day." Ella looked over the paper at Adam. "How bonkers is that?"

"It's got to be some sort of joke."

"I don't think so. There's a web address here." A little twinkle came into Ella's eyes. "Do you think we should apply?"

Adam was assaulted by an image of Jacob grinning at him with that same twinkle in his eyes. Jacob's voice seemed to echo in his ears, *Will you wrestle with us, Dad*? Adam rose abruptly from the armchair. "I'm going for a walk."

He hurried from the room, shoved his feet into trainers and half-ran through the porch. He could hardly bring himself to breathe the air in that small space. They'd had the tiled floor torn up and replaced, but still a bitter tang of blood seemed to linger like a smell nothing could get rid of. He pounded the streets of Walthamstow, head down, not feeling the warmth of the sun or noticing the sounds of life going on around him. The city that had once made him feel so alive seemed as cold and dead as his house.

CHAPTER 3

It was dark when Adam returned home. He padded upstairs, hoping Ella was asleep. He didn't want to talk, he just wanted to lie down and sleep. Not that sleep provided much respite. Rarely a night went by when he didn't wake reeling from a dream of Jacob. A sound caught his ear – a low sobbing. He quietly opened Henry's bedroom door. Henry's slim body was twisted into his duvet. He was clutching something to himself. Adam didn't need to look closer to know it was a stuffed bunny that had used to live in Jacob's bed. Just as he didn't need to look closer to know Henry was crying in his sleep. It had started after the funeral. Sometimes it went on for an hour or so. Others it continued all night. They'd taken Henry to a grief counsellor, but it made no difference. At first the heart-breaking sound had kept Adam and Ella awake. After a while, Ella had developed the capacity to zone out of it. But not Adam. Night after night, he lay awake listening to it. He'd tried wearing earplugs, but they didn't keep out the pain of knowing his son was in distress. The only thing that allowed him to blank his mind to that was physical exhaustion. So now every evening he would walk until he reached the point where sheer fatigue carried him off to sleep.

The house was quiet when it should be noisy and noisy when it should be quiet. Nothing there made sense anymore. Adam stripped off his sweaty clothes, dumped them in the dirty-washing basket and headed for bed. As he crept under the duvet, Ella switched on her bedside lamp.

"Sorry, I tried not to wake you," said Adam.

"I wasn't asleep. We need to talk."

"I'm tired."

"So am I, but there's something I have to say this to you."

Henry's sobs filtered through the wall, each one knotting Adam's stomach tighter. If he didn't go to sleep now, he knew he would move past exhaustion into a hinterland of gritty-eyed sleepless misery. But he knew too from the tone of Ella's voice that she wouldn't take no for an answer. He folded his arms and waited for her to continue.

"I think we should put the house on the market," she said.

"We've already talked about this, Ella. We can't afford to."

"Why not? We could move into rented accommodation."

"And how would we pay the rent?"

"We can use the equity."

Adam hissed through his nostrils. "Why don't I just chuck our money down a drain?"

"If you don't start writing again, we won't be able to pay the mortgage and we'll end up losing the house anyway."

Adam winced. "I will start writing again."

"That's not what you said earlier. You said you were starting to wonder whether you'd ever be able to write another word."

"And you replied, *Of course you will.*"

"Yes, but maybe it will take a change to make it happen."

Adam considered these words momentarily. "Do you remember why we bought this place? You wanted to bring up the boys in a proper home. If we sell it, we'll probably never get back on the ladder. Not in London."

"Perhaps you're right. I don't know. I do know something has to change." Ella glanced towards Henry's room. "For all of our sakes."

They lay silent, side-by-side but not touching, as they did every night now.

"Do you know what I think about every day?" Ella said suddenly. "A millimetre to the left and we would have lost both our sons."

She turned off the light and rolled her back to Adam. He thought about reaching for her, but it was like he'd forgotten how to. He stared at the darkness, listening and trying not to listen to Henry. The sound was as relentless as tinnitus. Giving up on sleep, he slid out of bed and went into the study. He booted up his computer and plugged in headphones. He exhaled in relief as music drowned out the sobs. With a familiar sense of dread, he opened the manuscript's Word file. His eyes played back and forth over the hated sentence in smaller and smaller movements until they were locked on one word – *blood*. In a dance he'd gone through countless times, he stabbed a finger at the 'backspace' button, but stopped before the sentence was fully deleted and rapidly retyped the words. They existed fixed in a moment when Jacob was still alive. Sometimes during the hours of staring at them, Adam pretended he still existed in that moment too. He imagined Jacob and Henry charging into the study. He pictured himself gathering them up in his arms, attacking their faces with kisses and feigning agony as they wrestled him to the carpet.

Tiredness and grief stung Adam's eyes. He closed the manuscript and removed the headphones. The sobs had stopped, but there was no point returning to bed. He was way beyond sleep. He headed downstairs and reached for the TV remote, but hesitated as his gaze came to rest on the newspaper. He picked it up and read the article about Fenton House. After a thoughtful pause, he returned to the study and typed the web address provided into the browser. It took him to a page that instructed him to 'Please answer the questions below in as much detail as possible.', then warned him that 'If you provide false information, you will be disqualified from the selection process.' The brusque paragraph was signed 'Niall Mabyn, Chief Executive, Personal Legal Services, Mabyn & Moon LLP.'

A bemused look came over Adam as he read the first question.

1: What is your favourite colour?

What sort of infantile question was that? 'I don't have one.' he typed. His bemusement intensified at the next question.

2: Do you bathe/shower every day?

'If possible.' he answered curtly, but as he worked his way down the list he found himself enjoying the distraction and responding in more detail.

3: Do you cover your mouth when you cough?

Answer: Yes. I'm a bit of a germaphobe.

4: Do you consider yourself a day or night person?

Answer: Neither. I like/dislike both equally depending on my mood and what's going on.

5: Do you own a mobile phone?

Answer: I must be one of the last people in the world not to own a mobile phone.

6: Do you own a microwave oven?

Answer: We did, but it broke and we haven't found the need to replace it.

7: Do you eat with your mouth open?

Answer: I try not to – my parents taught me it was bad manners.

8: Do you eat ethnic food?

Answer: If by 'ethnic' you mean Indian, Chinese etc, then yes I do. I love a really hot curry.

9: Do you like cake?

Answer: Doesn't everyone? My favourite is Victoria sponge.

10: How often do you vacuum and dust your home?

Answer: Whenever necessary. Usually once or twice a week.

11: Do you feed the birds in your garden/yard/local park?

Answer: My wife Ella and I put food out on a bird table. Our son Henry enjoys feeding the ducks in the park.

12: Do you prefer cats or dogs?

Answer: I like them both the same, except for the cat that kills birds in our yard.

13: Do you think it's possible for someone to disappear without a trace?

Adam frowned at the final question. It was the only one that had any obvious bearing on the newspaper article and it struck him as being a little sinister. He mulled it over before answering 'In today's world of forensic science and practically limitless forms of communication I don't think so.' As a tongue-in-cheek afterthought, he added 'More's the pity. I sometimes feel as if I would like to do just that.'

At the end of the questionnaire there was a separate section for personal particulars – name, age, gender, ethnicity, nationality, marital status, children, education, occupation, address etc. Adam provided the required information and read through his answers before hitting the submit button. The mostly nonsensical content of the questionnaire had strengthened his initial suspicion that this was an elaborate hoax – perhaps some sort of reality TV set-up.

He Googled Mabyn and Moon. A link took him to a website offering '...a full range of services in family, personal and business law'. There was a telephone number and an address in Helston, Cornwall.

An email alert flashed up. He navigated to his inbox. The email was from Mabyn and Moon – 'RE: Fenton House questionnaire'. His eyebrows lifted. Wow, that was quick. Was someone sitting up all night responding to applications? He doubted it. More likely it was an automated response.

'Dear Mr Piper,' began the email. 'I'm pleased to inform you that you have made the shortlist of potential tenants. You and your wife and child are invited to attend an interview at Boscarne Cottage, Treworder on Friday 29th July at 11:00 AM. Should you fail to attend, your application will be rendered null and void. Please print out this letter and present it upon arrival. Miss Trehearne and I look forward to meeting you. Yours sincerely, Niall Mabyn.'

The email looked believable enough, but Adam still wasn't convinced. No one effectively gave away a house of any kind, let alone one worth millions. There had to be a catch other than the supposed ghostly residents. Didn't there?

He printed off the letter, took it to the bedroom and tapped Ella awake.

"What is it?" she asked groggily, squinting at the alarm clock. "I've got to be up for work in a few hours."

"I applied for that house."

"What house?"

"The one in the newspaper. We're on the shortlist. Here, read this."

Adam proffered the printout to Ella. She switched on her bedside lamp. "I've been thinking about what you said," he told her as she read the letter. "Maybe you're right, perhaps we need a change of scenery."

"A haunted house wasn't quite what I had in mind."

"Don't tell me you believe in ghosts."

"Well no, not really, but I'm not sure I like the idea of living in a house where a family vanished."

"That was over twenty years ago. Other people must have lived in Fenton House since then and no one else has vanished."

"As far as you know."

"This could be perfect for us, Ella. If it's for real that is."

"What makes you think it's not?"

Adam told her about the questionnaire. "I mean, what a load of nonsense. It makes me wonder whether someone's having a laugh."

"Actually they kind of make sense to me," disagreed Ella. "It sounds like they're based on someone's likes and dislikes. Most probably Rozen Trehearne's. Apart from the last one. That one creeps me out."

"Perhaps it's meant to. They might not want anyone who's easily spooked to apply."

"In that case I should steer well clear."

"Oh come on, you're as tough as an old boot."

Ella smiled and frowned at the same time. "Is that supposed to be a compliment?"

"No. Just the truth. You're the only one who's kept it together these past few months."

"Only because I've had to. Believe me I feel like breaking down every day."

Adam tenderly took Ella's hand. "That's why we need to get away. We could book a cottage for the weekend."

"Just the two of us?"

Silence greeted the tentative suggestion. At first, after the accident, Adam could barely bring himself to let Henry out of his sight. Schooldays had been a torment of worry. His anxiety had eased as the months crawled by, but he still baulked at the thought of leaving Henry for so long. Looking into Ella's eyes, though, he saw an almost desperate appeal, a fear that if they drifted much further apart they would never find their way back to each other. "Just the two of us," he echoed. "Henry can stay with your parents. It'll do him good. It'll do us all good." He tapped the letter. "Even if nothing comes of this."

"OK, let's do it."

There was an excitement in Ella's voice that had been absent since the accident. It was almost enough to make Adam smile. She switched off the lamp. In the darkness, he kissed her hand and held it against his chest. He closed his eyes, and for the first time in nine months he didn't see Jacob. Instead he saw Fenton House as he imagined it to be – a brooding pile of towers, turrets and gargoyles straight out of a Victorian melodrama. In the instant before he fell asleep, from somewhere off in the distance, he thought he heard the murmur of the sea.

CHAPTER 4

The sun was climbing a cloudless sky. Adam squinted at the dashboard clock – half-past ten. They'd been travelling for nearly six hours. He'd taken the steering-wheel for the first half of the journey while Ella dozed in the passenger seat. They'd swapped over at Exeter services and he'd slept most of the way through Cornwall. Any opportunity to make a deposit in his overdrawn sleep bank was difficult to turn down, even if it meant missing out on the glorious Cornish landscape. They were passing a military airbase. Beyond razor wire fences were flat grassy expanses crisscrossed with runways and dotted with wind-socks, aircraft hangers, air-traffic control towers, lightweight planes, fighter jets and helicopters. At a gated entrance, a block of carved stone identified the airbase as 'RNAS Culdrose'.

"How much further?" he asked.

"About ten miles," answered Ella. "We've just passed through Helston."

At the far edge of the airbase a sign directed them to 'The Lizard'. The road undulated between thick hedgerows peppered with gorse, bracken and a profusion of wildflowers. The landscape beyond the hedges was a mixture of heathery heathland and lush green fields grazed by fat Jersey cows. A few miles to the east were the otherworldly giant satellite dishes of Goonhilly Downs. Maybe a mile to the west, glimpses of the sea shimmered in the summer heat. They passed a quaint pub, a holiday park of dated chalets, roadside signs advertising cream teas, ice-cream, pasties and locally produced cider.

"Do you think we should phone and find out how Henry's getting on?" asked Adam.

"No, he'll be fine. My parents will be spoiling him rotten." Ella rubbed Adam's arm. "Relax."

He lowered his window and drew in a lungful of faintly salty air. "God that smells good."

A sign for Treworder directed them onto a narrow lane with passing spaces every few hundred metres. 'No Parking' cones punctuated the roadside. After a mile or so, the lane began to wind its way down into a wooded valley. Trees overhung the road, dappling it with shadows. "Wonderful, isn't it?" said Adam. "No pollution, no traffic jams."

"I wouldn't speak too soon," said Ella as they turned a corner and found their progress blocked by a long line of cars.

"Bloody hell, I wonder what this is about?"

"You don't think they're all here for the same reason as us, do you?"

Adam frowned. "Surely not. It would take forever to interview this lot."

A man in a high-vis tabard was making his way along the queue, stooping his tanned face to each car. A blonde-haired woman got out of one and said something to him. He replied with a shake of his head, gesticulating for her to get back in. When he reached Adam and Ella, he informed them in a thick Cornish accent, "Carpark's full."

"Can we park in the village?" asked Adam.

"No chance, mate. It's mad busy down there."

"Why, what's going on?" asked Ella.

She and Adam exchanged a glance as the carpark attendant grumbled, "It's this bloody Fenton House thing. Don't get me wrong, it's been good for business, but personally I could do without the hassle."

"So what do we do?"

"You can wait for a space in the carpark, but I wouldn't hold your breath. If I were you I'd turn around and go somewhere else, come back another day."

"We can't do that," said Adam. "We have to be at Boscarne Cottage in fifteen minutes." He unfolded the printout.

The attendant glanced at it, then gave Adam and Ella a weighing-up look. "Tell you what. You can leave your car here and walk down into the village. Give me your key and I'll park it for you when there's space."

Adam looked at Ella as if to ask, *What do you think*?

"From London, are you?" observed the man. His manner suggested Londoners weren't his favourite people.

Adam had encountered the attitude before and sympathised with it. Wealthy Londoners buying second homes was a serious problem in this part of Cornwall, pricing locals out of the market and transforming villages into ghost towns during the winter months. He put on his best friendly smile. If they were going to live around here, he didn't want to get off on the wrong foot with the locals. "Is it that obvious?"

"You get so you can tell. At this time of year there are more of your lot around here than locals."

Ella unhooked the ignition key from the keyring and handed it over. The man motioned for them to follow him. As they got out, the blonde leaned from her car window and demanded to know, "Hey, how come they can leave their car here?"

"They're on the shortlist," the attendant told her.

The blonde's eyes widened. She looked at Adam and Ella. "Which of you answered the questionnaire?"

"I did," replied Adam.

"Can I ask you something?"

"Sure."

She beckoned Adam closer, her voice dropping. There were four children of varying ages crammed into the car with her. "What answers did you give?"

"I can hardly remember. Nothing special."

"I'll pay you." The woman pulled out her purse.

"I... no thanks," Adam said awkwardly.

Ella tugged at his arm. "Come on or we'll be late."

"Please," the woman's voice rose in desperation, "I'm a single mum living in two-bedroom flat."

"I'm sorry," said Adam, quickening his pace.

Ella shook her head sadly. "I wonder how many people there are like her here?"

"A lot I should think. If you had a choice between bringing your kids up in a shoebox of a flat or a supposedly haunted mansion, what would you choose?"

"The mansion of course, but she's not even on the list."

"That doesn't make any difference," commented the attendant. "There have been all sorts knocking on Miss Trehearne's door day and night begging to live in Fenton House. It got so bad she had to call in the police." He puffed contemplatively on a rollup. "Makes you wonder what the world's coming to."

It seemed to Adam that it showed the world was the same as it had ever been, except in one respect. "I suppose it shows people aren't all that superstitious these days."

The attendant grunted. "You reckon?" He thumbed over his shoulder at the blonde's car. "It's not just people like her we've had turning up. There are a hell of a lot of oddballs who want to live in that house *because* it's said to be haunted."

"Do you believe it's haunted?" asked Ella.

"I couldn't care less one way or the other. I'll just be glad when this lot buggers off." The attendant stopped at the entrance to a jam-packed, dusty carpark. "I'll be here all day. And if I'm not here, I'll be in The Smugglers. That's the pub down in the village."

"How do we get to Boscarne Cottage?" asked Adam.

"It's at the far side of the village. Believe me, you won't have any problem finding the place."

They thanked the attendant and continued down the hill. Cars were parked on every spare bit of pavement, forcing them – along with a steady trickle of other people – to walk in the middle of the road. Glimpses of a deep, densely thicketed valley showed through a hedge on their left. They rounded a corner and a dazzling view opened up in front of them. Whitewashed, thatched cottages were huddled together as if for protection at the end of the valley. Cliffs of black volcanic rock speckled with yellow lichen framed the sea. Gulls wheeled and screeched above a little fishing boat chugging into shore.

Adam took it all in. "Imagine waking up to that every morning."

Towards the bottom of the slope the road curved sharply to the left. On the corner a tiny cottage was perched at the beginning of a rocky promontory. A footpath led to a bench facing out to sea at the tip of the promontory. To the right, steps descended a granite sea wall to a patchwork of smooth boulders and wet sand. Families were dotted around the little beach. Children were digging in the sand and splashing in the clear, almost tropically calm sea. To the other side of the promontory a larger beach of pale grey shingles shelved shallowly into the sea. Seaweed, driftwood and plastic jetsam marked the high-tide. A small fleet of sun-bleached blue, orange, red and white fishing boats were lined up at the back of the beach. Several 4x4 vehicles and a rusty tractor were parked on a cobbled slipway. The beach was busy with people strolling along, looking at the boats, skimming stones, clambering on the rocks at its far end or simply enjoying the view.

Ella took a photo. "Henry would love it here," she said, sounding as if she was warming to the possibility of living in Treworder.

"So would Jacob," Adam reflected quietly. His gaze was drawn to a group of figures who were obviously not tourists working on their tans. Despite the heat, they were dressed in heavy black clothes. They looked as if they'd just stepped out of a goth nightclub. A woman with dyed bright red hair was twirling around as if dancing to music only she could hear.

The road ran parallel to the shoreline, passing between sturdy cob-walled buildings. There was a fishmonger offering 'Fresh Wild Fish'. A hole-in-the-wall cafe was serving 'Treworder crab and lobster sandwiches' to a long queue of customers. Perched over the cafe was a little art gallery, its windows overstuffed with driftwood sculptures and stained glass creations. Across the road was a gift shop selling buckets and spades, body boards, cheap footballs, ice-creams and such. Next door to it a Cornish flag dangled from the 'Treworder Pilot Gig Club'. A sign outside the club-house advertised 'Boat Trips'. At the midpoint of the street the cobbled slipway was flanked by fishermen's sheds with crab and lobster pots, containers of tackle and orange marker floats stacked outside them. At its far end, where the road looped away from the sea up the opposite side of the valley was 'The Smuggler's Inn', a three-storey slate-roofed building. A sign depicting a bearded smuggler with a barrel on his shoulder hung over its door.

Drinkers thronged a sun-baked beer garden, their numbers spilling out onto the road and slipway. The smell of cigarette smoke, sun-cream and alcohol permeated the air, mingling with the briny whiff of the sea. Some of the drinkers had the look of fishermen – rugged faces, broad shoulders, brawny arms. Others were obviously holidaymakers – shorts and t-shirts, sunburned faces. Many were of a type who wouldn't normally be found thereabouts on a sunny summer's day. There were more goths – faces caked with black lipstick and eyeliner, top hats and canes, long dyed hair. There was a little clique of scholarly characters – wire-rimmed spectacles, high foreheads, serious expressions. Another group were all wearing T-shirts with the spectral white logo 'Ghost Hunters' emblazoned across them. One of the 'Ghost Hunters' was filming the crowd with a camcorder. The eclectic mix gave the street an almost carnival atmosphere.

The crowd extended up the hill, clotting into a dense mass outside a detached cottage sunken behind a whitewashed wall. The atmosphere suddenly seemed less merry. People were jostling for space. Many looked tired and dishevelled, as if they'd been there overnight. Several were holding aloft handwritten signs. Some conveyed straightforward begging messages – 'HOMELESS with three mouths to feed. PLEASE HELP', 'Lost my job. Can't pay mortgage. Don't let my family end up on the street.' Others had stranger tales to tell – 'WIDOWER NEEDS TO SPEAK TO THE DEAD AND FIND OUT WHO RAN OVER HIS WIFE', 'The spirits of Fenton House are in torment. I have the power to set them free.'

Adam and Ella came up against a wall of bodies. "Excuse me," said Adam, attempting to squeeze past a woman.

She blocked his way, snapping, "Back off."

"I need to get to the cottage."

"So do we all."

A policeman was stationed inside the cottage's garden gate. Waving the letter in the air to attract his attention, Adam shouted, "We're here to see Miss Trehearne. We're on the shortlist."

A murmur went through the crowd. Dozens of pairs of eyes turned towards Adam and Ella.

"Hey!" gasped Ella as someone shoved her in the back in their eagerness to get to Adam. She staggered and would have fallen if the crowd hadn't suddenly closed in even more tightly around her.

A hand snatched at the letter, tearing off a corner. Adam thrust it into his pocket and put a protective arm around Ella. His heart began to beat fast. The surrounding faces no longer looked merely tired or desperate, they looked angry and resentful.

"Give me that letter," demanded a man, wielding a 'Jobless. Homeless. Hungry.' placard as if he would hit Adam with it.

The policeman forced his way through the crowd, inserting himself between the man and Adam. He escorted Adam and Ella to the small, neatly kept garden at the front of the cottage. The flowerbeds were a riot of rosebushes. A heavily scented wisteria climbed the cottage, fringing its sea-blue front door. 'Boscarne Cottage' was etched into a slate plaque beside the door. Curtains were drawn in little, leaded windows.

They halted in the shadow of the thatch that overhung the eaves by half-a-metre. "Are you alright?" Adam asked Ella.

Nodding, she said a touch breathlessly, "That was horrible."

"It's been like this for the last two days," said the policeman. "Can I see the letter?"

As Adam handed it over, Ella surveyed the faces beyond the garden wall. "It makes me feel awful. We've got a house. We might be taking the place of someone who hasn't."

"I didn't think it would be like this," said Adam.

"Would it have stopped you from applying?"

He considered the question, then admitted, "No. We need this just as much as any of them."

Satisfied the letter was genuine, the policeman knocked on the door. It was opened by a beanpole of a man in a pinstripe navy blue suit and matching tie. Everything about him was thin. Thinning white hair was combed in precise lines over a liver-spotted scalp. Thin lips were set in a deadpan line beneath an equally thin nose. He peered down at Adam and Ella with hawkish blue eyes. The policeman handed him the letter. He glanced at it and said in a brisk, business-like voice, "I'll need to see some ID." Adam and Ella showed him their driving-licences. The man stood aside to let them into the house, adding, "I'm Niall Mabyn of Mabyn and Moon solicitors. Miss Trehearne is expecting you."

CHAPTER 5

The solicitor ushered Adam and Ella along a gloomy flagstone hallway, stooping to avoid hitting his head on a low, beamed ceiling. The noise of the crowd receded to the edge of hearing as they entered a room cosily furnished with a floral three-piece-suite and thick rugs. Despite the summer heat, a fire crackled in a stone fireplace. A fat pug with a turquoise ribbon around its neck waddled over to sniff their ankles. Sunlight flooded through French doors overlooking a little walled back garden alive with sparrows and blackbirds feeding at a table and bathing in a wrought-iron bath.

A birdlike old lady in a long dress that matched the dog's bow occupied the armchair nearest the window. Her grey hair was pinned up in a bun. Her wrinkled cheeks glowed with rouge. Her lips – which were as red as holly berries – were drawn into a smile that stretched to her grey eyes. Bifocals were balanced on the end of her nose. She made Adam think of the Mrs Pepperpot stories he'd read the twins a few years ago.

She rose to greet the newcomers with a sprightly, "Mr and Mrs Piper, lovely to meet you. I'm Rozen Trehearne." Her voice was well-spoken with a soft Cornish burr. She extended a ringless, bony-knuckled hand. They shook it and she gestured them to the sofa. As Mr Mabyn perched himself in the other armchair, she indicated a teapot and a Victoria sponge on a coffee-table. "Would you like some tea and cake?"

"Thank you. That would be lovely, Miss Trehearne," said Ella.

"Please call me Rozen. May I call you Adam and Ella?"

"Please do."

Rozen poured tea into china cups and passed them to her guests along with a slice of cake each. She settled back in her armchair, sipping delicately from her own cup. The pug made round eyes and lolled its tongue at Adam.

"Edgar is an incorrigible beggar," said Rozen.

Adam broke off a bit of cake. "Can I give him some?"

"He's supposed to be on a diet, but seeing as it's a special occasion..."

Edgar snaffled the cake and whimpered for more.

"Shush, Edgar. Lie down," instructed Rozen.

The pug reluctantly retreated to the hearth rug. Rozen watched her guests eat and drink for a moment, before focusing her smile on Adam, "So tell me, Adam, why do you want to live in Fenton House?"

Adam could suddenly feel sweat gathering under his clothes, and not only because of what had happened outside or the warmth of the fire. His mind was back in that terrible moment – the crash of breaking glass, Jacob on the porch floor, blood spreading like... like... He blinked away from Rozen's gaze.

Ella answered for him, her voice as steady as ever. "There was an accident. We lost our eleven-year-old son, Jacob."

Rozen put a hand to her heart as if there was a pain there. "Oh you poor things. I'm so sorry to hear that."

"Thank you. It could have been even worse. Jacob's twin brother, Henry, was hurt too. He might easily have been killed. I thank god every day that he's still with us."

"Yes that's something to be thankful for, although I don't suppose it makes the loss of Jacob any easier to bear. Do you have a photo of them?"

Ella took one out of her handbag. It had been taken at their tenth birthday party. She'd carried it with her ever since. Henry and Jacob had an arm around each other and were beaming into the camera over a Star Wars cake. She'd said at the time, and many times since, that they'd never looked more beautiful.

Rozen peered at the photo through her bifocals. "What handsome boys. Which one is Henry?"

Ella pointed him out. Rozen studied Henry as if committing his features to memory before returning the photo. "So you're religious?"

"What makes you say that?"

"You said you thank god every day."

Ella smiled uncertainly. "I don't know if I'd say I was religious. I try to keep an open mind to the possibility of something... else."

"And what about you Adam?"

He shook his head. "I don't believe in any of it."

"What do you believe in?"

Adam's sad eyes looked into Rozen's cheerful ones as if he might find the answer there. "I don't really know."

"Do you believe in love?"

Adam flicked Ella a glance. She was looking into her teacup, but he could tell she was listening for his reply. "Family," he answered, skipping around the question like a rabbit narrowly avoiding a snare. "I believe in family."

"Family is love. That's what Mother used to say. I don't have a family of my own. Father died when I was very young and Mother wasn't a well woman. I cared for her until her death. By which time I was fifty-one. Far too old to learn how to share my life with a husband."

"What do you believe in, Miss Trehearne?"

"Rozen, please."

"Rozen."

"I believe in everything. A world of possibilities."

"Except for when it comes to yourself and marriage."

Rozen's smile reached a millimetre higher. "You're very perceptive, Adam."

"I'm a writer."

"So Mr Mabyn tells me. I'm afraid I haven't read any of your books."

"I don't imagine they'd be your sort of thing. They're a bit gruesome."

"Oh I don't mind that. I like something gritty. I suppose that's because I've led such a sheltered life. Are you working on a new novel?"

"No... Actually yes, but..." Adam trailed off awkwardly.

Ella came to his rescue again. "Adam has been having some problems since the accident. I suppose you could call it writer's block."

"I see," said Rozen. "And you're hoping a change of scenery will clear it. Well, if you'll forgive the pun, you've come to the right place. Writers, indeed artists of all kinds, have always been drawn to this area in search of seclusion and inspiration."

"We're not here just because of my writing," said Adam. "Our son has been having problems too."

Rozen spread her hands as if to say, *Of course.* "In many cultures twins are believed to be two halves of the same spirit. How does one recover from such a loss? But if Henry can make a recovery anywhere, then it's here. There's nowhere better in the world to be a child. The sea, the fresh air, the freedom. Tell me, Adam, how did you feel when you arrived here?"

"I suppose I..." He faltered as if admitting something shameful. "I felt OK."

"And when was the last time you felt OK?"

"Before Jacob died." As if justifying himself, Adam added quickly, "It's so beautiful here."

"Yes, it's beautiful. It's more than that though. There's a mystery here – not only in Treworder, but the entire peninsula – a magic that other places have long since lost." Rozen chuckled softly. "You must think I'm a batty old woman."

"No of course not."

"Yes you do, I see it in your eyes," Rozen said without a hint of offence. "And when I tell you about Fenton House you'll think it even more so. But if you decide to live here you'll soon find out I'm anything but."

"Decide," said Ella. "Does that mean we can live in Fenton House if we want to?"

"A final decision will only be made once all shortlisted applicants have been interviewed," Mr Mabyn put in matter-of-factly.

"Mr Mabyn is right," said Rozen. "I apologise for getting ahead of myself. From our brief conversation, I believe you to be very much deserving of Fenton House, but the final decision is not mine to make."

"Whose is it then?" asked Adam.

Rozen looked at him with a queer twinkle in her eyes. "It's time I told you something about Fenton House's history. The house was built in 1909 by Walter Lewarne, an industrialist who was born hereabouts and made his fortune in London. Walter lived alone. He was not a sociable man and never married. As I'm sure you know, Walter committed suicide. No one knows the exact reason why, but he was heavily in debt and facing bankruptcy. After Walter's death, my grandfather, Anthony James, bought Fenton House. Grandfather passed away in 1935. When my grandmother Nessa followed him in '37, their only child Winifred – my mother – and her husband Benedict Trehearne moved into the house with their young son George. I was born the following year and when war broke out a year after that Father enlisted and was sent to France. He never returned. But please don't think that means I had an unhappy childhood. Quite the opposite. Unlike many girls of my social standing, I wasn't sent away to boarding school. Mother employed home tutors. I suppose because she was lonely and wanted to keep her children close. We never discussed her reasons, but I was happy to be with her. She was a magnificent woman – beautiful, elegant, kind. And The Lizard was a paradise for me. I spent every spare minute exploring its coastline, learning its secrets."

Rozen fell silent, a distant look in her eyes as if she was enjoying old memories. She sighed contentedly. "We lived like that until the morning I found Mother collapsed in her bedroom. She'd suffered periodic bouts of ill health over the years and always managed to get through them. But not this time. She was diagnosed with pernicious anaemia. The condition had gone untreated for so long it had damaged her nerves. Her doctor wanted to hospitalise her, but she refused. She was an extraordinarily strong-willed woman. She was too weak to get out of bed for several months. We had to hire a live-in nurse and a nanny. I was eleven at the time. George was thirteen. When I was sixteen, I took over Mother's care. I looked after her for thirty-five-years. In 1989 she developed stomach cancer. Once again, she refused to go into hospital. Three months later she was dead and, for the first time in my life, I was all alone. Or so it seemed."

Rozen nibbled cake, letting the cryptic remark hang in the air for a moment before continuing, "At this point I should perhaps tell you about my brother George. He moved to London aged eighteen to attend university. After graduating he relocated to the south of France and we fell out of contact. At the time of Mother's death I hadn't spoken to him in several years. He returned for the funeral and the reading of the will. He brought his wife Sofia – a radiantly beautiful young woman – with him. She was twenty-four. George was fifty-three. They had a six-year-old daughter – Heloise. George was, I suppose, what you could call a playboy." There was no judgement in Rozen's voice. It was a simple statement of fact. "Father had put a considerable amount of money into trust for him, which he came into aged twenty-one. But that had long since been spent by the time of Mother's death. I'd seen the will. I knew George was to inherit Fenton House, and I was to inherit this." She spread her hands at the room. "A former cottage for workers at the house."

Once again, Rozen's voice was neutral. She appeared to harbour no resentment that the house had gone to George despite all the years she'd spent caring for her mother. "I assumed George would sell the house and return to France, but I was wrong. After the funeral, he moved in there with his family. I later learnt that he owed a large gambling debt to several casinos in Marseilles. George, Sofia and Heloise lived at Fenton House until 1996 when, again as I'm sure you already know, all three of them disappeared. They were simply there one day and gone the next. When, after several months, it became apparent that they weren't coming back, I took up residence in Fenton House once again."

A shadow seemed to fall over Rozen's face. The sparkle in her eyes dimmed. "Now you know a little about George, let me tell you about the day Mother died. It was the darkest of my life. There was no big final moment. No goodbyes were said. Mother had been in terrible pain, but that day she seemed quite comfortable. We were talking about something. I don't remember what. Midway through the conversation, she closed her eyes. At first I thought she'd dropped off to sleep, but then I realised she'd stopped breathing."

Rozen paused as if gathering the strength to continue. "When the ambulance took Mother away the house felt strange. Not in an eerie way. In an empty, hollowed out way. I felt as if my world had ended. I sat up the entire night with one thought on my mind – was there any point in continuing living? It was just before dawn when I saw something that answered my question." The light in her eyes flared back into life. "And suddenly, as if a veil had been lifted from my eyes, my grief was gone because I knew Mother was still with me."

"Did you see your mother's ghost?" asked Ella.

There was something in Ella's voice – something faintly hopeful – that drew Adam's gaze. She was holding the photo of the twins, unconsciously running her thumb back and forth over Jacob. Rozen beamed at her. "I'm afraid it's necessary that I don't tell you what I saw, my dear. What I can tell you is that from that moment on Mother spoke to me every day. Or rather she spoke to me every day that I lived at Fenton House."

"So why did you leave?" asked Adam.

Rozen responded with a question of her own. "Let me ask you something, do you prefer to spend time around old or young people?"

"It depends who the people are."

"That's a very diplomatic answer, Adam, and I appreciate the sentiment behind it. But if you're honest with yourself, I think you'll find you prefer to be around young people. People whose energy and vitality make you feel more alive. Well the dead are no different. It's a bit like reading a book. They don't want to look at someone who reminds them of what they are. They want to forget themselves. That's why Mother warned me I had to leave."

Ella frowned. "Warned you. Are you saying you would have been in danger if you stayed?"

"Not from Mother. But Mother's spirit isn't the only one that inhabits the house."

"How many others are there?"

"I don't know exactly. Nor do I know who they are."

"Are they..." Ella sought the right words, "evil spirits?"

"I can't say. I can tell you that they never harmed me."

"What about your brother and his family? Did they harm them?"

Rozen turned her palms upwards in a *Who can say?* gesture. "The prevailing opinion in the newspapers was that my brother's past had caught up with him and he was forced to find somewhere else to hide from his debt."

"Is that what you believe?"

Rozen looked thoughtful before replying in a careful tone, "I believe there are some things we are not meant to understand – things of and not of this world. George held no such beliefs. The only things he believed in were those he could see."

Adam let slip a sudden breath of incredulous laughter. He held up a hand. "I'm sorry, Miss Trehearne. I don't mean to be rude. It's just I'm struggling to take this ghost stuff seriously."

"I completely understand," said Rozen. "I'm sure I'd feel the same way if I hadn't lived in Fenton House. But please believe me, Adam, when I say that you should take this very seriously. If you are chosen, it may be that you live there for the rest of your life without ever experiencing anything, for want of a better word, supernatural. Or it may be that at some point, like me, you experience an awakening."

"What do you mean by awakening?" asked Ella. "Do you have some sort of..." again she sought the right words, "clairvoyant power?"

Rozen chuckled as if amused by the idea. "I have no special powers whatsoever, my dear. The house has the power."

"It's not built on a graveyard, is it?" Adam joked.

"Not as far as I'm aware." Rozen put down her teacup like a full-stop. "I think we've said all that needs to be said for now. It's time you saw Fenton house. That is if you're still interested in proceeding."

Adam and Ella looked at each other. Ella gave a nod and Adam said to Rozen, "We'd very much like that."

She smiled. "Good."

Mr Mabyn stood up and opened the French doors. "If you'd please follow me, Mr and Mrs Piper."

"Aren't you coming?" Ella asked Rozen.

"No, my dear. As I said, I'm not welcome there anymore. Perhaps we'll talk more afterwards. If not..." She extended her hand. "Goodbye Ella. Goodbye Adam. Thank you for your honesty."

CHAPTER 6

Still stooping as if to avoid invisible ceiling beams, Mr Mabyn led them to a gate in the back garden wall. Beyond it an alley sloped up between neighbouring cottages to a small carpark watched over by a constable. A sign on a farm-style gate read 'Private. Permit Holders Only'. Mr Mabyn ushered them into the back of a black Mercedes and folded his long frame into the driver's seat. The constable opened the gate and they pulled onto the lane about fifty metres up from the crowd. The lane climbed out of Treworder through a tunnel of trees. After half-a-mile of fields peppered with hay rolls, they came to a hamlet of thatched cottages and modern houses. The lane was blocked by traffic cones. A man in a luminous tabard moved them aside to allow the Mercedes through. They made their way along a road that ran parallel to the coastline until it met up with the lane where Adam and Ella were parked. Mr Mabyn turned onto an even narrower lane that snaked through fields sleepily grazed by cows and horses.

The lane curved back down towards the coastline. The deep blue banner of the sea unfurled itself again and windswept hedgerows curled wavelike away from it. The lane ended at rust-flecked double gates about three metres high and topped with spear heads. The gates were set in an almost equally tall stone wall. Swirling iron shapes evoked images of a stormy sea. A TV crew was set up outside the gates. A woman in a 'Ghost Hunters' t-shirt was speaking into a camera. Mr Mabyn lowered his window. "This is a private road," he informed them. "Please leave at once or I'll contact the police."

"We're happy to pay if–"

"Miss Trehearne is not interested in your money." The old solicitor's dour tone brooked no argument. He remained seated while the camera crew packed their gear into a van. Once they were gone, he got out and unlocked the gates. The hinges squealed as the gates swung inwards. He beckoned

Adam and Ella out of the car. He handed Adam a bunch of keys, singling out a large iron one. "That's for the front door. I'll be waiting here."

"Don't tell me you're scared of ghosts too, Mr Mabyn," smiled Adam.

No trace of humour showed on Mr Mabyn's face. "Ghosts do not concern me, Mr Piper. All that concerns me is carrying out Miss Trehearne's instructions. With that in mind, I must inform you that if you remove anything – even a single stone – from the house and gardens, you will be disqualified from the selection process."

As they started along a gravel driveway, Adam said to Ella, "You were right about the questionnaire. The birds, the dog, the Victoria sponge. And what are the bets that Rozen's favourite colour is turquoise?"

Tall sycamores marched up either side of the driveway. Lush lawns freshly mown into stripes were dotted with yews clipped into mushroom shapes and clumps of pale beeches. The borders blazed with red-hot pokers, hydrangeas, rhododendrons and foxgloves whose colours stood out strikingly against the vast blue backdrop. A faux-ruined wall with empty arched windows and half a doorway decorated one bank of a large lily pond. Tropical palms and ferns dipped their fronds into the water. After a hundred or so metres, the driveway widened into a circle with a fountain at its centre.

Adam and Ella stopped as one and stared speechlessly at Fenton House. It was three storeys of pale grey granite with a triple peaked slate roof, positioned so that its front overlooked Treworder and its back faced the cliffs stretching hazily towards Lizard Point. A circular tower topped by a stone spire stabbed skywards from the right-hand side of the roof. Above an arched porch and a metal-bound wooden door was a tall stained glass window like something from a cathedral. To either side were huge bay windows crowned by crenelated battlements. Gargoyles projected from the corners of the eaves. To the left-hand side of the house was an orangery whose vaulted glass roof glittered with condensation.

"It's..." Adam began. "I don't know what to say. Words fail me."

"It feels surreal being here, thinking this could be ours."

"I know."

"It doesn't look haunted."

"What does haunted look like?"

"I don't know, but not this. Maybe if it was a gloomy day I'd feel differently."

"It's just a house, Ella. A very beautiful house, but still only bricks and mortar. It needs a bit of work too."

Adam pointed out flaking window frames, green streaks beneath the gutters, slipped roof tiles. He reached to take Ella's hand. She looked down at his fingers curling into hers, then up at his face. He'd been grey with grief since the accident, but now there was a flush of sunburn on his cheeks. Or maybe it wasn't sunburn. The furrows that seemed to have been permanently etched between his eyebrows had faded to faint lines.

Ella squinted up at the circular tower. "That's where Walter Lewarne hanged himself. Can you imagine him dangling there with birds pecking at him?"

"He was in debt," said Adam. "So was George Trehearne. Pretty mundane stuff when you think about it."

He eagerly drew Ella onwards. They'd only advanced a few more steps when a robin landed in front of them. The bird puffed out its bright orange chest and twittered at them.

"It looks as if it's trying to ask us something," said Ella.

The robin turned away and bobbed along the driveway. It fluttered up onto the rim of the fountain – a stone bowl shaped like a church font with a column of lions' heads spouting water from their mouths at its centre. "It's going to have a bath," said Adam, but the robin turned to look inquisitively at them again.

"What a tame little thing," said Ella. "I wonder if Rozen used to feed it."

"Maybe she sent it to spy on us."

Ella smiled at Adam's playful tone. She'd wondered whether she would ever hear it again. She said to the robin, "I'm sorry little fellow, we haven't got any food for you."

As they approached the front door, Adam peered up at the stained glass window. It depicted a tree with deep roots and wide-spreading branches. His gaze moved to the gargoyles. One appeared to be some sort of imp or monkey, sticking out an obscenely long tongue. The other was a winged creature with a goat-like face and horns. "Now they're scary." He pointed to the winged gargoyle. "That one looks a bit like your mum."

"Hey." Ella nudged him in the ribs.

Grinning, he held up the key. "Shall we?"

He slid the key into an ornate lock, turned it with a clunk and opened the heavy door. They stepped into a pleasantly cool entrance hall every bit as impressive as the house's exterior. Two black wrought-iron chandeliers dangled from a high ceiling with fruit-and-foliage cornice-mouldings. Glossy parquet floors were covered by plush dark red and gold rugs that complemented the wallpaper. To the left was a broad, cantilevered staircase supported by stone pillars. To the right was a large white marble fireplace with a dark oak surround. The hall was flooded with a rainbow of light from the window. Beeswax polish scented the air.

Adam's gaze lingered on a painting in a gold-leaf frame above the fireplace – a portrait of a woman in a long black dress. Strings of pearls hung from her swan-neck. A white fur stole was wrapped around her slender shoulders. Her face was pale with thin red lips, a sharp nose and dark eyes bordered by even darker bobbed hair. Apart from her lips and a few muted touches of colour, the painting was almost monochrome.

"That's got to be Rozen's mother," remarked Adam. "The resemblance is unmistakable."

"She looks sad," said Ella.

"Wouldn't you be if I was killed in a war?"

"I bet she never loved anyone again after her husband died. You can see it in her eyes."

Adam gave Ella's hand a gentle squeeze. "Where shall we explore first?"

She drew him towards an arched door. It led into a dining room. A long sturdy oak dining table and fourteen chairs with barley-twist legs occupied the centre of the room. Two large tapestries draped the walls – one depicting a unicorn rearing on its hind legs, the other a winged lion in flight. There was another marble fireplace, its mantelpiece bookended by porcelain wolves. A door in the far wall led into a room furnished with a pair of stiff-backed sofas and several matching armchairs arranged around an elegant coffee-table. The walls were hung with desolate paintings of stormy seas and shipwrecks. A bay window overlooked the side garden.

"This must be the living room," said Ella.

Adam put on a posh accent. "Actually my dear I think you'll find it's the drawing room. That's where the ladies withdraw to after dinner, leaving the gentlemen to talk business and politics and other topics beyond the grasp of the female intellect."

Ella slid him a look that suggested he was skating on thin ice.

They returned to the dining room. A third door led to a large, sun-splashed room at the back of the house. French doors overlooked a patio, beyond which a long lawn sloped gently towards the sparkling sea. A grandfather clock adorned with carved wooden foliage ticked in one corner. There were more tapestries and paintings of mythical birds and beasts. A stag's head with immense antlers stared down from over a deeply recessed stone fireplace. In front of the hearth were a shabby but comfortable looking three-piece-suite and a brown, somewhat moth-eaten bearskin rug with the head still attached.

"This is the living room," said Adam.

"Actually I think you'll find this is more accurately called the sitting room."

Smiling at Ella's touché, he pointed to the stag's head and the bearskin rug. "I wonder if Walter Lewarne shot those?"

"Who knows, but they would have to go."

"Why? I like them." Adam stroked the bearskin. "It's beautifully soft. Just picture us curling up on it in front of a roaring fire."

They continued exploring. The next room was a wood-panelled games room with a red-baize snooker table, studded-leather armchairs and a walnut poker table. Then came a small, dark wood library with walls of dusty antique books – some so old their spines had disintegrated. There were shelves of morning and evening prayer books, along with fiction and poetry. "This lot must be worth a fortune," said Adam. "Keats, Shakespeare, Shelley, Poe... I could happily spend my days here just reading and looking at the view."

"What about writing your own books?"

"Maybe I wouldn't need to write anymore if we lived here."

Ella made a dubious noise. Adam had threatened to give up writing before, but they both knew it would never happen. As he'd said numerous times since his writer's block kicked-in – if there was one thing he hated more than writing it was not writing.

After the library came a study with a green leather-topped desk and a window facing the pond. Then a kitchen with a flagstone floor, a Rayburn, a jumble of cupboards, a well-used table, four mismatched chairs, a gaping fireplace and a big pantry. Then a laundry room with a twin-tub and a ceiling-mounted clothes drying rack. Then a broom-cupboard as big as their London kitchen. They lingered for a while in the sultry warmth of the orangery, admiring the exotic plants and flowers while dodging drips of condensation from the glass roof.

They almost missed the final downstairs door which was shrouded in shadows beneath the staircase. A brass plaque was inscribed with 'The Lewarne Room'. The door it was attached to opened onto a long, gloomy room. A galaxy of dust motes was suspended in the light bleeding through closed wooden shutters. The floor was tiled with a red fleur de lis pattern. Above wooden panelling, the walls and ceiling were papered with the same design. A red velvet sofa and armchair faced each other in front of an enormous stone fireplace. Silver candelabra with red candlesticks occupied a pair of pedestals at opposite sides of the room. There was a musty, closed-in smell, as if no one had been in there in a long time. The shutters squeaked as Adam opened them. The room glowed luridly in the sunlight.

"I think that's the first time they've been opened for a hundred years," he said. He ran his fingers over the lustrous green-and-black spotted pedestals. "This is serpentine. The rock that gives the peninsula its name. It's beautiful, don't you think?"

"Yes." Ella pointed to a pair of paintings in the alcoves that flanked the fireplace. "They're a bit sinister." One painting was of a mother and child. The child – little more than a cherubic baby – was being cradled towards its mother's milk-swollen breast. Its eyes were wide with anticipation. The mother's eyes were so heavy-lidded that she almost appeared to be sleeping. In the other painting the same child was being torn from its horrified mother's arms by a heavily muscled man. With one thick-knuckled hand, the man was wrenching back the child's head. With the other he was thrusting a dagger into its throat. A lacquered wooden panel above the fireplace was carved with four words. "They are no more," read Ella. "I wonder what that means?"

"It sounds like some sort of Biblical reference."

Ella shuddered. "I don't like it in here."

"It's definitely an atmospheric room."

Adam looked at a framed photo leaning next to one of the candelabra. A woman, a girl and a man were seated side-by-side on the room's red sofa. The waifish young woman was wearing a close-fitting black dress that came down to just below her knees. She held herself rigid-backed, chin high. Her lips were a straight line. Her bobbed wavy blonde hair was styled into a side-parting. She seemed to be looking past the camera. The girl was maybe twelve or thirteen-years-old. She was sitting equally stiffly in a red satin Alice dress. Her long light-brown hair was centre-parted. She had the same delicate but full-lipped features as the woman. Her big brown eyes were staring expressionlessly into the camera. Next to her was a stocky man in a stylishly cut grey suit and open-necked white shirt. In contrast to his companions, he was lounging against the cushions. He had swept back silvery-black hair, deep-set eyes, a squashed boxer's nose and a somewhat seedy smile. He exuded a kind of louche arrogance.

"This must be George, Sofia and Heloise," said Adam. He added sarcastically, "Happy looking bunch, aren't they? I wonder if they–"

"Don't," broke in Ella.

"What do you mean, don't? You haven't heard what I was going to say."

"You were about to make some jokey comment about what might have happened to them. But don't. Not here."

Adam held up his hands in mock innocence. He approached the other pedestal on which there stood a grainy black-and-white photo. A brass plaque on its frame was engraved with 'Walter Lewarne. 1915'. A slim man in a country gentlemen's three-piece suit was standing side-on in front of a tall arched mirror set between curtains. He was clean-shaven with almost femininely delicate, high-boned features and centre-parted short, dark hair. He was looking into the mirror rather than at the camera. There was a curl to his lips as if he was disgusted by what he saw.

"What does he find so interesting about his own reflection?" wondered Adam.

"I don't know, but I don't think he liked what he saw."

Adam approached the front exterior wall and traced his fingers along a spidery crack that threaded up from the wood panelling to the ceiling. "Looks like there's some movement in the walls here."

Ella made an uninterested, "Mm," and headed for the door. "Let's look upstairs."

Adam turned to follow her, but hesitated and cocked an ear. "Do you hear that?"

"What?"

"I heard a gurgling. Like running water."

"I don't hear it."

Adam listened again. The sound had disappeared beyond the periphery of his hearing. "Neither do I now."

They ascended the broad staircase past more tapestries. The landing was colourfully illuminated by a rear window the same dimensions as the one at the front of the house. The stained glass was a storm-tossed collection of glittering blue and turquoise. Looking back and forth between the windows gave Adam the impression that he was in a tunnel bookended by the land and sea. A wood-panelled, red-carpeted hallway stretched away from either side of the landing. There were eleven doors – five on one side and six on the other.

"Shall we split up?" suggested Adam. "Otherwise this will take all day."

"No chance." Ella hooked her arm through his.

He gave a smiling shake of his head. "If we're going to live here, you'll to have to get over this twitchiness."

"That's a big if."

"I don't think so. I got the distinct impression Rozen's made up her mind that we're the ones."

"She said the final decision isn't hers to make."

"Then whose is it? Her mother's?" Adam rolled his eyes as if to say, *Give me a break.*

Ella squeezed his arm sharply. "Please, Adam, I asked you not to talk like that here."

He pulled his arm free and peered behind a tapestry.

"What are you doing?" asked Ella.

"Looking for hidden microphones, because that's the only way anyone else will hear us."

"This obviously isn't some kind of reality TV setup. This is for real."

"Yeah, it's very real. Unlike all the nonsense about this place being haunted. If something's going to make me think twice about living here, it's not the stories Rozen told us. It's that she really believes they're true."

"What does that mean?"

"It means she's a vulnerable old lady and I don't want to take advantage of that."

"She doesn't seem particularly vulnerable to me. She seems as if–" Ella broke off, cocking her head as a bell began to toll. "Is that coming from inside or outside the house?"

"Outside, I think. There was a church in that hamlet we passed through."

"It doesn't sound like it's coming from that far away."

"Could be the grandfather clock."

A final *ding!* rang out more loudly than the preceding ones. "How many did you count?" asked Ella.

"Twelve."

"I counted thirteen."

"Well you must have counted wrong. Unless the clock's faulty. What were you going to say about Rozen?"

"I'll tell you later. Let's finish looking around."

The nearest door led into a bedroom cluttered with hefty oak furniture. There was a four-poster bed whose posts were fashioned into the same barley-twist as the dining room furniture. At its foot was a chaise longue. A full-length wall-mounted mirror occupied an alcove to one side of a granite fireplace. A stuffed peacock eyed them beadily from its perch on the mantelpiece. The walls were covered with amateurish paintings of animals – mainly birds – and framed flower pressings. In a corner there was an antique rocking-horse with a threadbare teddy-bear astride its saddle. On one of the bedside tables there was an antiquated rotary dial telephone. Windows opened onto a balcony overlooking the front garden.

"I get the feeling this was Rozen's room," said Ella, perusing the paintings.

Adam opened the windows and drank in the view. The garden wall only ran along the front. The rest of the garden was sheltered by a tall hedge, from beyond which came the soft, relentless sound of waves washing the cliffs. "It might be ours soon."

Ella's forehead wrinkled.

"What's that look about?" asked Adam.

"I'm just trying to imagine the three of us rattling around this house. Do we really need somewhere like this?"

Adam's voice was suddenly passionate. "It's not only about the house. Like Rozen said, there's a magic to this place. I'm not talking about something supernatural. I'm talking about fresh air and beauty. Henry could heal here. We all could." He took her hand again, drew her into an embrace and kissed her.

When Ella pulled her lips from his there were tears in her eyes. "You haven't kissed me like that in a long time."

The colour on Adam's cheeks had deepened. He kissed Ella again, his hands dropping to her waist. "I have an idea," he whispered. "Let's christen this room."

Ella let out a surprised little laugh. "No."

"Why not?"

"It wouldn't feel right."

Adam lowered his lips to her neck. She squirmed free. He made a playful grab for her and she danced away towards the door. Smiling, he lunged after her. With a squeal of laughter, she ran from the room. He chased her through the opposite doorway into a white marble bathroom with a roll-top bath at its centre. Ella darted around the bath and back into the hallway. Adam pulled up abruptly as he stubbed his foot on one of the bath's claw feet.

"Oh you're really for it now," he grimaced, limping from the bathroom. Ella was nowhere to be seen. The neighbouring door was open. "I'm coming to get you," he said in a sing-song voice, poking his head into the room. It was unfurnished except for a wall-mounted mirror. The next room was the same. Along with a mirror, the final room on that side of the house had a few items of furniture – single bed, chair, dressing-table, bedside table, wardrobe – all draped in dust sheets. "Ella, where are you?" He peered under the sheets – no Ella. He headed for the other wing of the landing. The furniture in the first four rooms was covered in dust sheets too. He was smiling at first as he lifted the sheets, but then a frown crept in.

"The game's over," he called. "Come out."

No reply.

"I promise I'll keep my hands to myself."

More silence.

The final room was an ostentatious bedroom that extended out from the back of the house with stone-casement windows on three sides. To the north east, Treworder's white cottages gleamed like jewels. To the south west was a sinuous line of cliffs and coves. A crystal chandelier dangled from the ceiling. A tall fireplace was set between stone pillars with cherubic figures floating up them. A red-silk canopied four-poster bed dominated the room, its corners topped with crucifixes. Adam peered under it. Nothing. His frown intensified.

"This isn't funny any–" he broke off with a gasp as hands encircled his waist.

Ella dug her fingernails into his flesh. "Did I scare you?"

"No."

She nuzzled his neck. "Admit it, you were a bit scared." She started to unbuckle his belt.

"I thought you didn't feel right about doing anything."

"I changed my mind."

Ella turned Adam towards her and pushed him onto the bare mattress. She slid off her jeans and underwear and straddled him. The mattress squeaked as she tilted her hips back and forth. "This bed sounds as old as it looks," he said.

"Shh," she murmured, quickening her movements. Her eyelids grew heavy, her soft sighs thickened into husky moans.

Adam bucked against her, his moans mirroring hers as she dropped forwards onto his chest. They held each other silently for a while, then she rose to pull her jeans back on.

"I think that's what they call a quickie," said Adam. He breathed deeply. "God, I feel more relaxed than I have done since..." He trailed off, not wanting to say what came next. A yawn pulled at his mouth. "What I'd like to do more than anything now is curl up with you and fall asleep."

"Mmm, I know what you mean."

Ella snuggled back into Adam, closing her eyes. Sighing, he shut his eyes too and felt the world drifting away. A delicious blankness settled over him.

A sound like stone grating against stone wormed its way into his consciousness. He opened his eyes slowly, almost warily. A robin was on the windowsill, pecking at something on the stone sill. Adam smiled, shaking his head at himself. What had he expected to see? Winifred Trehearne emerging through a wall?

Ella stirred and opened her eyes. "Is that the same bird?"

"I think so," chuckled Adam. "Did you enjoy the show little birdie?" He rose and tapped on the glass. The robin fluttered away.

Ella glanced at her wristwatch. Her eyebrows lifted. "Bloody hell, do you know what time it is?"

He shrugged. "Half twelve?"

"It's quarter to two. We've been in this house nearly two hours."

"I suppose time flies when you're having fun. We'd better get a shift on. Mr Mabyn will be wondering what's happened to us."

Adam started towards the door, but paused as Ella said, "Do you notice something about this bedroom? There are no dust sheets."

"Maybe Rozen kept this room ready for guests."

"It's also the only bedroom with no mirror."

"I think this was Walter's bedroom." Adam pointed out a 'WL' carved into the bedhead. He thought about Walter's expression in the photo. "As you said, he didn't seem to like his reflection very much."

Adam caught hold of Ella's hand and drew her from the room. They checked out the last door. A narrow wooden staircase climbed steeply into gloom beyond it. Adam pressed a switch and a bare bulb flickered into life. The creaking stairs led up to a long corridor lined with unvarnished doors. The first door opened into a small room furnished with an iron-framed single bed. A ceiling mottled with damp sloped down towards a little window recessed in a thick wall.

"This must have been where the servants slept," said Ella.

The neighbouring room contained a mouldy washbasin and toilet. Wasps buzzed around a honeycomb-shaped nest in a corner of the ceiling. Adam quickly closed the door. "That'll need sorting out."

"You're speaking as if we were already living here."

"Because I've got a strong feeling that we *are* going to live here."

"Listen, Adam, even if we're chosen I'm not sure–"

"I thought we were going to save this conversation for later," he interrupted, moving on to the next door which opened onto a jumble of dusty furniture.

"Look at this." Ella approached an arched door inlaid with ebony and ivory carvings of stars and planets. She traced her fingers over the intricate carvings. "I wonder if this leads to the tower."

"Only one way to find out." Adam turned the handle. "It's locked." He took out the bundle of keys and tried them all. "None fit." He waggled his eyebrows mischievously. "Maybe Rozen keeps someone locked up there. An insane illegitimate child or something."

Ella exhaled an unamused breath. "Crack one more joke like that and I'm definitely not living here."

"Sorry, I couldn't resist."

Her irritation faded as rapidly as it had appeared. It was so wonderful to see Adam smiling. She hooked his arm and pulled him onwards. The rest of the rooms contained more of the same –furniture, boxes of crockery, dust, cobwebs. Ella rubbed her nose. "It's making me want to sneeze. Let's get out of here."

They made their way downstairs and took a last lingering look at the entrance hall, then they strolled around the garden, hand-in-hand. A wooden gate was set into the hedge. Adam tried the keys again and, this time, found one that fitted the lock. A curving green tunnel brought them to a path cut into the cliff top. A vertiginously steep bank of grass, bracken and thorny plants tumbled down to a sheer wall of black rock. Gulls and cormorants sunned themselves on boulders jutting from the dark, deep-looking sea.

"I don't think I'd ever tire of looking at this," said Adam.

He reluctantly turned his back on the view and they returned to the front gates. Mr Mabyn held his hand out for the keys. "Sorry we took so long," said Ella as the solicitor locked the gates. "We lost track of time. It's an amazing house."

Mr Mabyn stooped into his car without comment.

"Can I ask you something about Miss Trehearne?" said Adam as they drove back to Treworder. Mr Mabyn nodded for him to go ahead. "Is she a well woman?"

"I'm not a doctor, Mr Piper."

"I appreciate that, Mr Mabyn, but the thing is..." Adam sought to put his thoughts into the same impersonal language the solicitor used. "We don't want to take advantage of someone who's not of sound mind."

"Even if I was party to any information concerning Miss Trehearne's health, I would not be in a position to reveal it to you." Mr Mabyn paused meaningfully before adding, "What I can say is that I'm duty-bound to serve my clients' best-interests."

The implication of the solicitor's words seemed clear enough – Rozen knew what she was doing.

CHAPTER 7

The chocolate-box cottages of Treworder trembled in the sun. The intense midday heat hadn't deterred those gathered outside Boscarne Cottage. If anything, the crowd had grown larger and more boisterous. Mr Mabyn parked up and they returned to the cottage via the back garden. Rozen smiled at them from her armchair. Edgar was snoring on her lap now. "So," she began expectantly as Adam and Ella seated themselves, "what do you think?"

"We love it," said Adam. He turned to Ella. "Don't we?"

"Yes."

"You don't sound convinced, my dear," said Rozen.

"I am. It's just…" Ella sighed. "Well, there was so much to take in. It's all a bit overwhelming."

"The house can have that effect, especially on people like you."

"What do you mean, people like us?" asked Adam.

"People in a heightened emotional state. I must say, the house seems to have agreed with you both. You look different. There's more colour in your cheeks."

A faint heat tingled up Adam's neck. Was that a suggestive note in Rozen's voice? Did she know what they'd been up to? He dismissed the thought. How could she possibly know? "I actually feel different," he admitted. "I don't mean I've had an awakening or anything like that. I just mean I'm excited at the thought of possibly living somewhere so wonderful."

Rozen beamed at him. "It sounds like you've fallen in love, which is exactly what I was hoping to hear. Fenton House needs someone like you. Someone who'll–" She broke off. "There I go, getting ahead of myself again. Mother always used to scold me for it, but it's a habit I've never outgrown."

Her bright little eyes moved between Adam and Ella. "What I need now is for you to help me see the choice to be made."

"Just tell us how," Adam said eagerly.

"What would help most is if you tell me what you saw and heard."

"We didn't see or hear anything out of the ordinary."

"The robin was a bit unusual," said Ella. She described how the bird had led them along the driveway and reappeared at the bedroom window.

"It's not so unusual when you consider that robins were Mother's favourite birds," said Rozen. "She did everything she could to encourage them into the garden, and I continued to do so after her death. They often stand on the window ledges waiting to be fed. Did anything else catch your interest?"

"The church bell. It seemed to strike thirteen times. Did you hear it?"

"No, my dear. But then I am going deaf in my old age."

"A number of things stuck in my mind," put in Adam. "In particular your mother's portrait and The Lewarne Room."

"Those things tend to stick in the mind of everyone who visits the house. The portrait was completed shortly after Father's death. No one can look in Mother's eyes without being touched by her grief. The Lewarne Room has remained unaltered since the house was built. Apart from an occasional bit of dusting, no one goes in there. I never liked the room myself. The paintings always made me uneasy."

"They made me feel the same way," said Ella.

"One other thing caught my interest," said Adam. "The locked door in the attic. Where does it lead?"

"To the observatory tower. No one's been up there in my lifetime. You may have heard of the Big Storm of 1920?" As Adam and Ella shook their heads, Rozen continued, "On February 16th of that year an Atlantic storm battered the peninsula with heavy rains and gale force winds. Several people lost their lives. The observatory tower was badly damaged. That was also the day Walter Lewarne took his own life. My grandfather had the tower sealed up."

"So is it dangerous? Could it fall down?" asked Ella.

"Part of it – albeit a small part – did after another violent storm in the winter of '74. It was a sword of Damocles dangling over our heads until the insurance paid out enough to reinforce the external walls. Unfortunately the money didn't extend to making the tower safe enough for use."

There was a little interval of silence. Rozen looked at Adam and Ella as if waiting for them to say more. Adam suddenly felt as if the house was slipping away from him. His mind raced for something – anything – that might stop it from doing so. "We made love," he blurted out. Ella threw him a startled look, but he continued in a confessional tone, "The sun shining through the stained glass, the sound of the sea, like Ella said it was all a bit overwhelming. We got carried away. I'm sorry. I know we shouldn't have, but... Well it happened and if that means we don't get the house then I suppose it wasn't meant to be."

Rozen's smile remained fixed in place. "There's no need to apologise. I'm not experienced in matters of the heart, but I can imagine how your child's death has affected your relationship. Whatever happened did so because that's what you needed and it's what the spirits of the house needed from you." She turned to the solicitor. "Mr Mabyn would you please show Adam and Ella into the dining room."

Adam and Ella followed the solicitor into a dining room crammed with antique furniture. "Please wait here until I return," he said, closing the door.

"Do you think I blew it?" Adam whispered to Ella.

She silently pursed her lips.

"Don't be like that, Ella. I had to say something."

She looked at him from beneath sloping eyebrows. "Are you really that desperate to live there?"

"This could be a new start for us. A chance to forget."

Ella's frown deepened. "I don't want to forget Jacob."

"That's not what I mean. I don't want to forget him either. But I do want to forget the past nine months." Adam glanced towards the door at the sound of approaching footsteps. "That was quick. Do you think that's a good or a bad thing?"

Ella didn't reply, as if uncertain what would constitute good or bad. Mr Mabyn poked his long face into the room and beckoned to them. They returned to the living room. Adam noticed that Rozen had applied a fresh coat of shiny red lipstick. He noticed too that the teapot and cake were gone. In their place was a slim document. Rozen pointed to it. "That's the contract. All it needs is your signature, Adam."

His heart leaped so high it almost cut off his breath. "You mean Fenton House is ours?"

"If you want it."

A half-choked laugh of delight escaped him. "Of course we want it. Just give me a pen and tell me where to sign."

"I think we should read the contract through first," cautioned Ella, wearing a sort of stunned smile.

"Ella's right," agreed Rozen. "Take it away with you. Read it carefully and think it over for a few days."

"I don't need–" Adam started to say, but fell silent at the look in Ella's eyes.

She levelled a searching gaze at Rozen. "Can I ask why us?"

"It's difficult to say exactly. Certain things you saw and heard. But most of all because it's clear to me that your family and the house would be a perfect fit."

Rozen held out her hand to Adam. He took it and she sandwiched his fingers between hers. "I apologise in advance for taking a liberty, Adam, but I want to ask you for something. May I kiss you?"

"I... err... yes." Adam bent towards Rozen. He somewhat awkwardly offered his cheek, but she pressed her lips lightly against his. They were warm and waxy. The whiff of rouge flew up his nostrils.

He drew away a little more quickly than he'd meant to. "Thank you, Rozen. I'm sure we'll be seeing each other again soon."

"I very much hope so. Goodbye again to you both and good luck whatever your decision."

"Goodbye Miss Trehearne," said Ella, still smiling, but with a trace of terseness in her tone.

Mr Mabyn escorted them to the back gate. He gave Adam his business card. "Once you've signed the contract send it to that address."

"You say that as if there's no question of us not signing," said Ella.

Mr Mabyn afforded her a dry glance that suggested the remark was not worthy of a response. "If you have any questions, you may contact me on the number provided. Please do not contact Miss Trehearne again until after you've moved into Fenton House." He pointed them along the alley in the opposite direction to before.

Ella held her tongue until they were out of the solicitor's earshot. "Can you believe that woman? Did you notice she'd put on fresh lipstick?"

"Yes."

"I think she was turned on by your confession. She's obviously attracted to you. Maybe that's what this whole thing is about – her finding a toyboy." Ella prodded the contract. "It's probably written into here that you have to service her needs once a week or something."

"Don't be ridiculous," said Adam. "She just wanted a kiss. She might not have kissed anyone since her mother died. Who knows, maybe she's never kissed a man before. Are you seriously begrudging her one little kiss?"

Ella was sulkily silent for several paces, then she muttered, "I suppose not."

Adam caught hold of her arm and turned her to him. Cupping the back of her head, he crushed his lips against hers. After a breathless moment, he drew away. "Does that make up for it?"

"I'll have to think about it," Ella replied with a provocative pout. "I may need some more convincing." Her voice was suddenly serious again. "If there's anything dodgy in this contract, we're not signing it. Agreed?"

Adam didn't respond until Ella gave his hand a sharp squeeze, then he nodded reluctantly.

CHAPTER 8

The cottage they'd hired for the weekend overlooked the harbour in Porthleven, a fishing village a few miles north of The Lizard. As Adam drove, Ella perused the contract. "Listen to this," she said. "On signing we assume full responsibility for the upkeep of Fenton House and all the land belonging to it. We're obliged to maintain said property in a good state of repair."

"That sounds reasonable," remarked Adam.

"What if something goes seriously wrong with the house? What if another storm damages the tower? It could cost us tens of thousands."

"So we'll sell our house. The money will keep us going until I sell my new book."

"You've got to finish writing it first."

Adam smiled nonchalantly, but there was an edge of tension in his voice. "Once I'm here the words will come. I'm sure of it."

"I hope you're right. There's one thing I know you're right about. We *will* have to sell our house. It's written into the contract that we can't use Fenton House as a second home. It must be our only residence."

"That's fine by me. The sooner we sell our house the better."

"I understand how you feel, Adam. Part of me feels the same way. But I also don't like the idea of burning our bridges."

"Fuck those bridges." Adam's voice was brittle with emotion. "If it was up to me, we'd never go back to Walthamstow again."

Ella stroked his shoulder like a mother comforting a child. Her gaze returned to the contract. "The signee along with their spouse or partner and any children must reside continuously in Fenton House. Basically if one of us moves out all of us have to. I find that a bit odd. What about when Henry goes to university? Will we have to leave too?"

"That's a long way off, Ella."

"Six years. It's not that far away."

"Even if we do only get to live in Fenton House for six years, I'd still sign without hesitation." Adam made a circular motion for Ella to move on to the next point.

"Our house is not the only thing we'll have to sell. Any furniture, ornaments and soft furnishings brought into Fenton House must be in a style sympathetic to it."

Nodding approvingly, Adam continued to motion.

"We may not remove any of the contents of Fenton House. We can move them around within its confines, with the exception of paintings, tapestries and mirrors. The Lewarne Room must not be altered in any way. We may redecorate the other rooms, but only after Rozen has given her approval. We may not make any structural changes. We may not enter the observatory tower. Well we know why that's in there. We may not allow anyone into the house to investigate or write about it and its past or present inhabitants. Nor may we publish anything of that sort ourselves. We may not..." Ella paused, raising an eyebrow. "Now this is strange. We may not bring in a priest or psychic to bless, exorcise or perform any other sacred ritual."

"Actually that makes perfect sense when you think about what Rozen believes."

"I suppose so, but that doesn't exactly put my mind at rest."

"Look, we've established that Rozen's an eccentric. Anyone would be who'd lived her life. So let's just take this contract with a big pinch of salt."

"No let's not." Ella's voice was soft but firm. "I know you fell in love with Fenton House the instant you saw it, but let's try to think about this without emotion. Who is Rozen Trehearne? What does she want from us?"

"She's a harmless old lady. And this isn't about what she wants. It's about what the," Adam put on a ghostly voice, "sp-ir-its of Fenton House want."

"I don't find that funny."

"Oh don't be like that, Ella. Think about us. Think about how much closer the house has brought us together already."

"I am thinking about that, but I'm also thinking about Henry. If there's even the slightest chance that this might put him in danger–"

"What danger?" Adam pointed at the contract. "Do you really think I'd sign that if there was any danger? We've also established that the mysteries of Fenton House aren't all that mysterious. Walter Lewarne killed himself because he was about to go bankrupt, and George Trehearne went on the run from French gangsters."

"I'm sure you're right, but..." Ella sighed. "Oh I don't know. It's impossible to make sense of all this."

"Then don't try to. Just go with it. Enjoy it. This is a once in a lifetime opportunity. If we don't do this, we'll spend the next forty or fifty years wondering what might have been. Or at least I will."

Smiling, Ella conceded, "I would too."

"Tell you what. Let's finish going through the contract then put it away and not speak about it until after the weekend."

"There's not much more to go through. Once every quarter a representative of Mabyn and Moon will pay us a visit to ensure we haven't broken any of the conditions. You can guess what will happen if we have. And finally, if we're still..." Ella trailed off, then said in a voice of quiet amazement, "Oh my god. If we're still in Fenton House at the time of Rozen's death we'll inherit the house and its contents."

Adam whistled. "Do you realise how much a place like that is worth?"

"It's got to be three or four million."

"And then some." Adam waggled his eyebrows. "That's just given me a really nasty idea."

"Adam! You'd better not be thinking what I think you are."

He chuckled. "That's how my mind works. I'm a writer. But seriously, how much longer before Rozen pops her clogs? Five, ten, fifteen years max?"

"Stop it." Ella made as if to tear up the contract. "I'm warning you, one more word and–"

"OK, OK." Adam made a mouth-zipped gesture.

CHAPTER 9

Adam and Ella barely left the cottage all weekend. They made love, drank wine, watched the sun extinguish itself in the sea, made love again and slept in each other's arms. It was as if they were in a bubble where the years between them falling in love and now didn't exist. But the instant they packed their bags into the car, the bubble burst. "It's been wonderful, hasn't it?" said Ella, reaching for Adam's hand.

"Yes," he replied, but there was a flatness to his voice. He got into the car without looking at her.

They spoke little during the long drive to London. Ella's attempts to make conversation met with an unenthusiastic response or no response at all. The familiar sadness filled Adam more with every passing mile. By the time they reached the M25 he felt as grey as the concrete supports of the motorway flyovers. They detoured into Hounslow to collect Henry from Ella's parents.

"Are you coming in?" Ella asked when Adam didn't get out of the car.

Despite his eagerness to see Henry, he shook his head. He'd avoided Richard and Linda as much as possible since the accident. Although they hadn't openly blamed him for Jacob's death, he sensed their silent accusation. Ella had assured him he was wrong, and he realised that he was probably just seeing his own guilt reflected in their eyes, but he couldn't shake the feeling.

"Just come to the door and say hello."

"I'm tired."

Ella sucked her lips as if unsure whether to be concerned or annoyed. "There's no talking to you when you're in this mood."

Adam heaved a sigh. "OK, I'll come."

They approached the front door and Ella knocked. The door was opened by a man with a smiling red face and grizzled grey hair. "Hi, Dad," said Ella, leaning in to kiss his cheek. She added a touch apprehensively, "How's he been?"

"Fine, except for a little incident last night."

Adam felt a pinch in his stomach. "A bad dream?"

Richard nodded. "It was nothing much. Linda settled him down soon enough."

Henry came into the hallway with his grandma – a trim woman from whom Ella had inherited her peaches-and-cream complexion and thick brown hair. There were dark smudges under Henry's eyes. His lips were set in the same sad line as Adam's.

Ella tried to smile but only succeeded in looking worried. "Have you had a nice time, darling?"

Henry replied with a barely-there nod.

"What about you?" asked Linda. "How did it go?"

"We'll talk on the phone later." Ella glanced meaningfully at Henry. As far as he knew, they'd gone to Cornwall for a weekend break, nothing more. "Say goodbye to Grandma and Grandad, Henry."

Henry kissed his grandparents. Richard put an arm around Henry's shoulders and carried his bag to the car. As Adam and Ella made to follow, Linda caught hold of her daughter's hand. She looked at Ella as if reading the fine lines on her face. "They offered you the house, didn't they?"

"I said we'll talk later."

Linda turned to Adam. "Please don't tell me you're seriously considering moving down there. Henry doesn't need any more upheaval. He needs stability."

Adam bit down on the impulse to reply that Ella and he would be the judges of what Henry needed. "Thanks for looking after him, Linda."

Ella disentangled her hand from her mother's. They hastened to the car before Linda could say anything else. Henry was sitting silently, staring ahead. Seeing the frown on his daughter's face, Richard asked, "What's the matter?" When Ella flicked her eyes towards her mother, he continued, "I know she sticks her nose in sometimes, but it's only because she cares."

Ella's frown faded into a sighing smile. She kissed her dad again and ducked into the car. Adam nodded a quick goodbye at Richard and headed around to the driver's side. Richard and Linda waved as the car accelerated away. Ella was the only one who waved back.

There was a quiet tension in the car as they crossed London. "The Lizard was amazing," Ella told Henry. "You'd love it."

Her words briefly snapped Adam out of his gloom. "You should see the beaches, Henry," he said enthusiastically. "All the kids down there go surfing."

"Isn't surfing dangerous?" asked Henry. Since the accident he'd become averse to doing anything even vaguely risky – his bike had gone unridden, his football had been left to gather dust. Adam had struggled to resist the temptation to encourage this new trait. He wanted to wrap Henry up in cotton-wool, but knew that in the long run it would do more harm than good.

"It can be I suppose."

The silence resumed and, as they neared Walthamstow, seemed to grow more oppressive. Adam took a longer route home to avoid Whipps Cross Hospital. As Ella and Henry got out of the car, Adam sat staring at the house – the front yard cluttered with wheelie bins, the net-curtain veiled windows. It all looked so small and drab after Fenton House. His gaze came to rest on the porch. It took all of his willpower to leave his seat. He fetched the bags from the boot while Ella unlocked the front door and punched in the alarm code. His pace quickened as he passed through the porch.

"I'll make us a cup of tea," said Ella, heading for the kitchen.

Adam took the bags upstairs and started to unpack. He stopped suddenly and sank onto the bed, face in hands. He stayed like that until Ella called him downstairs. Henry was staring expressionlessly into the TV, a plate of untouched toast on his lap. Adam sat down beside him. Ella took the cordless phone upstairs. Adam could guess who she intended to ring. He went to the bottom of the stairs and listened to her conversation.

"I just can't make up my mind, Mum," Ella was saying. "Henry's so unhappy. Adam too. It makes me think it would be for the best. But then I think about you and Dad and all our friends and Henry's school and my job..."

Adam returned to the sofa and turned off the TV.

"Hey, I was watching that," Henry complained.

"I need to speak to you about something important. How would you feel about going to live in Cornwall? It would be very different to here. We'd be living by the sea just outside a little village. There'd be no cinemas nearby, no shopping centres, obviously you'd have to go to a new school, make new friends. But we'd have a big house and garden. We'd be able to go to the beach every day in the summer. Does that sound good?"

Henry's face gave away nothing. "Do you and Mum want to live there?"

Adam resisted the urge to tell him how much he wanted that. "Forget what we want for now. If you don't want to live there, we won't. It's as simple as that."

"Would Grandma and Grandad be able to come and visit us?"

"Of course."

Henry's eyes dropped in thought. Adam held his breath as he waited for him to say something. He broke into a smile when Henry looked at him again and said, "Then I'd like to live there. When are we going?"

Adam cupped his hands against Henry's cheeks. "Soon. I hope." He glanced towards the ceiling. He couldn't hear Ella talking anymore. He switched the TV back on and went upstairs. Ella was staring out of the bedroom window. She turned as Adam approached, her soft brown eyes wide with indecision.

"Your parents would think differently about us moving away if they'd heard Henry crying in his sleep," said Adam.

"They have heard him."

"Not night after night. They're not thinking about what's best for Henry. They're just worried they won't get to see much of him if we move."

"Of course they are. They love him. They love all of us."

Adam inclined his head doubtfully. "Henry wants to go."

Ella frowned. "I thought we agreed to talk to him together."

"I..." A guilty hesitation came into Adam's voice. He'd known Ella would be irritated, but after hearing her on the phone he'd felt the need for some extra ammunition to tip the scales in Fenton House's favour. "I didn't pressure him into an answer. I made it clear it was his choice whether we stay or go."

"Oh so no pressure at all then." Ella turned back to the window.

Adam gently put his hands on her arms. "The same goes for you. You were right to stop me from signing the contract in Treworder. We all have to want this or it won't happen."

Ella leaned her head back against his chest, exhaling a long breath. "What if Fenton House really is haunted?"

"I'll tell you what house is haunted. This one. Everywhere I look I see Jacob." Adam's gaze travelled the room, passing over the patterned rug that Jacob had used to pretend was a road network for his cars, the bed where he'd loved to snuggle up between his parents. "Memories. That's all ghosts are, Ella. We have no memories attached to Fenton House, so for us it's not haunted."

"Just give me a little more time."

Adam kissed Ella's hair. "OK."

They went downstairs. Henry had nodded off on the sofa – something he often did these days. He found it easier to fall asleep to the noise of the TV than the silence of his bedroom. Adam and Ella exchanged a sad glance.

Adam lifted his son, carried him upstairs to bed, undressed him and laid the duvet over him. He watched Henry sleeping for a moment, noting the faint knot between his eyebrows, before returning downstairs.

"He didn't wake," he told Ella.

"He must be tired out."

"I know how he feels. I'm going to get an early night too. Are you coming to bed?"

"I won't be long. I need to think."

Adam trudged upstairs, weighed down by the thought of spending even one more night in the house. He wearily dumped his clothes on the carpet and got into bed. He closed his eyes not expecting sleep to come quickly – but, for once, it did. He dreamed of Fenton House. He could see it away in the distance, bathed in sunlight. He walked towards it, his pace quickening with every step, but it never seemed to get any closer. The light began to shrink into a circle until the house disappeared and only darkness was left.

Adam snapped awake to the familiar, gut-wrenching sound of Henry sobbing. He jumped out of bed and hurried to his son's bedroom. Ella was already in there, cradling and shushing Henry. The lines between Henry's closed eyes had deepened into crevasses. His freckled forehead shone with sweat and his body trembled as if he was in the grip of a fever.

Ella looked at Adam hopelessly. "He's been like this for twenty minutes. I don't know what to do."

"Yes you do," he said.

A brief silence passed between them, then Ella said, "Sign the contract."

CHAPTER 10

Day One

Adam and Ella took one final look around the house to make sure they hadn't missed anything. The wardrobes and drawers were empty, the bookshelves were bare, there were ghostly outlines on the walls where pictures had once hung. Most of the furniture was remaining behind, but still the place felt naked to Adam, stripped of personality, not a home anymore, just an anonymous house. He peered under Henry's bed. There was something lodged between the skirting board and a bed leg. He stretched to retrieve it. His heart squeezed. It was a Diecast red racing car that had been a favourite of Jacob's until he outgrew it. The bedroom walls were scarred with the tracks of its wheels.

"There's nothing in our room," Ella said from the landing. "What about in here?"

Adam quickly pocketed the toy. Ella had been on edge all morning, tearing up several times as they packed the car and trailer. He didn't want to set her off again. "Same."

Ella peered into the bedroom. From the way she sucked her lips against her teeth, Adam could tell she was struggling not to breakdown. He took her hand and drew her downstairs. Linda and Richard were sitting with Henry on the sofa. Linda's expression was a mirror of Ella's. Richard was pressing money into Henry's palm. "It's for his birthday," he explained.

"In case we don't see him," added Linda.

"You'll see him," Ella assured her. A strained note suggested they'd already been over this subject several times. "You're both welcome to come and stay whenever you want, for as long as you want. Aren't they, Adam?"

Adam pushed out a smile. "Of course." He felt a twinge of guilt. Richard and Linda were good people. They hadn't judged him when he was a penniless writer, and Ella was almost certainly right that they weren't judging him now. They deserved better than a forced smile.

"Thanks, Grandad," said Henry, pocketing the money. He kissed Richard and turned to do the same to Linda.

She hugged him. "I'll miss you."

Adam hid his impatience as he waited for Linda to release Henry. He felt a powerful impulse to get away from his old home and get to his new one, exacerbated by a nagging fear that Ella would suddenly change her mind about the move. Linda finally let go and rose to embrace Ella. Tears wobbled on both women's eyelids.

Adam couldn't resist any longer. "We need to get going."

"I'll call you when we get there," Ella told her mum. She ushered Henry out of the house. Richard and Linda followed them.

Adam was the last to leave. His footsteps faltered in the porch. He looked at the floor, seeing Jacob's pale, blood-speckled face. His lips formed four quiet words. "Bye my beautiful boy."

He shook himself free of the image and stepped outside. He locked the door and handed his house keys to Richard. Ella did likewise with hers. One set was to be passed on to the estate agents so they could show around potential buyers. Richard needed the other set to let in the house clearance company who were auctioning off the furniture. After another round of hugs and kisses, Ella and Henry got into the car. Adam pecked Linda's cheek.

"Look after them both," said Richard, gripping Adam's hand almost painfully hard.

Surely that goes without saying, thought Adam. He silently reproached himself. Within the space of ten months, Richard had lost a grandson and now his only child was moving hundreds of miles away. He had every right to be concerned. "I will."

Linda broke down and pressed her face into her husband's shoulder as the car pulled away. Ella's tears overflowed too at the sight. Doubts suddenly found their way into Adam's mind. *Are we doing the right thing? What if we're no happier in Cornwall than we are here?* Then the house disappeared from view and with it the questions. He exhaled as if a heavy weight had fallen from him.

"Well that's that," Ella said in a half-disbelieving tone. "We've actually done it. How do you feel?"

"I feel..." Adam sought for the right word – relieved? excited? yes, he was both of those things, but more than anything he felt... "lighter. How about you?"

"Right now I mostly feel guilty about my mum and dad." Ella glanced at Henry. He had headphones on and was staring into an iPad. "He seems OK."

"He'll be better than OK." As Adam said the words he was surprised to realise that he truly believed them. "We all will be. You'll see."

"I'm not sure the same can be said for my parents."

"They'll be fine too. We're moving to Cornwall not Australia. Once we're settled in, we'll invite them down. When they see Fenton House, they'll realise this is the best thing that could have happened." Adam's mood was so high that even the thought of Richard and Linda invading his cliff top sanctuary couldn't bring him down. He smiled at Ella. "Thank you."

"For what?"

"For saying yes. I love you."

"I love you too." A thickness came into Ella's voice as if she was fighting off more tears. "I do have one other feeling. I feel as if we've forgotten to bring something with us."

A sting of tears rose into Adam's eyes too. He took Ella's hand and held it tightly.

Once they escaped the congestion of London, the roads were relatively clear. Most of the traffic was travelling in the opposite direction. The end of the summer holidays was approaching. Many cars were packed with families returning home. Adam couldn't help but feel smug. No more over-before-you-know-it holidays for him. From now on life would be like one long holiday.

At the halfway point, Ella offered to take over the driving. Adam shook his head. He didn't want to stop unless they had to. It was late afternoon when they reached Helston. A narrow, sloping high-street wound its way up between an assortment of pubs, cafes, restaurants and little shops. At the top of the street, Adam parked up, got out and approached a door with formal black lettering edged in gold on it – 'Mabyn & Moon Personal Legal Services Est. 1975'. He pressed an intercom button and a woman's voice inquired, "Who is it?"

"Adam Piper to see Mr Mabyn."

There was a pause then, "He's on his way to you, Mr Piper."

The door opened and the solicitor loomed over Adam. "Good afternoon, Mr Piper. I trust you've had a pleasant journey." As usual, Mr Mabyn's manner was strictly business-like. "I'm to accompany you to Fenton House and instruct you on the use of the boiler, electrics and such."

Ella raised a hand in greeting. The solicitor responded with an unsmiling nod and stooped into his Mercedes. "As friendly as ever, I see," Ella said to Adam.

They followed Mr Mabyn out of the high-street. Minutes later they were passing the razor-wire fences of RNAS Culdrose. Adam glanced at Henry whose eyes were shut. "It's a shame he's asleep. He would have liked to see this."

"He'll have plenty more chances to," Ella smilingly reminded him.

The land opened out into rolling fields bleached by the long hot summer. Brilliantly blue glimpses of sea glimmered tantalisingly in the late August sun. Adam wound down his window. The air was crisper than the previous time they'd been there. He greedily drank it in and the tiredness of the journey dropped away. He had a vague feeling of the rest of the world receding, as if they were crossing into somewhere cut off like an island. He found himself smiling. How could he have doubted even for a second that they were doing the right thing?

He could feel his heart beating as they negotiated the narrow lane to Fenton House. He almost gasped when he saw the place. It was even more breath-taking than he remembered. Mr Mabyn opened the gates and they entered the avenue of sycamores, whose leaves seemed to whisper, *Welcome*. The garden was radiant with late-summer blooms. The stained glass window sparkled as if happy to see the house's new inhabitants.

Adam gently woke Henry and they got out of the car. "What do you think?" Adam asked excitedly.

Henry stared around himself. "Is this really all ours?" There was a look of dazed wonder in his eyes.

Adam laughed. "Yes, incredible isn't it?"

The heavy front door creaked as Mr Mabyn opened it.

Adam put an arm around Henry's shoulders as they followed the solicitor into the house. Henry gaped at the lofty ceilings, the grand staircase, the tapestries and paintings, the elaborately moulded plasterwork and arched doors. "You could fit our whole house into just this bit."

"*This* is our house now," said Adam.

"There's no mobile phone reception on this part of the peninsula," said Mr Mabyn. "There are two fixed-line phones in the house. One here." He pointed out a corded old phone in the hallway. "And another in what was Miss Trehearne's bedroom."

Mr Mabyn briskly made his way to the kitchen and opened a door concealed by a curtain at the back of the pantry. It led to a windowless bare-brick room. Chopped logs and kindling were stacked against one wall. The ceiling was a tangle of lead and copper pipes, many of which sprouted from a bulky rectangular boiler that looked as if it had been there since the house was built.

"The central heating runs off an oil-fired boiler," explained the solicitor, handing Adam a dog-eared instruction manual. "The oil tank is buried in the garden. I'll show you where. It's been filled recently and should supply your needs for several months. When it needs refilling, the cost will be yours to bear."

"How come they didn't build a basement for all this?" asked Ella.

"You would have to ask Walter Lewarne that question." There was no trace of humour in Mr Mabyn's response. Turning his attention to an ancient-looking fuse box, he pointed out the mains switch.

"Looks like it could do with a bit of updating," Adam said with understatement.

Mr Mabyn began to reel out the same line. "The cost of any repairs or improvements will be yours to–"

"Yes, we know," interrupted Ella. "If anything goes wrong we're up shit creek without a paddle."

The solicitor showed them the mains water stop-tap, then headed for the backdoor. His movements were verging on a jog, as if he was keen to spend as little time as possible in the house.

"I bet he gets invited to loads of dinner parties," Adam whispered to Ella.

"Shh, he'll hear you," she mouthed back, giving him a dig in the ribs for the sarcastic aside.

As they made their way around the side of the house, Mr Mabyn rambled on mechanically about the transfer of utility bills and other practicalities. Adam stopped and turned in amazement at a sound he hadn't heard in a long time. Henry was balancing along the low wall bordering the patio. Another little laugh escaped Henry's lips as he jumped to the lawn. Adam felt a swell of tears, not of grief but of joy. Smiling, Ella reached for his hand.

"If you'd please," Mr Mabyn hurried them along, "I have other business to attend to."

The oil tank was in a concrete pit accessed by a metal trapdoor. Nearby was a tap that operated a rusty sprinkler system. Mr Mabyn led them to a garage and a little cluster of adjoining outhouses that contained a plethora of tools, plant pots, composts, weed killers, fertilisers, insecticides, a lawn roller and a sit-on mower. "Do you wish to retain the gardener's services?"

"I'll be doing the gardening," said Ella.

Adam looked at her with raised eyebrows. "Are you sure? It's a hell of a big garden."

"I'll have plenty of time on my hands. If it gets too much, we can always hire some help to tide us over."

"And what about the cleaners?" inquired Mr Mabyn. "Miss Trehearne employs a local firm."

"I'll be doing the cleaning too," said Ella.

"In that case our business is concluded and I'll bid you good day." Mr Mabyn handed Adam the bunch of keys, turned on his heel and strode to his car.

CHAPTER 11

Adam and Ella watched Mr Mabyn drive out of the gates. Their gazes moved over the garden and house before landing on each other. Neither of them seemed to know quite what to say. Adam puffed his cheeks and broke the silence. "I suppose we'd better start unloading."

They each picked up a box from the trailer. As they carried them into the house, Henry asked, "Where's my bedroom?"

"Do you know I hadn't thought about that," said Adam. "Which bedrooms *are* we going to use?"

"Let's go and choose," said Ella.

Henry excitedly led the way upstairs, his eyes as bright as the stained glass windows. Adam and Ella found each other's hand again. "Wow, look at all these doors," exclaimed Henry. He ran to the nearest one. He took one look at the four-poster bed, the stuffed peacock and the animal paintings and said, "I don't want this room."

"I think this room would be good for us," Ella said to Adam.

"I preferred that other room. You know, the one where we..." Adam paused suggestively, "liked the view."

"Too many windows. It'll be cold in the winter. Besides, we've already discussed this. It's too far away from the bathroom and too close to..." Ella glanced upwards. She'd made it clear that she didn't want any of them to be sleeping under the observatory tower when the first winter storm swept in.

Henry checked out the neighbouring room, poked his head into the bathroom and moved on. The next room elicited another negative response. Unlike the deep reds and dark oak that dominated the rest of the house, the walls of the final room on that wing of the landing were sea blue and the furniture was made of pale plain wood. A leaded window overlooked the rear garden. There was a little stone fireplace flanked by a wardrobe and a wall-mounted long mirror. A painting of a rosy-cheeked sleeping baby hung above the single-bed's headboard. There was a plaque on the picture frame. Henry read the name etched into it, "Heloise."

"That was the name of a girl who once lived here," said Ella. "Perhaps this was her bedroom."

"Can it be my room?" asked Henry.

"Are you sure you want this room?" asked Adam. "It's the smallest one up here."

"That's why I like it." Henry pointed to the window. "Hey, look." A robin was perched on the window ledge, looking into the room.

"It's our little friend," said Ella. "We saw him last time we were here. Rozen – the lady we told you about – used to feed him."

"Can I feed him too?"

"We haven't got any bread. That's a point. We haven't got any food at all. I'd better go shopping."

They returned to the entrance hall. Henry peered into the shadows under the stairs. "The Lewarne Room," he read out loud. "What does Lewarne mean?"

A look passed between Adam and Ella. They'd told Henry nothing about Fenton House's strange history. All he knew was that they'd won a competition to live there. "A man called Walter Lewarne built this house," said Adam.

"I want you to stay out of there," said Ella.

"Why?" asked Henry. "What's in there?"

"Some valuable and very breakable antiques." Ella shepherded him out of the front door. Adam cocked an eyebrow at her. "You know how sensitive he is," she whispered. "Those paintings might upset him."

"And you know what little boys are like – telling him to stay out will only make him all the more curious to see what's in there."

Adam unhooked the trailer. Ella headed off in the car while Henry and he piled up bags and boxes in the entrance hall. After a few trips back and forth, Henry pulled a bored face. "Can I play in the garden?"

Adam hesitated to reply, thinking about the broad pond and towering cliffs. Rozen's words came back to him – *There's nowhere better in the world to be a child. The sea, the fresh air, the freedom...* Freedom. That was a big part of the magic. Possibly the biggest part. "OK, but be careful and don't leave the garden."

Nervousness prickled through Adam as he watched Henry run to the faux-ruined wall by the pond and clamber onto it. At the same time, it felt good to see him forgetting his fear. Keeping half-an-eye on Henry, Adam continued unloading. By the time Ella returned, the trailer was empty. "I picked up some bits and pieces from a little shop in Mullion," she said, taking the shopping into the kitchen. "The nearest supermarket is in Helston."

"Good. The further away the better."

Ella laughed. "I'll remember you said that when you're moaning about having to drive ten miles for that Columbian coffee you like."

He slid his arms around her waist. "Can you believe we're really here?"

"Ask me again in a few days." Ella wriggled free, approached the deep ceramic sink and turned on the cold tap. The pipes clanked and spluttered out yellowish water that cleared after a few seconds. She filled the electric kettle they'd brought with them and glanced around for somewhere to plug it in. "Huh, I was going to make us a cup of tea but..." She indicated a socket that had three round pin connectors instead of rectangular ones.

"Maybe there are some adaptors around here somewhere." Adam began rifling through drawers of dishcloths, tea towels, cutlery and kitchen utensils.

Ella opened a cupboard stacked with cups and saucers. "I wonder why Rozen left all this stuff behind."

"Her mum probably told her to."

Ella shot Adam a glance. "We agreed not to talk about that, especially not when Henry might hear."

"Sorry. I wasn't thinking. No adaptors but I found this." Adam held up a blackened whistling kettle.

Ella turned her attention to the old Rayburn. "Now all we need to do is work out how to use this thing."

Adam opened the oven's thick metal doors. One side of the stove's interior was piled with crumpled newspaper, kindling and logs. "It's already set. We just need to light it."

"I got these in case we wanted a fire." Ella produced a box of matches. She lit the newspaper. Crackling flames quickly took hold.

Henry came running into the kitchen. His face was flushed and sweaty. A bloody graze glistened on one of his elbows. Adam went cold at the sight. Suddenly, as if he'd stepped from a dream into a nightmare, he was back in the porch with Jacob and the blood. So much blood...

"What happened?" asked Ella.

"I fell over," Henry answered breathlessly.

She reached for his arm. "Let me see."

"It doesn't hurt. The robin came to see me. Can I have some bread for it?"

Ella cleaned the graze with a dishcloth. She opened a loaf and gave him a slice. "Don't feed it too much."

"Thanks, Mum." Henry exited the room as rapidly as he'd arrived.

"Slow down," she called after him. She shook her head with a bemused smile. "It's like someone flipped a fear on-fear off switch in his head." She turned to Adam and her smile faded at his tense face.

He sighed. "Will I ever be able to see blood without thinking about Jacob? Or think about Jacob without seeing blood?"

Ella stroked his arm.

They spent the next couple of hours putting their clothes in wardrobes and drawers and making up their beds. An evening chill crept in. Adam fired up the boiler. The bulky cast-iron radiators gurgled as hot water flowed through them. He set up his computer in the study and sat in the high-back leather chair behind the desk, resting his fingers tentatively on the keyboard. He noticed something digging into his thigh. He took Jacob's toy car out of his pocket and gently, almost reverently, placed it on the desk.

Ella chucked a pizza in the oven. They ate at rusty white furniture on the patio, bathed in lengthening shadows. Henry animatedly told them about the fish and frogs in the pond, the trees he'd climbed, the warren of burrows he'd discovered and how the robin had followed him everywhere. "I've given it a name. I—" He clammed up as if he'd said more than he meant to.

"What do you call it?" asked Ella.

"Just Robin."

Ella and Adam exchanged a glance. It was obvious Henry was lying. They didn't press the conversation further. It had been such a physically and emotionally exhausting day, but also a day full of promise and hope. They didn't want anything to spoil it.

After their meal, Ella took Henry upstairs for a bath. Adam stayed on the patio, drinking wine and watching the light fade on the sea. Ella poked her head out of a first-floor window and shouted for him. He tipsily made his way to Henry's bedroom. Henry was tucked up in bed, his eyelids already heavy with imminent sleep. Jacob's old grey stuffed bunny was propped on his pillow.

Adam bent to kiss his son's forehead. "Night, sweetheart. Sleep tight."

"Night, Dad. I love you."

"I love you too."

Ella switched off the light and they retreated from the room, leaving the door ajar and the hall light on. "Well that was easier than I expected," she murmured as they returned to the patio. "I thought he might be scared."

"It's all the running about. He's too tired to be scared. He seems better than he has done in months."

Ella pulled a *Let's wait and see* face. "What if he starts crying? We won't be able to hear him from down here."

"There's not much we can do about that tonight. If necessary, we can buy a baby monitor. Although I'm not sure what Henry would think of that."

Twilight was descending over the garden. A quarter-moon smiled through a veil of cloud. "I'll make a fire," said Adam, wrapping a blanket around Ella's shoulders.

He filled a wicker basket with kindling and logs from the boiler room. He arranged the wood on a bed of screwed up paper in the sitting room fireplace and put a match to it. Ella came through the French doors with the wine glasses. Her eyes gleamed orange-gold in the glow of the flames. The firelight picked out the soft contours of her face, the gentle curves of her breasts and hips. Adam took the glasses off her, set them down on the hearth and ran his hands up her body.

"Aren't you tired?" she murmured.

"Yes, but not too tired."

His lips found hers. His tongue parted them. He drew her down onto the bearskin rug. She shifted uneasily away from its curving yellowed teeth.

"It won't bite, but I might," teased Adam.

They undressed and moved against each other – not fast like the first time they'd made love in the house, but without urgency until they climaxed together. Ella rested her head on Adam's chest and they lay like sedated animals. He stared into the fire, his mind blissfully empty. He sat up suddenly, glancing around.

"What is it?" asked Ella.

"I need a pen."

"There's one in my handbag."

Adam found the pen, grabbed a scrap of paper and wrote *'The blade slid between her ribs. She fell onto the bed with a soft thump, blood blooming like a rose on her chest.'* He read the words aloud. "What do you think?"

"I like it, but I've said that plenty of times before and it hasn't stopped you from rewriting it."

Adam frowned at the words he'd written, then nodded as if he'd made up his mind. "This is the one."

Ella smiled cautiously. "Let's go to bed."

They gathered up their clothes and headed upstairs. They paused on the landing, listening for any sounds from Henry's room. Silence. They glanced at each other, hardly daring to hope.

Adam opened the balcony doors in their bedroom, letting in the moon and the murmur of breaking waves. Ella got into bed and massaged her shoulders. "I'm aching all over."

"You'd better get used to that feeling if you're going to do the housework and gardening."

"It'll do me good. I've spent too many years at a desk."

Adam slid under the duvet. Ella kissed him and switched off the lamp. He gazed around the moonlit room. His eyes came full circle to Ella. She was already asleep. A strong urge – almost a compulsion – came over him.

"Winifred Trehearne are you here?" he asked.

He'd only meant to whisper, but his voice seemed so loud that he glanced nervously at Ella. She didn't stir. He listened to the house. The only sound he heard was the creak of cooling wood. Chuckling under his breath, he closed his eyes and focused on the lulling murmur of the sea.

CHAPTER 12

Day Two

Adam awoke to the chatter of gulls. For the first time in months, he'd slept the night through without disturbance. He wondered if he'd been so tired that he simply hadn't heard Henry crying. Or was it possible that Henry had slept through too? He was tempted to wake Ella and find out if she'd heard anything, but she looked so peaceful he couldn't bring himself to. He got out of bed and went onto the balcony. The breeze was sighing in the sycamores. A pink glow was dividing the sea from the sky. He thought of the dreary view from the bedroom in Walthamstow and promised himself he would never take this one for granted. He wanted to watch the sunrise, but his mind wouldn't allow him to. It was whirring with words demanding to be let out. He put on his dressing gown, left the room and padded to Henry's door.

Henry was sleeping soundly. Adam hardly dared breathe for fear of disturbing him and spoiling the image.

He crept away. The house was cold, but not unpleasantly so. A sense of stillness hung over it as soft as the light trickling through the windows. He sat down at the study desk and made to turn on his computer, remembering as he did so that he couldn't plug it in. Until he got his hands on some adaptors he would have to go old school. He reached for a pen and a ream of printer paper and jotted down the sentence that had come to him last night. Others followed, slowly at first, but with gathering speed until he was writing in a fast scrawl. Usually he worked in a tightly controlled style, but this was almost a stream of consciousness. It was as if a dam had cracked inside him and all the words that had been held back were gushing out. He lost himself totally in the story, leaving behind all the grief and guilt of the past ten months.

He looked up with a start as Ella entered the room. She placed a steaming cup on the desk. "Sorry for interrupting. I thought you might need some caffeine."

"Thanks."

"You looked like you were really back in the groove."

"I was." Adam put down his pen and flexed aching fingers. He flipped back through the paper. He'd filled over twenty pages. Many of the words were semi-legible, sentences rose and fell like waves. "What time is it?"

"It's almost eight."

He shook his head in astonishment, unsure what to make of this see-sawing from one extreme to the other. "All this in two hours. I've never written so fast. If I keep going like this I'll have the first draft finished by the end of next week."

"There's no rush. Better to go slow and get it right. That's what you always say."

"Yeah, but I'd be crazy not to take full advantage of this while it lasts. I could dry up again."

"I'm sure that won't happen. It's just going to take a while to get your confidence back."

Adam took Ella's hand and feathered his thumb over it. "How do you always know what to say to me?"

She smiled. "Because I know you better than you know yourself."

Adam sipped his coffee, looking at her over the rim of the cup. Her eyes were clear and the surrounding skin was less dark. "You look as if you slept well."

"I woke a few times worrying about Henry. I looked in on him once but he was fast asleep."

"He was the same when I poked my head around his door before starting work. Do you think it means–"

"I don't know," broke in Ella.

It would take more than one night of unbroken sleep for her to allow herself to believe Henry had shaken off his night terrors. Just as it would take more than one wildly productive writing session for Adam to believe he'd truly broken through his block.

"What about you?" asked Ella. "How did you sleep? Any bad dreams?"

"Now that you mention it, no." Adam greeted the realisation with strangely mixed feelings. He despised the gut-wrenchingly lucid recurring dream in which he saw Jacob die over and over again. He usually faced sleep with dread because of it, but there were also times when he closed his eyes in the hope that it would come. No photograph could capture his son's face so perfectly.

Ella's face reflected Adam's uncertainty. "That's a good thing, isn't it?"

He gave her a smile and nodded. "Is Henry awake?"

"Yes, he's playing in his room. I'm going to take him up some breakfast."

"I'll do it. I need a break."

They went to the kitchen. A pan of porridge was bubbling on the Rayburn. Ella ladled some into a bowl and put it on a tray alongside a glass of orange juice. Adam took the tray upstairs. The morning sun glowed in the rear windows. Birds were chirping over the barely audible but ever-present sound of the sea. His smile vanished as he neared Henry's door. He stopped so abruptly that the juice slopped over the tray. Henry repeated the words that had halted Adam in his tracks.

"Come here, Jacob. Don't be scared. I won't hurt you."

As if afraid of what he might see, Adam tentatively opened the door. Henry was stooping by the open window with one hand stretched towards a robin on the threshold of the sill. As Adam entered, the robin fluttered away. Henry jerked around as if he'd been caught doing something naughty.

"Was that Robin the robin?" asked Adam.

"Yes." The quickness of Henry's reply gave away his lie.

"Sorry for frightening him off." Adam set the tray down on the bed. He watched his son gulp down the juice and set to work on the porridge. He stroked the soft curls at the back of Henry's head. "Are you alright?"

"Uh-huh. Can I go out in the garden?"

Adam nodded.

Henry handed back his empty bowl and bolted from the room. His footsteps echoed along the hallway and down the stairs. Adam sat for a while with a line between his eyebrows before following him. Ella was busy sorting through the kitchen cupboards, making space for the crockery they'd brought with them. She smiled at Adam. "Henry just came through here like a whirlwind. He said he's going to find his friend. I assume he means Robin."

Adam wondered whether he should tell Ella the robin's real name. He decided against it. He knew she would insist on talking to Henry about the robin. Henry had been so unhappy for so long. If it made him happy to call the robin Jacob, then why not let him do so without the awkwardness of having to explain himself? What harm could it possibly do beyond that which had already been done?

Adam took a bowl of porridge to the study. He sat staring at the toy car, his mind too full of Jacob for writing. Voices outside attracted his attention. Ella had thrown on some clothes and was chasing Henry around the lawn. She caught him and they collapsed in a laughing heap. The smile returned to Adam's face. He headed upstairs and set a bath running. After soaking away the aches of the previous day, he went in search of Ella and Henry. Ella was in the orangery, trimming dead fronds from a palm tree. A fine mist bloomed from the hose system that snaked across the richly black raised beds and around the terracotta pots.

"How about a walk into Treworder?" he suggested. "I'd like to introduce Henry to Rozen."

Ella pushed her lips out uncertainly. "There's so much to do in the house."

Adam caught the note of unease in her voice and guessed what it was about. He glanced around to ensure they were alone. "Don't worry, I'll speak to Rozen first and make sure she knows not to say anything to Henry about the house's *other* residents."

"OK. You lock up. I'll find Henry."

"He's going to find out sooner-or-later, Ella. Probably sooner. He starts school in a few days. Someone's bound to say something."

"I know and we'll talk to him before then. I just want him to settle in first."

Adam made his way around the ground floor locking doors and closing windows. It hardly felt necessary. The house was so hidden away. The only people who passed anywhere near it were hikers on the coastal path. Ella and Henry were waiting at the back gate. Henry was clutching a bunch of flowers. "I picked them for Miss Trehearne," he said.

"That's really thoughtful of you," said Adam, unlocking the gate. They descended through the tunnel of hedge and turned left onto the narrow cliff top path. The sun sparkled on the white tips of waves far below. Gulls soared gracefully on currents of air high above. Maybe half-a-mile offshore a fishing boat bobbed on gentle swells.

Henry reached for his mum's hand despite his newfound bravery. "It's a long way down."

"You walk between Mum and me," said Adam. "And remember to watch where you're putting your feet."

The well-worn path followed the contours of the cliffs, undulating like the sea. It curved around a corner sheltered by gnarled gorse, passing a semicircular sign bearing the oak leaf logo of The National Trust. "Satan's Saucepan," read Adam. "Sounds ominous."

They emerged from the gorse at the rim of a dizzyingly deep bowl-shaped indent several hundred metres in circumference. The steep sides of the bowl were carpeted in coarse grass and tangles of bracken. Its base was a jumble of boulders. Waves rolled through a towering rock arch, bubbling and hissing on the boulders.

"It looks like boiling water," said Henry.

The path curved around the landward rim of the bowl. At the far side, it swung inland through a small carpark. A lane snaked down past cottages huddled into the valley side and joined the road they'd entered Treworder by on their previous visit. Henry peered over the sea-wall at the deserted little sandy beach. There were a couple of dog walkers on the larger shingle beach to the other side of the rocky promontory. A few people were sauntering around between the art gallery, gift shop and fishmonger.

"It's a bit different to the last time we were here," remarked Adam.

"Thank god," said Ella.

"Can we go to the beach?" asked Henry.

"After we've seen Miss Trehearne," said Adam.

They strolled along the seafront. Henry eyed-up the fishing boats, obviously itching to go exploring. Adam uneasily recalled the crowd that had been gathered around the corner from The Smuggler's Inn. He half-expected to see a few desperate characters still loitering, but the street outside Boscarne Cottage was empty. At the whitewashed garden wall he said to Ella and Henry, "You wait here. I'll see if Rozen's in."

He knocked and, after a brief wait, Rozen opened the door. She was wearing what appeared to be the same turquoise dress. Her smile was in place, but her rouge and berry-red lipstick were absent, revealing a sallow complexion and thin lips. She touched her cheek as if conscious of this.

"Hello, Rozen. I thought you might like to meet my son. We can come back another time if this isn't convenient."

"No, no, Adam. Now is fine." Rozen gestured for them to come inside.

As Ella and Henry approached, Adam lowered his voice and said quickly, "We haven't told him about your mother yet. We'd appreciate it if–"

"I won't breathe a word," Rozen assured him. She turned her attention to Ella. "So lovely to see you again." A twinkle played in her eyes as she looked at Henry. "And you must be Henry. What a handsome boy. Just like your father."

Blushing, Henry held out the flowers. "These are for you."

"They're beautiful." Rozen reached for the bouquet, but hesitated. "Did you pick them from Fenton House's garden?"

"Yes."

Her smile held firm, but the twinkle flickered like a candle in a breeze. She pointed to the doorstep. "Just put them there."

Henry did as she said. They followed her through to the living room. The pug eyed them from the rug and yawned as if bored by the sight. "Come and say hello, Edgar," said Rozen. Edgar struggled upright and shuffled over.

Henry bent to stroke him. "He's cute."

"And extremely lazy," said Rozen. "Would you like something to drink?"

"No thanks," said Adam. "We just wanted to say how grateful we are for what you've done for us."

"Thank you for choosing us to live in your house," said Henry.

"It's not my house anymore, darling boy," pointed out Rozen. "And I didn't choose you. Your dad is a very special man. It's because of him you're living in Fenton House. Do you like it there?"

"Yes."

"We all like it there," said Ella.

Rozen directed an ear-to-ear smile at her. "So it's won you over too."

Ella returned the smile. "I admit I wasn't convinced this was the right move for us, but now we're here, I feel... Well, I feel at home."

"I can't tell you how glad I am to hear that." Rozen held out a thick-knuckled hand. Ella took it. Rozen gave a gentle squeeze and let go.

"If you ever need anything – help around the house or whatever – just give us a call," said Adam.

"Thank you, Adam, I will."

There was a moment of silence. As if he'd done his duty, Edgar trundled back to the rug and flopped down.

"We'll leave you both in peace," said Ella.

Rozen accompanied them to the front door. As they stepped outside, she touched Adam on the arm. "May I speak with you alone for a moment?"

"Of course." Turning to Ella, Adam added, "I'll catch you up."

Ella gave him a quizzical glance, but followed Henry out of the garden.

Rozen smiled after Henry. "Perfect. Absolutely perfect," she said, seemingly as much to herself as to Adam.

"You were right, Rozen. This place really seems to be working its magic on him. He's already like a different boy. We thought he might be scared of such a big house, but he's not at all."

"And he has no reason to be. Mother will look after him. She always wanted a boy of her own."

Adam made no reply. What was there to say to that?

Rozen pointed to the flowers. "I can't accept those."

"I assumed it was OK to take flowers from the garden."

"It is, but I've taken everything that was mine from there. The rest is for someone else."

"I understand."

"Do you?"

"Well, to be honest, no. I'm not sure I ever will either, but if that's how you want it to be, then that's how it'll be." Adam retrieved the flowers. "Bye for now, Rozen."

"Bye Adam. Say hello to Mother for me."

"I... I will do."

Ella and Henry were turning from view by The Smuggler's Inn. Adam hurried to catch them up, pausing to put the flowers in a bin. He didn't want to have to explain to Henry why Rozen had returned them. He caught up with Ella and Henry in front of the pub. "What was that about?" asked Ella.

"I'll tell you later." Adam thumbed at the pub. "Fancy a bit of lunch?"

Beyond a little beer-garden a door with a porthole led to a cosy bar – beamed ceiling, stone fireplace, half-a-dozen small round tables, barstools lined up at the counter. The walls were crowded with photos of Treworder's fishing fleet and the men who operated it. Loops of rope hung from the beams as if on stormy nights the room rocked like a boat at sea. The bar was empty except for a man enjoying a quiet pint and a newspaper at one of the tables. A tonsure of greying hair encircled the man's shiny bald head. Black-rimmed glasses were balanced above a neatly trimmed goatee. He looked up from his paper and his gaze lingered on the newcomers as they bought drinks and took them to a table. Adam recalled seeing a group of similar scholarly-looking characters outside the pub on the day of the interview, but couldn't be sure if the man had been amongst them. In London he would have ignored him, but here it seemed like the right thing to smile and nod hello. The man took it as an invitation to stand and approach them.

"Am I right in thinking that you're the new residents of Fenton House?" he inquired in a softly spoken Scottish accent.

"That's us," said Adam.

"Welcome to Treworder. I'm Doug Blackwood."

Doug extended his hand and Adam shook it. "Adam Piper. This is my wife Ella and my son Henry."

"Nice to meet you. I'm relatively new to these parts myself. I moved down from Edinburgh in June."

"It's a beautiful place to retire to," said Ella.

A smile pulled at Doug's goatee. "Do I really look that old?"

"Oh I'm sorry, I just assumed–"

Doug wafted away her apology. "I came here to work." He laughed as Ella's eyebrows lifted. "You look surprised. Perhaps you're wondering what sort of work an old boffin like me would find in these parts. Do you mind if I join you?"

"Not at all," said Adam.

Doug fetched his pint and drew up a stool. "I'm an author."

"Oh really," said Ella. "Adam's an author too."

"I suppose that's one of the few benefits of being a writer," said Adam. "You can work wherever you want."

"Actually that's not true for me," said Doug. "Unlike you, I don't write fiction. I have to go where my subject demands. In this case that means spending a few months in Treworder. Which is no great hardship."

A faintly cautious note entered Adam's voice. "How do you know I write fiction?"

"Well, you see, I have a professional interest in Fenton House. I'm researching a book on local history and I'm particularly interested in–"

Doug broke off as six black-clad figures piled noisily into the room. There were four men in an array of long leather jackets, tight trousers and thick-soled boots. One was wearing a top hat from below which flowed raven black hair. A black cane with a silver knob was balanced on his shoulder. His arm was wrapped around a willowy twenty-something girl in a laced-up bodice, short skirt and torn crimson fishnets. She had a pretty, white-powdered face. Thick black mascara highlighted her big blue eyes. Her short feathery hair was dyed the same colour as her tights. Adam thought back to the redhead dancing on the beach. Was this her? She was holding hands with a busty older woman in a velvet cape and a skirt short enough to reveal lacy stocking-tops. Laughing shrilly, the women shoved the top-hatted man. He stumbled against Adam.

"Careful," said Adam as his beer slopped over the brim of his glass.

The man stared at him briefly over the top of red-lensed sunglasses before turning to approach the bar counter.

The barman greeted him with a shake of his head. "I'm not having you lot bothering my customers again. You're barred."

"Oh what the fuck?" said the redhead.

"Watch your language. There's a child present. Now please leave."

The redhead flicked the barman the finger and twirled out of the door. Her companions followed, laughing. The top-hatted man rapped the floor with his cane, theatrically removed his hat and bowed to the room.

"Sorry about that," the barman said to Adam. "Do you need a towel?"

"No thanks. I'm fine."

"They've been hanging around for weeks," said Doug. "Treworder attracts certain types. It's–"

"Excuse me a moment, Doug," broke in Adam. With a meaningful glance at Henry, Adam said to Ella, "Will you order the food? I'll have the crab salad."

Ella said to Henry, "Come on, let's go to the bar."

Adam gestured for Doug to follow him outside. The goths were on the beach now. The women were skipping along the shoreline, arm in arm. "I was going to say it's an uneasy relationship," said Doug. "People like them bring money into this area, but at the same time they make a lot of locals uncomfortable." He pointed towards Satan's Saucepan. "In the past eight years five people have jumped to their deaths from those cliffs. That's sort of what my book is about. Not suicide per se, but the way in which areas exploit their folklore for economic gain, and in doing so sometimes end up writing new tragic pages into their histories."

"My son knows nothing about the history of Fenton House and I want to keep it that way for now."

"Yes, I'd guessed that. I had no intention of talking about the haunting in front of him. I just wondered if it would be OK for me to have a look around the house and perhaps take a few photos."

"I'm sorry, but that's not going to happen."

"I'd be very discreet. We could do it when your son was out of the house."

"It's not that. There are certain clauses in the contract we signed for Fenton House. One being that we don't allow anyone like you in to investigate it."

Doug's bushy eyebrows lifted. "Why do you think Miss Trehearne is so keen to keep people like me out of the house?"

"You'd have to ask her. I really don't have any answers for you. As far as I'm concerned, Fenton House is just… Well, just a house, nothing more."

"So you don't believe in paranormal phenomena?"

"No. What about yourself?"

"That's not an easy question to answer. I've seen things in my life that can't be logically or scientifically explained, but I've not seen anything that definitively confirms the existence of the supernatural. Look, I know I can't go inside Fenton House, but surely that doesn't mean you can't talk to me about it." Doug wrote his address and telephone number on a beermat and gave it to Adam. "It would be a great help if you could give me your general impressions of the house."

"I already have done."

Adam went back inside. Doug followed, but didn't sit down. He tucked his newspaper under his arm and swilled back the remainder of his pint. "Thanks for the chat." With a glance at Adam, he added, "Hopefully we'll have a chance to chat again soon."

"I'm sure we will," said Ella. "It's a small place."

CHAPTER 13

After lunch they headed to the beach. Henry ran down to the sea's edge and skimmed stones across its rippling surface. The goths were nowhere to be seen. Adam and Ella watched Henry from the back of the beach. Adam recounted his conversation with Doug, leaving out the part about the suicides. Then he told her about his parting words with Rozen.

A shadow touched Adam's expression. "In some ways I wish I was like Rozen. It must be comforting to believe there's something after all this. At the same time I feel sorry for her. It's as if she's been so focused on death that she forgot to live her life. Can you imagine what it must have been like for her all alone in that house?"

Ella hugged her arms across herself as if she felt a sudden chill. "I'd rather not."

Henry splashed along the waterline and clambered up some rocks to a wave-smoothed platform. Adam ran to climb after him and they sat with their legs dangling over the water, watching tiny darting fish. Adam looked into Henry's enraptured eyes and felt the shadow lift. He tousled his son's hair. "We'd better get back to the house. There's a lot to do."

They were sweating and out of breath by the time they completed the climb to Satan's Saucepan. Adam stared into its shadowy depths, wondering what it would be like to jump from the cliffs. Would the fall be fatal? If not, the sea would soon finish the job. Where would the currents take you? Would they carry you out to nameless depths never to be seen again? Or would they wash you up in some nearby cove? He hoped it was the former. He didn't want Ella or Henry stumbling across the corpse of a jumper.

As they entered the garden, Henry raced off ahead. Ella's gaze swept over the imposing house and the flower-starred garden. She gave a shake of her head. "I keep getting this feeling, like if I pinch myself I might wake up."

Adam playfully nipped the flesh of her hip. She dodged out of reach, laughing. He caught hold of her hand and they headed for the backdoor. Ella busied herself in the kitchen. Adam stoked the Rayburn and asked, "Do you mind if I get back to my writing?"

She shook her head, smiling at his eagerness. He hurried to the study. The urge to write was on him powerfully again. The world outside his head melted away as he set to work at the same feverish pace. Scenes flew by like things half-glimpsed from the corners of his eyes. A sudden loud crash burst in on his thoughts. His stomach like a knot of ice, he sprang to his feet and raced from the room. He almost bumped into Henry in the hallway.

"Are you alright?" Adam asked anxiously.

Henry nodded, looking sheepishly from under his eyebrows. Ella appeared from the direction of the kitchen. "What was that noise?"

"I knocked something over," Henry admitted.

"Where?"

"In The Lewarne Room."

Ella frowned. "I told you not to go in there."

Henry lowered his eyes. "Sorry, Mum."

Adam put a hand on Henry's shoulder. "Come on, let's inspect the damage." His tone was more relieved than angry.

One of the shutters in The Lewarne Room had been opened. A streak of sunlight intensified the reds of the tiles and wallpaper. Adam's gaze lingered briefly on the muscular man burying the dagger in the infant's throat, before moving to a fallen serpentine pedestal. The candelabra and Trehearne family photo lay next to it. He dropped to his haunches. The pedestal appeared to be undamaged, but one of the floor tiles was chipped.

"This thing weighs a tonne," he grunted, lifting the pedestal upright. "How did you manage to knock it over?"

"I was running and I... I dunno I just..." Henry trailed off guiltily.

"What were you even doing in here?" asked Ella.

Henry shrugged. "Just playing."

"No real harm done," said Adam. "But we're going to make a rule. From now on, no running in the house. OK?"

"OK, Dad."

As Adam picked up the candelabra and photo, he noticed a dent in one of the wooden wall panels. "Did the pedestal fall against the wall?"

"Yes."

Adam ran his fingers over the dent, wondering if he could get away with sanding and re-staining the wood. The panel shifted ever so slightly at his touch and a breath of cool air tickled his hand. He hovered his palm along the edge of the panel. "There's a draught coming through here." He placed both hands on the panel and pushed. It moved a few millimetres inwards. "I think this thing is hinged."

"Maybe it's a door to a secret passageway," Henry said excitedly.

Adam pushed harder. There was a squeak of wood rubbing wood, followed by a whisper of escaping air. A slender gap appeared at one edge of the panel, then the movement stopped. He leaned all his weight against it, but it was almost as if someone was pushing back against him. "I think there's something blocking it."

"I'll help," said Henry, shoving at the panel. It gave way with a sudden creak and both he and Adam toppled through it. They landed on their hands and knees, stirring up puffs of dust from a flagstone floor.

Adam blinked and coughed.

"It *is* a secret passageway," exclaimed Henry.

They were in a narrow brick passageway that ran parallel to the room. A metre-and-a-half or so above them was a ceiling of rough plaster and cobwebby beams. To the left wooden stairs rose steeply into darkness. Adam shivered as a current of dank air caressed his right cheek.

Henry jumped to his feet. "Let's go exploring."

Adam caught hold of him, fearing that his newfound courage might cause him to race off into the darkness.

Ella peered into the passageway. "What was blocking the panel?"

"I think it was just stiff. Who knows how long it's been since it was last opened. We need matches."

Ella hurried away to fetch them. Adam lit the candlesticks and held out the candelabra. The flames swayed in the draught. Their flicker revealed another set of stairs nine or ten metres to the right. These were stone and went downwards. A brass handle set in a small rectangle of wood at head height on the opposite wall caught his eye. He pulled the handle and the board came loose, revealing a pinprick of light. He pressed an eye against it and found that he was looking through a peephole into the study. He turned and discovered a peephole looking into The Lewarne Room too. He ducked back into the room and searched for the hole. It was camouflaged by the fleur de lis pattern.

"I wonder how many more peepholes there are?" Ella said uneasily.

"Let's find out."

"I'll stay here if you don't mind. I'd prefer it if Henry did too."

"Oh Mum," whined Henry. "Please let me go with Dad."

"This is an old house, Henry. It could be dangerous."

"Your mum's right," agreed Adam. "I'll have a look around and if it's safe you can come with me next time."

Scrunching his face in annoyance, Henry reluctantly ducked out of the passageway. Adam glanced from side to side, wondering which way to go. He decided to explore the lower passageway first and work his way upwards. Cobwebs brushed his face and shrivelled away from the candles. He found a peephole to the library. Next to it was a wooden panel inset with a brass button. He pressed the button and there was the ping of a spring being released. A bookshelf swivelled inwards, then began to close of its own accord. He realised that he'd probably broken The Lewarne Room panel's mechanism by forcing it open.

He descended the stairs to a corridor with granite block walls. His footsteps fell dead on mossy flagstones. Water seeped between the joins in the right-hand wall, drawing rusty orange streaks. It pooled in rivulets that appeared to drain away through the base of the opposite wall. He touched a finger to the water, then dabbed it to his tongue. It had a strong taste of iron. He recalled hearing the faint sound of running water when they first looked around the house. He'd thought there might be a leaky pipe, but this suggested the cause was something more substantial – perhaps some sort of natural underground water source.

The corridor passed beneath what Adam judged to be the entrance hall. A second stone stairway led upwards to another passageway. More removable rectangles of wood let him look through peepholes into the dining, drawing and sitting rooms. He located another button – this one in a plaster panel, its external side concealed by a tapestry in the sitting room. Two thirds of the way along the passageway was a flight of wooden stairs that mirrored those by The Lewarne Room. They creaked as he climbed to a passageway that branched off at a right-angle. Long black velvet curtains covered opposing sections of wall. He drew them back, unveiling two-way mirrors that spied on the sheet-draped furniture in the front bedrooms to the right of the landing. The mirrors were fitted with latch locks that allowed them to swing open on hinges.

A third staircase ascended to the attic. A passageway so low that Adam was forced to stoop led both ways along the eaves. He went left first. There were no peepholes to the attic rooms. The passageway turned left at the outer right-hand wall. Yet another flight of stairs returned him to the first-floor, passing below the underside of the attic stairway.

The passageway dead-ended at a blackened brick wall. Adam guessed it to be the chimney stack for the bedroom where Ella and he had made love on their first visit to the house. To its left was the concave interior of one of the stone pillars that flanked the fireplace. A peephole provided a direct line of sight to the four-poster bed. There was no button, but when he pushed the pillar it slid on hidden runners smoothly away from the wall. The peephole was secreted in a cherub's eye. A handle allowed him to pull the pillar back into place. He returned to the attic passageway and headed in the opposite direction.

At roughly three-quarters of the way along the eaves, a passageway branched off to the right. He carried straight on past it and came to another right turn. Stairs descended to the first-floor where a curtained mirror gave a view of and access to Henry's bedroom. He could guess now where the other passageway led.

Something on the floor caught his eye. He bent and picked up a book with a hardback red cover and a frayed spine. 'This book belongs to Heloise Trehearne. Aged twelve.' was written in black on the first page. The 'twelve' had been crossed out and replaced with 'thirteen'. He turned the page and found himself looking at colourful detailed drawings of flowers. 'Chamomile at Kynance Cove' was written underneath a flower with a yellow face and delicate white petals. A fuzzy-golden flower was identified as 'Carline Thistle at Coverack'. There were more flowers on the following pages, along with birds – including several robins – rabbits, foxes, badgers, fish, insects, shells, rocks and gems, all from various places on the Lizard Peninsula.

Tucking the book under his arm, Adam returned to the unexplored passageway. As he suspected, yet another stairway descended to the first-floor. The mirrors in his and Ella's bedroom and the neighbouring room served the same purpose as all the others.

A final set of stairs brought him back to The Lewarne Room.

"You were gone a long time," Ella said as he emerged through the secret panel.

"Mum was getting worried," added Henry.

"The passageways are a bit of a maze, but they don't seem to be dangerous," Adam told them. "There's water leaking through a wall underneath the house."

"That sounds as if it would be expensive to fix," said Ella.

"It probably would be, but I don't think we need worry about it. Whatever the cause is, I'd say it's been going on for a long time."

"Where do the passageways go?" asked Henry.

"They form a circuit of the house. There are secret panels and peepholes everywhere."

"Cool!"

"What about in our bedroom?" asked Ella.

"The mirrors in the bedrooms are two-way."

"What kind of person puts in two-way mirrors? Walter Lewarne must have been a real *pervert*." Ella mouthed the final word silently. She wrinkled her nose. "I don't like the thought of someone being able to creep around and spy on us. Mind you, I don't suppose anyone but us and Rozen know about the passageways. That's if she even knows."

"There is one other person who knows about them," said Adam. He handed the book to Ella. "I found that near Henry's room."

"Heloise Trehearne," read Ella.

"She's the girl on my bedroom wall," said Henry. "Who is she?"

"I told you, she used to live here," said Adam. "She's Rozen's niece." He didn't elaborate. The last thing he wanted was to spook Henry with stories of missing people. He set about closing the damaged panel as best he could.

"You said you'd show me the passageways," protested Henry.

"I will, but not now."

"When then?"

"Maybe tomorrow if you're a good boy. I want you to promise that in the meantime you won't go in them alone."

Henry sighed sulkily. "I promise."

"Good lad. Now go and play outside."

As Henry left the room, Ella said, "He'll go in those passageways the first chance he gets."

"I know. That's why I'm going to block this panel shut from the other side."

"Maybe it's not only him we have to worry about." A wry twist appeared on Ella's lips. "Perhaps you weren't so far off the mark when you joked about hidden cameras. I've got this picture in my mind of Rozen sneaking around in there."

"Come off it, she's almost eighty."

"Just because she's old doesn't mean she doesn't have urges. She might be into all sorts of kinky stuff. For all we know, she could have been watching us last night."

"Oh please," laughed Adam.

Ella jabbed him in the ribs. "This isn't funny."

He pulled her into an embrace. "Actually it's quite revealing. I didn't know you had such a sordid imagination. Tell the truth, you secretly like the idea of being watched."

She pushed him away, smiling herself now. "You wish."

"Look, if it'll make you feel any better, I'll go into the village tomorrow and talk to Rozen about the passageways."

Ella frowned as if she wasn't comfortable with the thought of Adam talking to Rozen alone.

"Don't worry, if she tries anything, I think I'll be able to fend her off," teased Adam.

He dodged away laughing again as Ella aimed another jab at him.

CHAPTER 14

Adam searched through the oil-smelling gloom of the outhouses until he found what he was looking for – a couple of lengths of wood and a saw. In a little crook at the back of an outhouse, he came across a perfect circular nest of twigs. Fragments of fragile turquoise eggshells were scattered over the floor below. He carefully pocketed them.

He returned to The Lewarne Room, measured the wood to the width of the passageway and cut it to length. He wedged the lengths between the closed panel and the opposite wall. Then he left the passageway via the library. He tried to open The Lewarne Room panel. It wouldn't budge. Next he pushed wardrobes in front of the mirrors in Henry's and his and Ella's bedrooms.

He went in search of Ella and found her sipping wine on the patio while perusing Heloise's book. "These drawings are beautiful," she said. "Heloise clearly loved The Lizard."

Adam poured himself a glass of wine. "You say that as though she's dead. For all we know she's alive and well and has a family of her own."

"I hope you're right." Ella ran a finger down the inside of the book's spine. "I think a page has been torn out here."

She handed the book to Adam. There was a rough edge along the spine. The following page was blank. Adam held it up to the fading sunlight. A faint impression of letters was visible on the page. "Have you got a pencil?"

Ella went into the house and returned with a pencil. Adam lightly shaded it over the blank page, revealing a neat, unbroken trail of words. 'Dear Aunt Rozen,' he read out. 'Please will you help me? I don't know what to do. Two Frenchmen came to the house today to see Daddy. I could tell that he was scared of them. He took them into The Lewarne Room. I know that I should not have done so but I went into the secret passageways and spied on them.

They spoke to Daddy in French. I do not remember much French but they said argent lots of times. Argent means money in English. Daddy kept nodding and saying je suis desole which means I am sorry. After the men left he called Mummy and me into the room and told us that he has decided to sell the house. I started crying. I told him that I don't want to leave Fenton House. I want to stay here with Grandma. He said Grandma is just bones in a grave. But you and I know that is not true. Why doesn't he believe us? Please don't let him sell the house and take me away from my Grandma and my flowers and robins. I love you and know you will help me.'

There was a moment of silence as Adam finished reading. "Wow," said Ella, puffing her cheeks. "I'm not sure whether that puts my mind at rest or freaks me out even more."

"At least we know for certain that there was nothing strange about the disappearance of George and his family."

"Do we? George needed to sell this house to pay his debts, but that obviously didn't happen or we wouldn't be sitting here now."

"This house had been in his family a long time. Perhaps he couldn't bring himself to sell it."

"Hmm." Ella sipped her wine, her forehead creased with uncertainty. "George doesn't strike me as the sentimental type."

"Me neither, but who knows, perhaps he held onto the house for Heloise."

"Then where is she?" wondered Ella. "Why hasn't she come back here to claim this place for her own?"

Adam shrugged. "Maybe she will one day."

"Which would leave us up the proverbial creek without a paddle."

Adam smiled. "Quite possibly, but you know what? Right now I couldn't care less about the future. I'm just happy to be here with you and Henry. If Heloise was to reappear a week or ten years from now, then we'll deal with it." He reached for Ella's hand. "As long as we're together we can deal with anything."

Smiling back, Ella leant in to kiss Adam. They remained like that for a long moment, their cheeks flushed by the setting sun. When they drew apart, Ella glanced at the book. "Are you going to show that to Rozen?"

"Do you think I should?"

"She might want it as a keepsake."

Adam shook his head. "She won't take anything else from the house, remember?"

"Yes, but this is different."

Adam made a doubtful noise.

"What about the police?" said Ella. "They might be interested to see it."

Adam frowned. "I don't see how it could be of any help to them. Besides, I wouldn't do anything like that without speaking to Mr Mabyn first."

Henry came sprinting across the lawn to the patio. "I'm starving," he said. "What's for tea?"

Adam and Ella both smiled. Henry had shown no enthusiasm for food since Jacob's death. It was good to see that his appetite had returned.

They ate their evening meal on the patio, watching swifts dart and swoop overhead. All Henry talked about was the passageways. He was full of excited speculation about what they'd been used for. In his mind, secret passageways were associated with smugglers, pirates and hidden treasure.

"This house was built just before the First World War," Adam pointed out. "Hundreds of years after there were any pirates in these parts."

"I think we should save the rest of this conversation for the morning," put in Ella.

"Aww," said Henry.

"Mum knows best," said Adam. Getting Henry over-excited before bedtime was a sure way to bring on his night terrors.

They stayed on the patio until Henry was half-asleep in his chair. Adam carried him upstairs. "You're getting too big for this," he puffed as he lowered Henry into bed. Henry sleepily changed into his pyjamas and Adam tucked the duvet around him.

Adam kissed his cheek. "Sleep tight. I love you."

"I love you too, Dad. And I love this house. I never want to leave here."

"Me neither." Adam remembered about the eggshells. He gave them to Henry and told him about the nest. "I wonder if it belongs to your friend."

"I'll go see if he's there in the morning."

"Don't touch the nest," cautioned Adam. "Robins will abandon a nest if they think it's been discovered. I learnt that from *my* dad."

Henry put the speckled shell fragments on his bedside table and curled up with the stuffed bunny. Adam headed downstairs. Ella was washing up in the kitchen. "He's gone straight off to sleep," he told her.

"He's not bothered by the passageways then?"

"Are you kidding? He thinks they're the best thing ever."

"Where are you going?" asked Ella as Adam opened the backdoor.

"For a walk."

Ella looked at him uneasily. "Don't go far."

Adam smiled. "Stop worrying. There's nothing to be afraid of."

Returning his smile, Ella nodded as if to say, *I know*.

Adam strolled around the garden like a king surveying his little kingdom. He stood for a while watching moonlight glitter on the sea, then he headed round to the front of the house. Bats flitted between the ghostly elms. His footsteps slowed as he caught a sound – a throaty moan. Stepping from the gravel driveway to the grass, he slunk to the gates and peeked around a gatepost. A black van was parked in the lane. The moan came again, drawing his eyes to two shadowy figures on the ground by the van. By the pale light of the moon, he made out a woman's even paler face. It was the redheaded goth. She was straddling the long-haired man, rocking back and forth, her skirt hitched high.

"Faith," the man breathed huskily, running his hands up over her hips. "Faith."

Was that the redhead's name? Adam wondered whether he should tell the couple to get off his property. Or should he just sneak away and leave them to it? He did neither. As the redhead's movements grew more urgent, a throb of arousal gathered in his groin. Her breathing took on a staccato rhythm. She tossed her head back as if in worship of the moon. Finally she slumped against her lover. She lay on him for a few breaths, then stood up and smoothed her skirt down. She flicked a glance at the gates. Adam quickly drew back behind the gatepost, his heart racing. There was the sound of the van's doors opening and closing. The engine started up. Without switching on its headlights, the van reversed along the lane.

Adam returned to the house, his footsteps urgent. Ella was still drinking wine on the patio. In the soft light trickling through the French doors, she looked as if she'd barely aged a day since they first met.

"What's that look on your face for?" she asked.

In reply, Adam bent to mash his lips against hers. He dropped to his knees, pulling her legs apart and kissing her inner thighs. His fingers sought out the buttons of her shorts. His head was reeling. He felt drunk with arousal. Shooting a glance at Henry's bedroom window, Ella said, "What if he sees us?"

"He's fast asleep."

Adam started to pull Ella's shorts down, but she pushed his hands away. "Let's go inside."

She rose and headed for the French doors. He caught up with her in front of the fireplace, snaking his arms around her midriff. "You don't get away that easily."

She glanced up at an oil painting of a centaur whose eyes camouflaged a peephole. She pressed back against Adam, shuddering as he slid a hand inside her shorts. Her gaze strayed to the painting again. Heaving a sigh, she drew away from Adam.

"What's the matter?" he asked.

"I'm sorry, I'm just not feeling it."

"It's the peephole, isn't it? I saw you looking at it."

Ella nodded. "It makes me feel like I'm being watched."

"The only people in this house are you, me and Henry." Adam smiled mischievously. "Oh and Winifred, but I don't think ghosts need peepholes to see through walls."

"How many fucking times do I have to tell you not to joke about that?" snapped Ella, batting Adam's hands away as he reached for her again.

"Oh come on, Ella, don't be so uptight."

"I'm going to bed," came her terse reply. Without looking to see if Adam was following, she turned and left the room.

He bit his lips in frustration. He knew the desire tingling through his veins wouldn't allow him to sleep. He needed an outlet for it.

He took his glass and a bottle of wine to the study, picked up his pen and poured everything out onto the pages. When he was done, his hand was warm with sweat but he felt cold inside. His gaze came to rest on the Diecast car. Suddenly Rozen's request to say hello to her mother didn't seem quite so absurd.

"Hello Jacob," he said, gently touching the car. His hand rested there for a moment, then he rose and went upstairs.

He looked in on Henry and watched his peaceful, sleeping face for a minute before heading to bed. Ella had fallen asleep with the light on. He felt a twinge of guilt for teasing her about Winifred. She stirred as he got into bed. "I'm sorry," he murmured, kissing her hair.

Snuggling up to him, she said, "Forget it. Turn off the light."

CHAPTER 15

Day Three

Something was tapping Adam's shoulder. His eyelids parted reluctantly. He found himself squinting up at Henry. The cold grey light filtering through the curtains seemed unreasonably bright, causing his brain to throb against his skull. He glanced at Ella's side of the bed. It was empty. "What time is it?"

Henry shrugged. "Can we explore the passageways now, Dad? Please can we?"

Adam winced at Henry's wheedling tone. "I want to hear what Rozen has to say about them first."

"But you said you'd show me them this morning."

"No I didn't."

"Yes you–"

"Enough with the backchat or you can forget about exploring the passageways," Adam cut in more sharply than he'd meant to.

Screwing his face up sullenly, Henry trudged from the room. A pang of remorse passed through Adam. His hangover wasn't Henry's fault. He rose and opened the curtains. The sky was overcast and misted by drizzle. He went into the bathroom, swallowed two paracetamol and took a bath, then dressed and descended to the kitchen. A soothing heat flowed from the Rayburn. He boiled the kettle and made a strong coffee. Ella appeared from the garden, her hands dirty with soil. "I was wondering when you'd surface," she said. "How are you feeling?"

"Like I drank too much wine."

"What's wrong with Henry? I saw him sulking in the garden just now."

"I was a bit sharp with him. He was pestering me about the passageways. I'll apologise to him when I get back from Rozen's."

"I'll be interested to hear what she has to say. Not just about the passageways, but about that too." Ella pointed at Heloise's book. "And I'm telling you this, Adam, if I don't like her answers, we're packing up and leaving. Agreed?"

Even after only a few days, it tightened Adam up inside to think of life without the silence and space of the house or the sight and smell of the sea. "I honestly don't think there's anything sinister to it."

"Agreed?" persisted Ella. "Or would you rather I start packing right now?"

Adam sighed. "Agreed."

He put Heloise's book in a bag, gave Ella a peck on the cheek and headed out the backdoor. As he made his way along the coastal path, a salty breeze cleared away the clouds and his headache. By the time he reached Boscarne Cottage, he was smiling at the thought of the previous night. His sex drive had been in hibernation for the best part of a year. Was there any surprise that it had woken up ravenously hungry?

Rozen answered the door in her usual turquoise dress. Adam wondered if she had a wardrobe full of identical dresses. Smiling, she wordlessly motioned him inside. The living room was sleepily warm. A log crackled on a bed of coals. Edgar lay so still on the hearth rug that he might have been stuffed with cotton-wool. Rozen insisted on pouring Adam a cup of tea before settling down in her armchair. "I'd like to think you dropped by for the pleasure of my company," she said. "But I can see you've got something on your mind."

"Why didn't you tell us about the secret passageways?" Adam asked, watching closely for Rozen's reaction.

She showed no surprise. "So you've found them. May I ask how?" Her smile broadened as Adam told her. "It sounds like someone wanted you to find them."

"Henry's clumsy. So is Jacob. They're always–" Adam's voice died.

His eyes grew distant. They returned to the room as Rozen asked, "Are you alright?"

Adam heaved a sigh. "Even after all these months, I still sometimes use Jacob's name as if he was still alive."

Rozen offered a nod of sympathetic understanding. "Mother's been dead for almost thirty years and I do the same."

"Yes, but for you it's different."

"Is it? Just because I could speak to Mother didn't take away the pain of knowing she's dead."

"So what does take away that pain?"

"Let's not dwell on such sad questions. You asked another question which I haven't yet answered." Rozen's eyes twinkled with delight. "Well my answer is – where would have been the fun in telling you about the passageways?"

Adam managed a smile although his headache was threatening a comeback. Such an answer was unlikely to satisfy Ella. "Ella's having second thoughts about the house. I was hoping you'd tell me something that would put her mind at ease."

"I could tell you that Mother asked me not to reveal the existence of the passageways, but I'm not sure that would help."

"No, I don't think it would. How did you discover the passageways?"

"Quite by accident. Much like Henry. I was seven-years-old. I was playing in the library one day, climbing on the shelves, pretending they were cliffs. I used to love nothing better than making believe I was an explorer searching for hidden treasure."

"Henry's the same way."

"All little children are, if given the space to let their imagination run free. Anyway, all of a sudden a bookshelf pivoted on its axis to reveal the passageways. I'd accidentally touched the release mechanism. I went a few steps into the passageway. I was too scared to go any further. Suddenly there was a click and I found myself in total darkness. The shelf had shut behind me. I was terrified, frozen to the spot. I started screaming. I don't know how long I was trapped in there for. It seemed like hours. Then the shelf opened and I was flinging myself into Mother's arms. When I calmed down, she made me promise not to go back into the passageways. She too had found them as a child, but hadn't explored them. She said she was claustrophobic. It wasn't until after she died that I found out the truth. There's something in the passageways."

"What? Ghosts?"

"No. The passageways have a power all of their own. Mother sensed it herself as a child. Some children are susceptible, or perhaps it would be more accurate to say, open to its influence. Others aren't. I was one of those others. I kept my promise until lure of the unknown became too great. Then I returned to the passageways armed with a torch and a ball of string. This time, I wedged the shelf open and tied the string to it. I fed the string out as I explored the passageways. I soon realised there was no need for it. The passageways run in a circle that takes in every floor of the house and brings you back to where you started."

"I know. I went all the way round."

"And how did you feel?"

"I felt curious as to why they were built."

Rozen nodded as if she'd expected that answer. "All I can tell you is what was handed down to me by word of mouth from Mother, who in turn had heard the stories from her own mother. Walter Lewarne was reputed to be something of a recluse, but as is usually the case the truth was more complicated. For the most part he preferred his own company, but when the mood took him he threw lavish parties – masquerade balls where the high-society of London drank endless champagne and danced to an orchestra until the sun came up. Locals weren't invited. Nor were local servants employed to tend to the guests. Somehow a rumour started that drinking wasn't the only vice indulged in at the parties." Rozen's eyes gleamed like grey gems. "It was said that in the small hours of the night guests danced in the moonlight naked except for their masks."

Adam thought about Faith's moonlit face, her eyes and mouth wide with pleasure. He became conscious of Rozen looking at him intently and resisted an urge to blink away from her gaze. "So Ella was right. She thought Walter might have been a bit of a…" *pervert* was the word Ella had used, but that didn't seem appropriate, "libertine."

"I'm merely telling you what I know. You may draw your own conclusions. As you can imagine, in a small community like this the rumours caused quite a scandal. Perhaps because of that, over the years, Walter came down into the village less and less. Even so, the rumours persisted. There was talk of strange characters coming and going from Fenton House and a light was often seen burning in the observatory tower all night long."

"What sort of characters?"

"I couldn't say. But it was said by those who saw Walter at the time that his face had grown haggard and his once black hair had turned grey." Rozen rested back in her armchair sipping tea to indicate she'd finished her story.

"Is there anything else you haven't told us about Fenton House?"

Rozen smiled coyly. "Let me ask you something, Adam? Why did you come to Treworder?"

"You know why. To make a fresh start."

"That's part of it, but I don't believe it's the whole reason. I believe you're searching for something that was stolen from you."

"And what's that?"

"The same things the world steals from most of us long before childhood ends – mystery, wonder. You want to believe there's more to the world than your eyes can see."

Want to believe. Those words made Adam think of Jacob's funeral. He wanted to believe what the vicar had said was true – that there was a light beyond life – but when he thought about death all he saw was darkness. A sigh swelled his chest. "Doesn't everyone want to believe that?"

"No, I don't think they do. There are those who spend their entire life afraid of anything beyond their understanding. My brother was one such person. He would rather have destroyed himself with gambling than accept the possibility that this world is only a passageway to something else."

The mention of George reminded Adam of the other thing he wanted to speak to Rozen about. He took out Heloise's book. It was obvious from way Rozen's mouth dropped open that she recognised it. "Where did you find that?" she asked, her voice hushed as if it was a sacred artefact.

Adam told her, handing over the book. She trailed her fingers tenderly down its cover. "I gave this to Heloise on her twelfth birthday. I never expected to see it again."

"I thought you might like to see her drawings. They're really quite beautiful."

"I taught Heloise to draw, but she soon proved to be a far more talented artist than me."

As Rozen turned the pages, her smile took on a sad quality that made Adam reluctant to mention what he'd found in the back of the book. He knew though that Ella would follow through on her threat if she didn't get the answers she wanted. "There's a page torn out. Heloise wrote you a letter."

Rozen found the missing page. The sadness in her smile deepened as she read the shaded-in words. When her eyes lifted to Adam they were filmed over with tears. "It's as I always suspected. George's past finally caught up with him."

"So you didn't know about the letter?"

"Heloise never gave it to me. I imagine that she couldn't bear to worry me with it. She was the sweetest little girl you could ever hope to meet. I don't have much money, but I would have done anything in my power to help her." Rozen's gaze returned to the illustrations as she continued, "She used to come to visit me most days. We would sit for hours chatting about the things she'd seen on the peninsula. And she would bring me pressed flowers, shells, fragments of serpentine. I've still got some of them."

Setting aside the book, Rozen stood and approached a sideboard. She took a metal tin from a drawer and opened it. Inside was an assortment of objects that could be found on the peninsula's beaches and cliff tops. As Adam pored over the tin's contents, Rozen said, "Heloise was fascinated by what things are made of. I had another pug back then. Victor. One time I found her poking around inside his mouth. When I asked what she was doing, she said she was looking for what made his bark. We used to talk about Fenton House too. Heloise started to see Mother not long after moving here. Mother would come to her at night and they would talk. They became very close. Heloise grew to love Mother just as much as I did. It was Mother who showed Heloise the passageways. Heloise used to hide from George in them when he was in one of his drunken rages. George loved to drink Champagne. That was another of his vices."

Falling silent, Rozen sat misted by memories for a moment. Regaining her bright-eyed smile, she passed the book back to Adam.

"Ella thinks I should give it to the police," he said.

"What good could possibly come of that?"

"That's what I said to her."

"I would prefer not to reopen old wounds, but you must do as you see fit."

Adam looked uncertainly at the book. Another question sprang to mind. "Why do you think George didn't sell the house?"

Rozen spread her hands. "Another mystery. I know this. Heloise loved Fenton House. Perhaps he held onto it for her, but she never came back for it. Don't worry, Adam, the house is yours. Nothing will change that now, unless you break the conditions of the contract."

Adam rose. "Thank you, Rozen. I think what you've told me will really help put Ella's mind at rest."

"It was my pleasure. I always enjoy our conversations." Rozen walked him to the front door. "Will you do something for me, Adam?"

He hesitated to reply.

She laughed softly. "Don't worry. I'm not going to ask for another kiss. When you get back to the house look in all the mirrors. Look as closely as you can. And next time we speak, tell me what you saw."

CHAPTER 16

As Adam climbed the steep valley side, he thought about Rozen's request. He hadn't looked in the mirror much since Jacob's death. He didn't like what his reflection revealed – features marred by grief and guilt. As he entered the garden, a tiny red-breasted shape fluttered to the path. He smiled at it. "Hello."

The robin flapped a few metres towards the house and landed again, swivelling its head to eye him beadily.

"What is it? Do you want me to follow you?"

As if in reply, the robin opened its black beak and trilled at Adam. He stepped towards the bird and it fluttered away.

"Where are you leading me?" he laughed. "Do you want feeding? Is that it?"

The robin landed on a peak of the orangery's glass roof. Ella was kneeling on the terracotta tiles inside the open door, pressing earth into a plant pot. She looked up at Adam, wiping sweat from her forehead with the back of her hand.

"What a clever little thing you are," said Adam.

"Who me?"

"No, the robin. It led me to you."

Ella glanced at the bird. Her gaze returned to Adam. "So what did Rozen have to say?"

"Apparently her mother didn't want her to tell us about the passageways."

"Why?"

"She didn't say. Basically, it was more of the same supernatural claptrap. I think she just enjoys being mysterious. You were right about Walter

Lewarne." Adam recounted Rozen's story about Walter's wild parties and the ensuing fall-out.

Ella shook her head. "That's what too much money does to you. It makes you think you can behave however you want."

"Since when did you become such a prude?"

"I'm not, but when you start perving on people through two-way mirrors I think it's time to stop and take a good hard look at yourself."

Adam chuckled. "I think you're probably right."

Ella glanced at Heloise's book. "And I see you were right about Rozen not wanting the book. What did she say about it?"

"She says Heloise never gave her the letter."

"And you believe her?"

"I don't see any reason not to. She was genuinely upset when she read the letter."

"Either that or she's a good actor."

"Why would she lie?"

"I don't necessarily think she is lying. I just think she's being economical with the truth."

Adam nodded agreement. "Exactly. Like I said, she gets a kick out of being mysterious. Rozen's not crazy or dangerous. I'll tell you what she is – she's a sad, lonely old woman looking for something to liven up her last few–"

He fell silent as the robin broke into a high-pitched *seee-seee, seee-seee.* "It sounds frightened," said Ella, looking up at it curiously. "Maybe there's a bird of prey nearby."

Adam's eyes searched the sky. There was nothing to be seen, not even a gull. The robin continued its urgent warbling cry. "I think it's hungry," he said. "I'll get it some–" He broke off as the bird took flight and fluttered in rapid circles towards the lawn.

"What's it doing now?" wondered Ella, stepping outside.

"Let's find out."

They followed the robin along the side of the house. It landed on the windowsill of The Lewarne Room. Its *seee-seee* grew even more insistent.

Adam frowned. "Where's Henry?"

"He was over by the pond a while ago."

Adam looked towards the pond. "He's not there now. Henry! Henry!" he shouted and received no reply. He glanced at Ella. They both looked at the robin again, then at the window. "You don't think he's…"

"Yes, I think that's exactly where he is," said Ella, hastening towards the front of the house.

Adam knew his hunch was right when he saw that the door to The Lewarne Room was open. The secret panel was open too.

"I thought you wedged it shut," said Ella.

"I did." Adam poked his head into the passageway. The wooden braces lay dislodged on the flagstones. There was no sign of them having been bent or broken. Pursing his lips in puzzlement, he straightened to fetch matches from the kitchen. Upon returning, he lit both candelabra and passed one to Ella.

Ella went left, Adam went right, each of them calling for Henry. Shadows played like overexcited children as Adam hurried through the passageways. He found himself imagining what Walter might have seen through the mirrors – naked bodies contorting as they murmured dark secrets of desire. He shook off the images. The passageways had a power alright, but it had nothing to do with the supernatural.

He quickened his pace as an orange glow flickered on the walls at the top of the final flight of stairs. He frowned disappointedly when Ella stepped into view and shook her head at him. He replied with a shake of his own head. They briefly split up again to search the uppermost passageway. Henry was nowhere to be found.

"If he's not in the passageways, where the hell is he?" wondered Ella, worry ratcheting her voice up a notch.

"I'll check out the attic," said Adam. "You search the bedrooms."

They exited the passageways via one of the latched mirrors. Adam worked his way through the gloomy, stuffy attic rooms. No Henry. "If you're hiding up here, Henry, you'd better come out right away or you're going to be in big trouble," he warned.

Silence.

He returned to the first-floor. Ella threw her arms wide in exasperation. "He's nowhere."

They hurried downstairs and searched the ground floor in vain. "I'm starting to get really worried," said Ella.

"Let's just stay calm," Adam replied, although his stomach was churning. "We haven't properly searched the garden yet."

Ella's gaze darted past him as the kitchen door opened. "Henry," she exclaimed, relief and anger blending in her voice. "Where have you been?"

Henry's freckly face was a picture of innocence. There were cobwebs in his hair. "I was playing outside."

Adam brushed the cobwebs from Henry's hair and displayed the evidence to him. "Where did these come from?"

"I don't know."

"There's no point lying, Henry. We know you've been in the passageways. How did you force open the panel?"

Realising the game was up, Henry gave his parents a look of wide-eyed appeal. "I didn't force it. I just put my hand on it and it opened."

"You shouldn't have been anywhere near that panel," reprimanded Ella. "You promised, remember?"

Henry nodded, lowering his eyes contritely. "I only went a short distance into the passageways." His voice dropped as if he was admitting something shameful. "Then a noise scared me and I ran outside."

"What noise?"

"The bell."

"What bell? I didn't hear a bell." Adam looked at Ella. "Did you?"

"No."

"It was really loud," persisted Henry.

"Where was it coming from?" asked Ella.

"I don't know."

"It was probably the grandfather clock," said Adam. "But whatever it was, it doesn't change the fact that you broke your promise. I want you to go to your room and stay there."

Henry pushed his bottom lip out. "Aww, for how long?"

"Until I say you can come out."

Henry looked pleadingly at Ella, but she folded her arms. He turned and sullenly stamped up the stairs.

A smile played over Adam's lips. "I know I shouldn't be, but I'm sort of happy he's being naughty. I feel like I've got my mischievous little boy back."

"Just so long as he doesn't make a habit of breaking his promises."

"He won't. I'll give him a little time to think about what he's done, then go up and have a word with him." Adam glanced towards the shuttered window. The robin was gone. "What about that robin? Do you think it was really trying to tell us Henry was in the passageways?"

"Who knows? Robins are clever birds." Ella eyed the secret panel curiously. "What I'd like to know is how Henry got that open."

"This is an old house. There's bound to be movement in the walls as they heat up and cool down. That's most likely why the braces came loose."

"And what about the bell? It must have come from inside the house otherwise we'd have heard it."

"Like I said, it was probably just the clock."

Ella made a doubtful noise.

"What does that mean?" asked Adam. He chuckled in realisation. "Oh come on, Ella, don't tell me you're starting to believe Rozen's ghost stories? We've already been through this. Rozen's a lonely old woman. I'm not entirely convinced that even she believes all the nonsense she comes out with."

"Oh she believes it alright."

"Does she though? What if that's why we're here? Maybe she needs us to make it real for her. Well I for one choose not to play that game. And as for this," Adam motioned to the secret panel, "there was no harm done."

"This time. Forget the supernatural crap, you said it yourself, Adam, old houses can be dangerous places."

"There won't be a next time. I'll nail the panel shut."

Ella wrinkled her forehead, accepting Adam's answers but clearly not satisfied by them. "Where are you going?" he asked as she turned to head upstairs.

"To see Henry. I don't want him cooped up in his room."

"We need to punish him, Ella."

She gave Adam a sad sidelong look. "He's made so much progress in the past few days. Are you willing to put that at risk?"

Adam thought about it briefly, then sighed and shook his head. Ella was right. Henry had been through more than any child should ever have to. So what if he'd broken his promise? The most important thing was that he didn't get sucked back down into his grief. That was where the real danger lurked.

CHAPTER 17

Adam fetched a hammer and nails from the outhouses. As he was returning to the house, Henry came pelting out of the front door. Adam called to him. He wanted to tell Henry how much he loved him, let him know he'd only been angry because he was worried. Henry put his head down and sprinted off in the opposite direction. Adam decided against going after him. Henry was probably still sulking. They would talk later when he'd calmed down.

Adam nailed the lengths of wood across the panel from the inside and exited via the library again. The nails protruded into The Lewarne Room. He bent them down with the hammer. Ella entered the room.

"How was he?" asked Adam.

"Fine as soon as he realised he wasn't grounded. I'm going shopping in Helston." Ella kissed Adam on the cheek. "I shouldn't be too long."

He waved her off and returned the hammer to the outhouses. He caught sight of something that made him frown. The nest had been dislodged from its crook and was upside down on the floor. A robin lay motionless beside it. There was no visible sign of injury, but when he picked the bird up its head flopped brokenly backwards. A cat must have come in through the open door and killed it, he reasoned. It wouldn't have been difficult for a cat to reach the nest which had been built perilously close to the floor. Another thought occurred to him – Henry knew where the nest was. Could he have killed–

Adam cut the thought off, disgusted at himself for allowing it to enter his mind. Henry would never do something like this! He would be devastated when he found out that Jacob was dead. *Jacob.* The name brought a lump to Adam's throat. He stared uncertainly at the dead bird. Was it really necessary for Henry to be told? If indeed this was Jacob, surely it was better for him not to know. There would doubtless be some tears when the robin's absence was noticed, but that would be nothing compared to the potentially disastrous effect of knowing it had been killed.

Adam picked up the nest and balanced it back in its crook. He reached for a spade and left the outhouse, pausing at the door to make sure Henry wasn't nearby. He dug a hole behind the outhouse and laid the robin in it. Tears pushed up behind his eyes as his mind flashed back to watching Jacob's coffin disappear behind the curtains at the crematorium. He quickly filled in the hole.

He went in search of Henry and found him throwing stones into the pond. "What are you up to?" asked Adam.

"Nothing." There was a moody downturn to Henry's lips.

"Do you want to go for a walk?"

"Not really."

"Come on. I'll buy you an ice cream."

Henry puffed his cheeks, but followed his dad to the back gate. They turned right towards Lizard Point. Henry went in front with Adam following closely. The mellow afternoon sun warmed their faces. The coconut scent of gorse blossom perfumed the air. Crickets chirped. Gulls skimmed and dived. Cormorants spread their bat-like wings. The path wound around shoulders of grass and bracken, descending into coves where ribbons of sand glistened and little thatched cottages hid from the world. A *pfft* sound like pressure escaping a steam valve attracted Adam's attention. He tapped Henry on the shoulder and pointed as the shiny black back of a killer whale emerged from the waves. Henry's sullenness slid away and his eyes widened delightedly. They passed a lifeboat station with a limpet-speckled boat ramp. Rusty funicular tracks climbed the cliffs behind it. The landscape took on a more exposed aspect. Endless ranks of waves seemed to be trying to pound the cliffs into submission. Tanker ships lined the horizon.

A lighthouse within a fortress-like compound of white walls loomed over the path.

Henry pointed to a large black funnel flaring from a corner of the compound. "What's that?"

"A fog horn."

They came to a windswept carpark with a gift shop and a café. The shop was cluttered with lamps, lighthouses and other decorative objects carved from serpentine. Beyond the café, the path sloped steeply down to the sea, passing a few dilapidated boat sheds and ending at a small crescent of pebbly sand. Sharp rocks jutted menacingly out of the sea. And then... Then there was nothing but blue, seemingly extending into infinity.

"This is pretty much where England ends," said Adam.

They watched waves being shredded by the rocks. Adam breathed in the air and held onto it for as long as possible.

They climbed to the café and sat on a terrace overlooking the minefield of rocks. Adam watched Henry wolf down his food, marvelling at what a difference the past few days had made. Henry's cheeks were fuller and had a healthy glow. His head was no longer hunched down as if cringing away from something. Sitting there between the blue of the sea and the gold of the sun, it was almost possible to imagine the past ten months had been nothing but a terrible nightmare.

When they got back to the house, Ella was unpacking shopping bags in the kitchen. Henry told her about the killer whale. She smiled at his excitement, and Adam smiled because he knew Henry's happiness would do more to put her at ease than anything he could say.

Adam headed for the patio and kicked off his trainers. Ella poured them each a glass of wine. "You look like you enjoyed yourself too," she said.

He smiled. "I feel like I really connected with Henry for the first time in months."

Ella was silent. Glancing at her, Adam was surprised to see a cleft between her eyebrows. "What's wrong?" he asked.

"I know it's stupid, but I keep getting this feeling like something bad is going to happen and spoil everything."

The lifeless robin returned to Adam's mind. He'd been uncertain whether to tell Ella about the grim discovery, but now he decided against it. He curled his fingers into hers, saying softly, "No it's not stupid. Bad things happen. We know that better than anybody. But right now life is good. Let's just enjoy this moment while it lasts."

"I wish I could, Adam, but my mind's so full of things that need doing. Did you call Mr Mabyn about the book?"

"No."

"Then I'd better do it."

Ella went back into the house. She returned after a few minutes. "Rozen had already called him," she told Adam. "He said he'll call round for it sometime in the next day or two. Where is it by the way?"

"I think I left it in the kitchen."

"Well it's not there now."

"It'll be around here somewhere. Maybe Henry moved it." Adam reached for Ella's hand again. "Relax, it'll turn up."

Ella sipped her wine. The cleft between her eyebrows faded away – but not entirely.

After putting Henry to bed, Adam and Ella made love with the bedroom windows wide open and the sea murmuring accompaniment to their moans. Afterwards, Adam went to the bathroom. He remembered Rozen's request – *When you get back to the house look in all the mirrors. Look as closely as you can.*

He peered into the mirror. A face that was sliding into middle age stared back – the jawline wasn't as defined as it had once been, the crow's feet were more pronounced, the grey hairs more numerous. Yet it seemed to him that some of the marks of grief had been soothed away by the past few days. He moved closer so that he could see the tiny broken veins, clogged pores and other blemishes unnoticeable at a glance. He looked closer still, until everything blurred and a vague ache gathered in the centre of his forehead. It was like with his writing – sometimes the closer you got, the less you saw. He found himself picturing Rozen staring back at him from the other side of the mirror.

Smiling at the absurd image, he made his way around the bedrooms looking in the mirrors – no apparitions or strange lights, just his own world-weary face. Ella was snoring softly by the time he got into bed. He curled up against her and swiftly followed her down into sleep.

CHAPTER 18

Day Four

Adam awoke to the dawn chorus, his mind buzzing with ideas. Padding from the room, he headed for the study and set to work. The sun climbed over the cliffs, changing the sky from pink to blue. A movement outside the window pulled him out of his interior world. Henry was walking barefooted in his pyjamas from the direction of the outhouses. It was still early for him to be up. Adam wondered uneasily whether Henry was searching for the robin.

He opened the window and called, "What are you up to?"

Henry gave a little start. "Nothing."

"Couldn't you sleep?"

Henry shrugged. "I slept OK."

There was something evasive in his manner, but Adam thought it best not to press the matter. He didn't want to prompt an awkward conversation about the robin's whereabouts. "Come inside and I'll make breakfast."

Adam went to the kitchen and set about firing up the Rayburn. Henry came in and sat at the table. Adam boiled them two eggs each and made toast. As they ate, Ella appeared in her dressing gown and kissed them both on the head. "It's going to be a nice day," she said, peering out of the window. "Shall we go to the beach?"

"I should work," said Adam.

"You've got all the time in the world to work, Adam. This is the last weekend of the summer holidays."

Ella made a picnic and they packed it into the car along with towels, suntan lotion, a football and a kite. Ella had been told that the nearby beach of Poldhu Cove was worth a visit. They stopped in the pretty little village of Mullion to pick up a newspaper, a windbreak and a cheap plastic bucket and spade. Poldhu Cove was a half-moon of golden sand strewn with grey pebbles and hemmed in by tumbledown cliffs. A path wound through grassy dunes past a beach-hut café. At the centre of the beach a shallow stream rushed down to the sea. Surfers and body boarders rode the foaming surf that dashed itself against the beach and encroaching rocks.

Adam set up the windbreak while Ella laid out the towels and Henry made sandcastles. They sunbathed, chatted and read. Adam and Henry had a kick-about and flew the kite. After that they all raced to the sea. Ella and Henry splashed and chased each other with a look on their faces that almost made Adam believe anything was possible.

They returned to Fenton House sandy and sunburned. After showering, they headed off in different directions – Henry to the garden, Adam to the study, Ella to the orangery. After a while, Ella poked her head around the study door. "How's it going?"

"Great. I've never written this fast before."

Adam gathered up the wad of paper that had accumulated on his desk. "Wow," said Ella. "You really have been going some. Can I read it?"

"Sure, but don't expect too much."

Within seconds of Ella leaving the study, Adam was lost in his writing again. It had used to take him a while to get going after being disturbed, but now it was as easy as diving into a swimming pool. The pen flowed across the pages with little or no effort. He almost felt as if he could close his eyes and it would continue of its own accordance. A cramp in his fingers eventually forced him to take a break. He rose to make himself a cup of tea. The sound of music drew him to the sitting room. Ella was on the sofa with the manuscript.

She cocked a curious eye at him.

"What are you giving me that look for?" he asked. "Don't you like it?"

"No, it's good. In fact, I think it's some of your best work. It's just so different to what you normally write."

"Is it?"

"You know it is. You wrote it."

"Yeah but I wrote it so fast I can't actually remember all that much about it. What's so different?"

Ella puffed her cheeks as if uncertain where to begin. Henry came running breathlessly into the room, his trainers squelching, his clothes sodden.

"I thought we agreed no running in the house," said Adam. "You're soaked."

"I fell in the pond."

Ella's voice rose in alarm. "That pond's deep. You could have drowned."

"I can swim."

"Not if reeds get tangled around your ankles. I'm beginning to think we shouldn't let you in the garden on your own."

Henry's face crumpled in dismay. "You can't do that."

"We can do whatever we want where your safety is concerned," put in Adam.

"It's not fair!" Henry hurled the words at them, whirled around and stormed into the hallway.

"Get back here," Ella yelled.

She started to rise, but Adam said, "I'll speak to him."

He followed Henry upstairs. Henry was removing his shorts in his bedroom. "I'm getting changed," he snapped. "Don't look."

Adam turned away, smiling at his son's sudden self-consciousness.

"You can turn around now," said Henry. He'd put on dry clothes and was smoothing down his hair in the mirror.

A vague awareness came to Adam that something was different about the room. "We worry about you."

"I'm not a baby. I'm nearly twelve."

Adam stroked his son's hair. "You'll always be our baby."

Henry shied away from him.

"Don't be like that, Henry. We love you. That's all it is."

"No it's not."

Adam frowned at Henry's resentful tone. Was Henry referring to his brother's death? What else could he mean? "You're right," Adam said gently. "But is it any wonder we're over-protective after everything we've been through?"

"Every time I try to have fun you go mad at me."

"Are you still sulking about yesterday?"

Henry's silence was as good as a yes.

"Why do you think we came to live here?" continued Adam. "We want you to enjoy yourself. Yesterday you broke a promise. Today I'm going to give you a second chance to prove you can keep a promise. If you promise to do as you're told from now on, you can carry on playing outside on your own."

Adam waited for a response, but Henry refused to look at him. He sighed. "If you don't want to be treated like a baby, Henry, then don't act like one. I'll be downstairs if you want to talk." He turned to leave but hesitated, realising what was different – the wardrobe had been shifted away from the mirror. "Did you move the wardrobe?"

"No."

"Don't lie, Henry. You've been trying to get into the passageways again, haven't you?"

"No."

"And what about Heloise's book? I suppose you didn't move that either?"

Henry's face scrunched up indignantly. "I haven't touched that stupid book."

Holding in his own annoyance, Adam pushed the wardrobe back in front of the mirror. "Don't move it again. Do you hear me?"

Henry huffed his breath, but nodded.

Adam returned downstairs. "What did he have to say for himself?" asked Ella.

"Not much."

"This behaviour isn't like him."

"I think I know what's upsetting him." Adam told Ella about the dead robin.

She pursed her lips sadly. "Poor little thing. Henry was probably searching for it by the pond. I'd better go talk to him."

"I don't think you should. He doesn't need to know it's dead."

Ella wrinkled her face as if unsure she agreed. They sat silently drinking their wine. Adam looked at the view without seeing it. He couldn't get Henry's angry face out of his mind. He knew only too well that anger could be another expression of grief. It had taken him months to climb out of his own pit of self-recrimination. He didn't want Henry to fall into that same trap.

By the time they all sat around the kitchen table for their evening meal, Henry seemed to have gotten over his mood. "I'm sorry," he said. "I promise to do as I'm told."

Ella smiled. "We don't want to spoil your fun, sweetheart. We only want what's best for you."

"Shall we retire to the sitting room?" Adam asked, putting on a posh accent that brought a smile to Henry's face too.

It was a cooler evening. Adam lit the fire and they played board games on the rug as the garden fell into darkness. When Henry started yawning, Ella took him upstairs.

Adam stretched out, sighing contentedly. Despite the run-in with Henry, it had been a good day. Ella reappeared. "What's up?" Adam asked when he saw her frown.

"I can't find Henry's stuffed bunny anywhere."

Adam's stomach gave a twist. He still thought of the bunny as belonging to Jacob. As a toddler, Jacob hadn't been able to sleep without it. Even as an eleven-year-old, he'd kept it in bed with him every night. Since Jacob's death, Henry had grown similarly attached to it. "I'll have a look around."

"There's no need. Henry doesn't seem bothered."

Adam's eyebrows lifted. "I suppose that's a good thing. Our little boy's growing up."

He opened his arms to Ella. She snuggled in, saying a touch sadly, "Sometimes I wish I could just press pause on him."

"Me too. I was watching you and Henry in the sea today and I wanted to grab that moment and never let go." Adam stretched out a hand and closed it on air. Sighing, he let his hand fall to the rug. Ella picked it up and kissed his fingers one by one.

CHAPTER 19

Adam and Ella lay talking about the day and watching the flames leap up the chimney. When the fire had burned down to embers, they went to bed. As Adam drifted off, his thoughts kept returning to the stuffed bunny. Jacob had used to chew on its floppy ears. One time not long after the accident, Adam had lain with the bunny clutched to his nose and the smell had been so strong it was almost like he was holding his son. Tears threatened to find their way between his eyelids, but before they could do so the memory dissolved into sleep.

He fell into a dream in which Henry was walking in his pyjamas on the lawn. Adam opened the window and called to him, "What are you up to?"

"Nothing," replied Henry.

Couldn't you sleep? Adam opened his mouth to ask, but something caught his attention. Henry's fingers were dirty as if he'd been digging in dirt.

Adam awoke with a start as if something had disturbed him. For an instant he seemed to see a shadow-wreathed figure at the end of bed. He jerked upright, his hand darting for the lamp. The light revealed an empty space. Had Henry been standing there? No. The figure had been taller than Henry.

He stiffened at a sound – a faint creak as of footsteps on floorboards. "Ella," he hissed.

"What is it?" she mumbled sleepily.

"I think I heard someone moving around."

Ella sat up, suddenly wide-awake. "I don't hear anything," she whispered.

Adam got out of bed, cracked open the door and cocked his ear at the silence. Nothing disturbed it. He glanced towards Henry's door. It was slightly ajar as usual.

"Where are you going?" Ella asked as he tiptoed from the room.

"To check on Henry."

Adam crept along the hallway and made out the dim shape of Henry in bed. He returned to Ella. "He's fast asleep."

"So what did you hear?" she wondered worriedly.

"I'm going to have a look downstairs."

Ella reached for the rotary dial phone at the bedside. "If you're not back in five minutes, I'm calling the police."

Adam padded to the stairs, pausing halfway down them to listen – silence except for the beating of his own heart. The beating intensified to a pounding when he saw the orange glow bleeding from under the sitting room door. He smiled at his jumpiness. It was only the fire. He opened the door and took a shocked step backwards. It wasn't the fire! Four candles were lit on the floor. Beside each candle stood a figure dressed all in black – two women and two men. Adam recognised three of the figures. Side on to him, with her back to the fireplace, was Faith. Facing her from a couple of metres away was the busty older woman. Faith's lover and another man formed two more sides of a square. The bearskin rug had been rolled up and moved to one side.

For a second there was stunned silence. Then the older woman shouted, "Run!"

All four figures fled towards the open French doors. Adam automatically gave chase. Faith tripped over the rug and fell to her knees. He grabbed her arm. She sprang to her feet, attempting to yank herself free. They reeled around like drunken dancers, then she broke away and darted into the hallway. Adam regained his balance and went after her. She ran into The Lewarne Room, slamming the door in his face. He thrust it back open. The room was as black as the night. He flicked on the light, expecting to find Faith halfway out of the window. She was nowhere to be seen.

"My wife's phoning the police," he said breathlessly.

No reply.

He edged forwards, craning to peer around the armchair and sofa. His eyebrows bunched together. No Faith. He stooped to peer up the chimney. Nothing but soot and cobwebs. He spun around at the sound of footfalls. Ella appeared at the door, clutching the stuffed peacock as if ready to bludgeon someone with it. "I heard a shout."

"A girl ran in here."

"What girl?"

"The one from the pub. The redhead."

"Well where the hell is she then?"

Adam spread his hands as if to say, *You tell me.*

Ella looked around herself nervously. "She can't have just disappeared."

"Maybe she snuck out behind me."

"I'd have seen her."

"Well she didn't go out the window." Adam motioned to the closed shutters. "Which leaves only one other possibility."

Both of their gazes moved to the secret panel. There were empty holes where the nails had protruded through the surrounding wood. The panel swung inwards at a gentle push. Once again, the lengths of wood lay on the flagstones beyond.

"You're not going in there after her, are you?" asked Ella.

"No way. I'll leave that to the police."

"I've already phoned them. They're on their way here. Do you think she knew about the passageways?"

"Even if she did, how did she get the panel open?"

They silently pondered these questions, then Ella said, "One of us will have to open the gates for the police."

"We'll all go." Adam grabbed a poker from the fireplace and they hurried upstairs to Henry's room.

Ella tapped Henry awake. "Nothing to worry about, darling," she told him as he blinked bemusedly. "We just have to go outside for a little while."

"Why?"

Instead of answering, Ella helped Henry into his dressing gown and ushered him from the room. As they made their way to the front gates, Adam's gaze flitted around in case Faith's companions were lurking in the garden. He half-expected to find the black van parked in the lane, but there was no sign of it. He opened the gates. Ella laced her arms protectively around Henry's shoulders. After fifteen or twenty minutes, the lane was illuminated by blue flashing lights. A pair of police cars pulled up and a constable got out. "We received a report of a break-in at this address."

Adam told him what had happened.

"Doesn't sound like a burglary," commented the constable.

"I think–" Adam broke off, glancing at Henry. Motioning for the constable to follow, he moved out of his son's earshot. "I think they were performing some sort of ritual. The girl I chased is called Faith. At least I think that's her name."

Two constables searched the garden. Two others went into the house. One by one, lights came on in the windows. A constable eventually returned and informed them, "The locks on your back gate and French windows have been forced. We've searched the house and the passageways. We didn't find anyone. Could you come with me, Mr Piper? There's something I'd like you to have a look at."

"What is it?"

"I'm hoping you'll be able to tell me."

With this cryptic remark, the constable led Adam to the sitting room and pointed out a symbol chalked on the floorboards. There were three concentric circles. The largest was about two metres in diameter. Within the innermost circle a cross had been drawn, like a rifle sight. Along the outside edge of the largest circle were four words, each one lined up with a point of the cross – 'Adonai', 'Agla', 'Tzabaoth', 'Tetragrammaton'.

"I've no idea what this is," said Adam. He heaved a sigh. He could just imagine Ella's reaction to the symbol. He could almost hear her saying, *I can't stay in this house. I want to go back to London.* The thought of it weighed down his feet as he returned to the garden.

"What did they show you?" asked Ella.

Adam tried to keep his voice light. "Just some nonsense. It's quite amusing really."

"Amusing?" Ella frowned as if she suspected Adam was being disingenuous. Manoeuvring Henry into Adam's arms, she went into the house. With another sigh, Adam followed her.

"Wait here," he said to Henry in the entrance hall. He went into the sitting room. Ella was staring at the chalked symbol with deep ridges on her forehead.

"I don't see what the hell is amusing about this," she said.

"No, you're right. It's not funny. It's tragic. But these people... Well, they're misguided but harmless."

Ella looked at Adam sharply. "They broke into our house in the middle of the night. Who knows what they're capable of?"

"Oh come on, Ella. You can't honestly think they meant to harm us. As soon as they saw me, they took off like startled rabbits."

Ella chewed over Adam's words and her frown lines became a little less pronounced. She glanced towards Henry. "I hope this doesn't set off his night terrors."

"He'll be fine. We'll tell him it was just some idiots messing around – which it was."

"I'm going to need statements from all three of you," a constable informed them.

Henry gave his brief statement first, then Ella put him back to bed. When she returned, Adam broke off from speaking to the constable and looked askance at her.

"He seems OK," she told him.

Adam smiled with relief. "He's a lot tougher than we give him credit for."

After signing their statements, Adam and Ella drank tea to chase away the chill night air. A pale blue light was diluting the darkness by the time the police were finished taking photos and dusting for prints. Adam locked the gates behind the departing police cars and returned to the house. Ella was staring uneasily into The Lewarne Room.

"Faith and her friends must have seen the nails and opened the panel," said Adam. "That's probably what woke me up."

"Probably," agreed Ella, although her tone suggested Adam's theory did little to reassure her. She looked at him curiously. "How do you know the girl's name?"

"I..." Adam stumbled sheepishly over his answer. "I overheard her and one of the men talking in the lane the other night."

"Why didn't you tell me?"

"It didn't seem important. They were only there for a minute." He shifted the conversation back to the previous subject. "Shall I nail the panel shut again?"

"What's the point? It clearly doesn't want to stay shut."

"It's a piece of wood, Ella. It doesn't have a choice in the matter."

"Leave it as is for now in case the police need to go in the passageways again."

The meaning behind the words was clear – Ella wasn't convinced they'd seen the last of Faith and her friends.

They scrubbed away the chalk symbol, scraped the candle wax off the floorboards and rolled out the rug. Ella insisted on dragging a sideboard across the French windows – which the police had temporarily secured with screws – for added peace of mind. They headed back up to bed. Neither of them closed their eyes.

"I'm not sure if I can sleep in this house," Ella said after a while.

Adam had been expecting her to say some such thing. "Tomorrow I'll call a home security firm. We can get extra locks put in, maybe even an alarm."

Ella sighed. "I wanted to get away from London so that we didn't have to worry about that kind of crap anymore."

"This is a bit different."

"Yes, it's worse. We're being specifically targeted."

"Not us. The house. The police said nothing like this has happened before. So this may well be the one and only time it ever happens." Adam put his arm around Ella. "Close your eyes."

She reluctantly did so. "Do you think they'll catch them?"

"I'm sure they will. There are only a handful of roads off the peninsula."

Ella's breathing slowly softened into sleep. Adam slipped into a fitful doze, troubled by a dream in which a gradually widening crack appeared in the wall at the foot of the bed. A sound issued from the crack – a ringing that started low but grew in volume until it rattled his bones.

CHAPTER 20

Day Five

Adam awoke to bright sunlight. For an instant, the ringing seemed to follow him out of his dream. Then it was replaced by Ella's voice. "Did you get much sleep?" she asked, stepping into the room from the balcony.

"Some." Adam didn't return the question. The smudges under Ella's eyes already provided the answer. "Is Henry awake?"

"He's in the bathroom. I'm going to take him into Helston. He needs new school trousers and shoes. He's grown so much recently."

"I'll contact Mr Mabyn and check we're OK to fit new locks."

Henry came into the room in his dressing gown and sat on the bed. "Morning, sweetheart," said Adam. "Are you alright?"

Henry nodded.

"It's OK if you're scared," said Adam.

"I'm not scared, Dad."

"Good, because there's nothing to be scared of. The people who broke into our house last night aren't bad people, they're just very silly and the police will make sure they never come back here. Now give me a kiss."

Henry kissed Adam's cheek.

"Thanks, I needed that," smiled Adam.

"Go and get dressed," Ella said to Henry.

When they were alone again, Adam said to her, "What about you? Are you alright?"

"I'm not sure." Ella's eyes strayed to the wardrobe that covered the mirror. "We'll talk later."

She stooped to give Adam a peck and left the room. A sigh found its way past his lips. He didn't want to talk about this later, or anything else that would inevitably lead to the topic of returning to London. Ella needed to understand that this was their home now. There was no going back. He knew it would be counter-productive to spell things out to her in such black-and-white terms. He would have to tread softly with her for a few days. He comforted himself with the thought that if she was buying school clothes for Henry that surely meant she was swaying more towards staying than leaving.

The car started up and pulled away. Adam dug out the number for Mabyn & Moon. A secretary answered his call and put him on hold. A moment later, Mr Mabyn's clipped voice came through the receiver. "What can I do for you, Mr Piper?" Adam explained the situation and the solicitor replied, "I understand your concerns, but the contract states very clearly that no structural changes may be made. That includes changes to locks and such like. All I can do is speak to Miss Trehearne and find out if she'll give permission."

Adam thanked the solicitor and hung-up. He made tea and toast and took it to the study. The view through the window brought to mind his dream about Henry walking in his pyjamas on the lawn. Had Henry's fingers been dirty for real that morning or only in the dream?

Adam made his way to the outhouses. He'd packed down the earth over the robin, but now it looked as if someone had dug it over. He dropped to his haunches and scooped up the loose earth. The robin was where he'd buried it, fifty centimetres or so down. He sucked in a sharp breath. Next to the bird the stuffed bunny lay like a murder victim. Several long rents had been slashed into it and its button eyes had been torn off.

As if afraid of doing further damage, Adam gently lifted the bunny to his nose. The smell of Jacob was gone. All it smelled of was damp earth. Anger surged inside him. It picked him up and carried him back to the house. He put the bunny on his desk and picked up his pen. After a moment he threw it down. All he could think about was Henry. How could he have mutilated Jacob's bunny? Why would he do such a thing?

The phone rang. Glad for the distraction, Adam answered it. "You may fit new locks," Mr Mabyn informed him, "but you must provide me with copies of the keys. Miss Trehearne is strongly against fitting an alarm."

"The locks should do the job," said Adam, thinking more about Ella than about how secure the house was.

"If it's convenient, I'll stop by later to pick up Heloise Trehearne's book."

"Ah well, we seem to have misplaced the book. I suppose that's one downside of living in such a big house. It's easy to lose things."

Displaying his usual unwillingness to engage in small talk, Mr Mabyn said, "Please let me know when the work is completed and I'll arrange a visit to inspect it. Good day, Mr Piper."

With that, the solicitor hung-up. The phone immediately rang again. This time it was the constable who'd taken Adam's statement. "We've arrested two suspects," said the constable.

"Who are they?"

"I can't give out that information. What I can tell you is that we have a forty-four-year-old woman and a thirty-eight-year-old man in custody."

That meant Faith and her boyfriend were still at large. "What about the other two?"

"We have their van. So in all likelihood they're still in the area."

Adam didn't like the sound of that. "Should we be concerned?"

"These people aren't violent criminals. I'm sure they're not a threat to you, but just be on your guard."

Adam asked about home security firms and the constable gave him a number. After calling and arranging for an engineer to visit the following day, Adam's thoughts returned to Henry. He abandoned trying to write and busied himself about the house, resetting the fireplace, watering the orangery, cleaning the kitchen, wrestling with the twin-tub, preparing a meal. At midday, Ella and Henry returned with bags of shopping.

"Something smells good," she said, smiling thanks as Adam took the bags off her.

They ate a subdued lunch in the kitchen. Ella couldn't stop yawning. Adam stared at Henry as if trying to work out what was going on in his head. Henry hummed to himself, happily working his way through a bowl of soup. When he was finished, he asked if he could play outside.

"So long as you stay in sight of the house," said Ella.

Henry rushed out the backdoor as if he was late to be somewhere. Adam told Ella about his conversations with Mr Mabyn and the constable. "Well at least the locks are something," said Ella. "I'm not surprised Rozen didn't go for the alarm."

"Why?"

"Because it would stop her from sneaking around here at night."

Adam studied his wife's poker-face. "You know, sometimes I can't tell when you're joking."

Ella watched Henry through the window. "I don't like the thought that those other two might still be in the area."

"Me neither, but the police don't think we've got anything to worry about."

Arching an unconvinced eyebrow, Ella took a piece of paper from her handbag and unfolded it on the table. "Does that look familiar?"

The paper was a printout of the concentric circles that had been chalked on the sitting room floor. "Where did you get this?"

"An internet café. It didn't take long to find this online. It's a symbol used for summoning diabolical spirits."

"Diabolical spirits. What does that even mean?"

"It means those goths think there's something evil in this house. Not just ghosts, but something demonic."

Adam let out a snort of laughter. "Oh give me a break." He tapped the printout. "Has Henry seen this?"

"Of course not."

"Good."

"Is that all you've got to say?"

"What do you expect me to say? This just proves what I said last night. Those idiots probably pulled this crap from the same website as you. As far as I'm concerned, this is the end of the matter." As if putting an extra full stop on the conversation, Adam opened the Rayburn and tossed the printout into the flames.

"I spoke to my mum and dad. They think we should go back to London."

"Of course they bloody do," Adam shot back. "They never wanted us to come here in the first place." Seeing the tension in Ella's eyes, he softened his tone. "Look I know you're upset, but this house will be like Fort Knox by the time I'm done. So stop worrying." He ducked into the fridge, grabbed a lemon and mixed up two gin and tonics. "Come on, let's take these outside and enjoy the last of the sun."

Ella looked at Adam as if unsure whether to accept his appeasement offer, then she took her glass and they headed for the patio. Adam raised his face to the sun. "Our backyard in Walthamstow will be in the shade now. Remember how we used to sit out there shivering?" He smiled wryly as Ella gave him a sidelong glance. "Yeah, I know I'm being obvious." He made a sweeping gesture. "But seriously can you imagine giving all this up to go back to that?"

Ella sighed. "Not really, no."

Adam rested his hand on hers. "This is just a little hiccup. A few weeks from now we'll have forgotten all about it."

"Hey Dad, look at me!" shouted Henry. He was dangling upside down from a branch a couple of metres above the lawn.

"Be careful," Adam called back.

Henry laughed, swinging precariously with only his legs hooked over the branch. "Get him down from there," Ella said to Adam.

He rose and hurried across the lawn. Henry's legs suddenly lost their grip. With a cry of alarm, he fell into his dad's outstretched arms. Adam staggered under his weight, recovered and set him on his feet.

He looked sharply at Henry. "What's the matter with you?"

There was an insolent gleam in Henry's eyes. "I'm just having fun. You said you want me to have fun."

"You could have broken your neck." Adam put his hand on Henry's shoulder and guided him firmly towards the house. "I want to talk to you about something."

They went into the study and Adam picked up the mutilated bunny. "Well, what have you got to say?" he demanded.

Henry treated Adam to an accusing look of his own. "I saw you burying the robin. Why didn't you tell me it was dead?"

"I didn't want to upset you."

Henry thrust his chin out angrily. "You should have told me."

"Maybe, but that's no excuse for doing this to your brother's bunny."

"Stuffed toys are for babies. I told you I'm not a baby."

Adam shook his head. "That's not a reason." He pointed at the cotton wool bulging through the rents in the bunny. "This..." He sought for the right words, but all he could think to say was, "This was Jacob's favourite cuddly toy."

"So what?" exclaimed Henry, tears filling his eyes. "I hate him! I hate Jacob. He was always hitting me and I never hit him back, except once and... and..." He trailed off into deep, shuddering sobs.

Tears welled into Adam's eyes too. He drew Henry into an embrace and stroked his hair. "It's OK, shh."

Henry's sobs gradually subsided. He looked pleadingly up into his dad's eyes. "I'm sorry, Dad. I don't really hate Jacob. It's just that sometimes when

I think about what happened I get so angry. I just wish I could forget all about it."

"I know," soothed Adam. There were times when he wished he could erase what happened *that* day from his memory, just as there were times when he feared that wish would come true.

"Are you going to tell Mum about the bunny?"

"We'll keep this between us, but in future if you feel like this will you speak to me?"

"Yes, Dad. I promise."

"Don't say it unless you mean it."

"I do."

"Good. And I promise not to keep things from you. You're right, Henry. You're not a baby anymore. Tell you what, there's a load of scrap wood in the outhouses. Why don't we build a treehouse?"

Henry's eyes lit up. "Really? Do you mean it? Can we start right away?"

Adam nodded. "You fetch the wood out. I'll be over in a short while."

"Thanks Dad."

Adam smiled as Henry gave him an extra-tight hug. Then Henry turned and raced out of the study. "No running in the house," Adam shouted after him. He sighed at the futility of trying to get anything to stick in an eleven-year-old's head. His gaze returned to the bunny. He stared at it sadly for a moment before putting it in a desk drawer and heading to the patio.

"Don't you think treehouses are a bit dangerous?" Ella said when he told her why Henry was scurrying back and forth with armfuls of wood between the outbuildings and an oak tree.

"We've got to start trusting him more, Ella. That's what this behaviour is all about."

"In that case, we should tell him about the ghosts."

"I'm not sure that's a good idea."

"He starts school tomorrow. It's better he hears it from us than from one of the other kids at school."

"I don't want to upset him, especially not after last night." Adam thought about the promise he'd made and felt like a hypocrite, but he was loath to risk turning Henry against Fenton House. If Henry decided he didn't want to be there, then they were as good as gone.

Ella looked at him as if she could read his mind. "OK, Adam, we'll play it your way for now."

He felt an urge to get away from her knowing eyes. Gin and tonic in hand, he rose and headed over to Henry.

For the rest of the afternoon, Adam and Henry worked on the treehouse. By teatime, they'd constructed a platform cradled in the oak tree's lower branches and reached by a makeshift ladder nailed to its trunk. Henry wolfed down his food and asked, "Can I go back outside?"

"For a short while," said Ella. "I don't want you in bed late."

Henry pelted off to the garden. Adam went to the study and threw himself into his writing, the words coming like rain from storm clouds. It was dark when he broke off and went in search of Ella. He found her in the sitting room.

"Henry's in bed," she told him.

Adam felt a flutter of anxiety. "I think I'm more nervous about tomorrow than he is."

"Kids are adaptable. He'll soon make new friends."

"That's the thing. We never had to worry about him and Jacob making new friends because they always had each other."

Ella glided her hands over Adam's neck and massaged his shoulders. "Mmm, that feels good," he said.

She kissed his ear, murmuring, "Let's go to bed."

They headed upstairs. Ella went into the bathroom. Adam paused halfway through undressing, his gaze sliding across to the wardrobe. A sliver of mirror was exposed. Hearing the bathroom door, he quickly shoved the wardrobe fully in front of the mirror and got into bed.

CHAPTER 21

Day Six

It was still dark when the urge to write dragged Adam out of bed. After several hours, Henry came into the study. He was wearing his school uniform. His hair was neatly brushed. Smiling, Adam beckoned him closer and kissed his cheek. "Be good."

"I will, Dad."

"It's time to go," called Ella.

Henry turned to leave, but Adam kept hold of his hand. He thought about the mutilated bunny. *It's no bad thing*, he told himself. *He's just trying to let go.* "Remember what we spoke about yesterday, Henry. If anything upsets you, tell me and we'll deal with it together."

Adam waved Henry and Ella off, calling after them, "Good luck!" Ella left the gates open for the home security engineer. Adam had only just sat back down at his desk when a white van pulled up. He showed the engineer where the goths had broken in. While the engineer set about surveying other potential points of entry, Adam made himself breakfast. He was eating on the patio when the crunch of gravel signalled Ella's return.

"How did it go?" he asked as she came into the kitchen.

"He seemed to take it all in his stride."

The engineer presented them with a quote for installing new locks and repairing the French doors and the back gate. They agreed the price and arranged a date for the work to be done. Then, for the first time since their weekend away, they found themselves alone. "It's so quiet here," Ella said as if she'd only just noticed.

"We should do something to take our minds off Henry."

She arched an eyebrow at Adam. "Oh yes, and what do you have in mind?"

He laughed. "Not what you're thinking. I was about to suggest a walk on the beach."

"Sounds good."

They left by the back gate. Fluffy white clouds scudded across the sky. A cool wind was chopping up the sea and whistling through the rock arch. Ella stopped so abruptly that Adam bumped into her.

"What is it?" he asked.

She pointed to the far side of Satan's Saucepan. A tall figure dressed all in black was heading rapidly in their direction. "Is that one of the men who broke in?"

A jolt of adrenaline quickened Adam's pulse. "Yeah, I think it is." He pulled Ella behind him and shepherded her back along the narrow path. Glancing over his shoulder, he saw that the man was catching them up.

"Hurry up," he said to Ella.

"I'm going as fast as I can."

Realising they wouldn't make it to the gate, Adam pressed the house keys into Ella's hand. "Go and phone the police."

Her eyes flitted to their pursuer and back to Adam. "What about you?"

"Go," he urged.

She continued on her way. Nervous tremors ran through Adam as he turned to face the fast approaching figure. There was a thick growth of stubble on the man's chin. His raven black hair was dishevelled as if he'd been sleeping in a ditch. Adam held up his hands, palms out. "I don't want any trouble."

The man stabbed a finger at him. "Where the fuck is she?"

"Who?"

"You know who! My girlfriend. Faith."

"How am I supposed to know where she is? She legged it at the same time as you."

The man transferred his finger to Fenton House. "She never left that place."

"My wife's calling the police."

"Where's Faith?"

"I told you, I don't know."

"Bullshit! Faith saw you watching us fuck. Does your wife know you get your kicks out of perving on people? Maybe I should ask her."

A wave of anger swept over Adam, propelling him to grab the man and thrust him towards the brink of the path. The man cried out, wind-milling his arms. Adam held him there for a second then, shocked by the realisation of what he was doing, he pulled him away from the edge.

"You tried to kill me," gasped the man, staggering backwards, his eyes round with fear.

"Stay away from my family!" warned Adam as the man turned to run back towards Treworder.

Adam's legs trembled under him as he returned to the house. Ella rushed out of the backdoor. "Are you OK?"

He nodded. "He's gone."

"The police are on their way." Ella drew Adam inside and locked the door. "What happened?" she asked as he dropped heavily onto a chair.

"He wanted to know where the girl who went into the passageways is."

"How would we know that?"

"That's what I told him, but he's convinced she's still in the house."

Ella's eyes darted around as if she expected to see Faith skulking nearby. "What if he's right?"

"The police searched the house. She's not here."

"It's a big place. They could have missed her."

"Even if they did, why would she still be hanging around?"

Creases clustered on Ella's forehead. "Faith and her friends came here to find something, right? Perhaps she found it."

"What are you suggesting?"

"I don't know, but don't you think it's odd that she hasn't contacted her boyfriend?"

"Not really. I imagine she's not best pleased with him for running off and leaving her behind."

A testy note came into Ella's voice. "You've got an answer for everything, haven't you?"

Turning her back on Adam, she left the kitchen. Sighing, he went after her. She stared pensively out of the dining room window.

"I don't want to argue, Ella. Seriously, though, what's more likely?" Adam gestured to the garden. "That this girl's out there somewhere hiding from the police and her boyfriend? Or that she's fallen into the clutches of some sort of demon ghost thingy?"

A faint smile found its way onto Ella's lips. "When you put it like that..."

Adam put his arms around her and held her silently as they waited for the police. They glanced skyward at a *whump-whump* sound. A blue helicopter emerged from the clouds. They went into the garden and watched the helicopter circle above Treworder. A police car pulled into the driveway and a constable informed them, "We've arrested a man fitting the description you gave us."

Ella puffed out a breath. "Thank god for that."

"I'm going to need a statement."

They went inside and sat at the kitchen table. Ella spoke first while Adam wondered how much he should say about what had taken place on the cliff tops. Another police car showed up. A constable poked his head through the front door and called his colleague outside.

It became clear to Adam that the decision had been taken out of his hands when the first constable returned and said, "I'm sorry to tell you this, Mr and

Mrs Piper, but the man we arrested has made some very serious accusations. He believes you've kidnapped his girlfriend and are holding her in this house against her will."

"That's insane," exclaimed Ella.

"I agree, but we'd like to search the house again."

"Search all you want," said Adam. The constable stared at him intently. Guessing what was coming, Adam squirmed internally.

"He's also claiming that you, Mr Piper, watched him and his girlfriend engaging in sexual intercourse outside your front gates five nights ago. And furthermore that when he threatened to expose this, you attempted to throw him off the cliffs."

"The second part of that is nonsense," Adam replied.

"What about the first part?" Ella asked, frowning at him.

Adam gave her a sheepish glance. His gaze returned to the constable. "Yes, I saw them. I could hardly miss them."

"And what exactly happened on the coastal path today?" inquired the constable.

Adam told him, leaving out the part where he grabbed the man. He could feel Ella's eyes on him as he signed his statement. The constable thanked him, left them alone and called his colleague into the house to begin their search. Ella stared at Adam for a moment longer before pointedly standing and leaving the room. He followed her out of the front door. When they were well out of earshot of the house, she turned with a flushed face and said, "Five nights ago. That was the night you came on to me outside. I wondered what got you so worked up. Now I know."

"What are you angry with me for? I didn't ask them to go at it like dogs in the lane."

"No but you didn't say anything to them either, did you?"

"What the hell was I supposed to say?"

"You should have told them to get off our land. Maybe then they wouldn't have broken in."

Adam reached for Ella's hand. "You're right. I'm sorry."

She pulled her hand away. "What happened on the coastal path?"

"I told you what happened."

Ella tapped her ear. "Do you hear that? That's my bullshit detector going off. You were shaking so badly you had to sit down when you got back to the house. Something happened between you and that man. Something more than just words."

Adam's voice dropped low. "He got in my face so I pushed him. I wasn't about to tell the police that and get charged with assault."

Ella looked at him as if she didn't recognise him. "Since when do you go around pushing people and lying to the police about it?"

"I was protecting my family. That's what matters to me." Adam reached for Ella's hand again. "That's *all* that matters to me."

This time, she left her hand in his, her eyes swaying between uncertainty and understanding.

A constable shouted to them from the front door, "There's a phone call for you. Sounds urgent."

Adam and Ella exchanged a glance. The same question was in both their gazes – *What now?*

They hurried into the house. Ella picked up the phone. "Hello... Yes, this is Ella Piper." Her face creased. "What kind of incident?" The lines sharpened. "What? Are you sure it was Henry?"

"Is Henry OK?" Adam asked worriedly.

Ella nodded, holding up a hand to quiet him. "Of course. I'll be there as soon as possible." She put the phone down and looked at Adam as if she could barely process what she'd been told. "That was Mrs Taylor, the head teacher at Henry's school. Apparently Henry's hurt one of the boys in his class."

"Hurt how? Was it an accident?"

"I don't know but it sounds bad. The boy's been taken to hospital."

Adam's eyes widened. "Bloody hell."

Ella grabbed her handbag and rushed outside. Adam made to follow, but she motioned for him to stay where he was. "Someone needs to be here in case the police find anything," she said, before getting into the car and speeding off without a wave.

Adam remained on the doorstep long after she was gone, unsure what to do with himself. The constables were busily searching every nook and cranny. Eventually Adam headed to the kitchen and made a sandwich, but it sat uneaten in front of him. His mind was whirring. There had to be some sort of mistake. Henry wouldn't hurt anyone – at least not deliberately. Would he?

"No he wouldn't," he told himself out loud, but an image lurked like a stalker at the back of his mind – the dead robin, its head lolling brokenly. Had Henry killed it after all?

He went to the study and forced himself to focus on his work, but the few words he managed felt dead on the page. A constable called him into the hallway and said, "That girl's definitely not in this house. Not unless she's hiding under the floorboards."

The constable thanked Adam for his cooperation, promising to be in touch if there were further developments. The thunk of the front door closing was followed by a silence that seemed to grow until Adam's breathing sounded loud in his ears. He glanced around and for the first time found himself wondering, *Is this the right place for us*?

Almost as soon as the thought came, it was replaced by another – an inspiration! He returned to the study and this time the words came fast and full of life.

CHAPTER 22

The afternoon was wearing towards evening when Adam became aware of voices – Ella and Henry were back! He jumped up from the desk and hurried to them. Ella's face was etched with strain. Henry had lapsed into his familiar hunched up posture. He stared at the floor as if he couldn't bring himself to meet Adam's gaze.

"You've been hours," said Adam.

"There was a lot to discuss," Ella replied wearily.

"So come on. Tell me what happened."

"Just give me a minute. I need something to drink."

"I'll make you a cup of tea."

"No. I need something stronger."

Ella went to the kitchen. Henry trailed after her, his head sinking even lower. She poured him an orange juice and herself a glass of wine. After a large mouthful, she sighed and briefly closed her eyes. "OK, so I've been talking to teachers, social workers and police all afternoon."

"Police," Adam echoed apprehensively.

"I've spoken to more police in the past few days than even when Jacob–" Ella broke off with a grimace.

"I didn't mean to hurt him," Henry piped up, directing pleading eyes at Adam. "But he wouldn't stop teasing me."

"About what?"

From the *What do you think?* look Ella gave him, Adam guessed the answer before Henry replied, "He said our house is haunted. I told him to shut up, but he kept calling me ghost boy. And then the other boys started saying it, so I..." He fell silent, hanging his head again.

"He pushed him over," Ella said in a pained voice. "The poor boy hit his head and was knocked unconscious."

Adam was momentarily too gobsmacked to speak. "How is he?"

"They're saying he could have neurological damage."

"What does that mean exactly?"

"How the bloody hell should I know?"

Adam pressed his fingers to an ache between his eyes. "So what happens now?"

"There's going to be an investigation. Henry's been suspended, but I don't see how he can ever go back to that school. For that matter, I don't see how we can stay in this area."

"Whoa!" Adam put up his hands. "Let's not get ahead of ourselves. This is bad, but it's not *that* bad."

"Not that bad?" Ella repeated in disbelief. "Our son almost killed someone."

"He pushed someone who got in his face." Adam added meaningfully, "It happens."

"Oh so that makes it alright, does it?"

"Of course not. He obviously has to be punished, but let's keep this in perspective. Ninety-nine times out of a hundred that boy would have walked away unhurt and we wouldn't have even heard about it."

"So how do we punish him?"

"Well for starters you're grounded," Adam said to Henry. "That means you don't go out of this house unless it's absolutely necessary. And don't think being suspended means you can laze around. You're going to be doing schoolwork every day on top of whatever chores your mother and I can find for you."

"But I didn't even start it!" protested Henry.

"No, but you certainly finished it."

Henry looked accusingly at his parents. "Why didn't you tell me this house is supposed to be haunted?"

Adam's tone softened with self-reproach. "Perhaps we should have, but we didn't want to scare you."

"I wouldn't have been scared because ghosts aren't real." An uneasy edge came into Henry's voice. "Are they?"

"Of course they're not. I'm sorry, Henry. It's my fault. I should have realised you wouldn't be silly enough to be scared. But that doesn't excuse your behaviour. You know what I'm going to say now, don't you?" Adam pointed towards the stairs. "Go on, go to your room. And this time you will be staying there for the rest of the day."

"I'm hungry."

"I'll bring you up something to eat," said Ella.

Henry sloped from the kitchen.

Feeling Ella's eyes on him, Adam said, "Go on say it. Say I told you so."

"Playing the blame game is the last thing on my mind right now," she said. "You should have seen the way they all looked at me at the school. I felt like a criminal." She heaved a sigh. "Christ, what a day."

"The police didn't find that girl. So we can at least put that behind us."

A sharp dismissive gesture made it clear that Ella no longer gave a shit about any of that. "Sometimes I think we're cursed."

"I'd hardly call this house a curse."

"To hell with this house! I'm talking about us. Our family." Ella snatched up the wine bottle, took it to the patio and dropped onto a chair.

Adam followed and laid his hands on her shoulders. "We'll get through this. We've got through far worse."

"I don't want to have to keep getting through things," she said bitterly. "Why can't life ever be easy?"

Adam had no answer to that. They were silent for a while. Ella finished her wine and poured another glass.

"Somehow I managed to get some work done this afternoon," said Adam. "Do you fancy reading it?"

Ella shook her head. "All I want to do is get drunk and forget today ever happened."

"That's why you should read it. It'll take your mind off all that."

"Alright, but don't expect to get much sense out of me."

Adam fetched the new material. Ella settled back with the pages in one hand and her wine in the other. Adam made a sandwich and took it up to Henry. He was surprised to find Henry asleep. He quietly set down the sandwich on the bedside table and studied his son's face. Adam's own face was troubled as he left the room.

He returned to the study with the eagerness of someone seeking the refuge of a make-believe world. He hadn't been working for long when Ella stormed into the room and threw his manuscript on the desk as if it offended her.

"Is that really what you think of your son?" she demanded to know.

Adam looked at her bemusedly. "What do you mean?"

"I mean it's pretty obvious where the inspiration for this crap came from. The boy's the killer, isn't he? The boy who just happens to have curly hair and freckles like Henry."

"I'm not sure who the killer is yet. I'm just following where the story leads."

"Well I'd say your subconscious is trying to tell you something." Ella jabbed at the manuscript. "That's the last I'm reading of that."

She left the room, slamming the door behind her. Adam stared at the manuscript with a line like a knife cut between his eyebrows. Was she right? He thought about the boy Henry had pushed over. He thought about the dead robin and mutilated bunny. He thought about Jacob bleeding to death at Henry's feet. He heard Henry's voice – *It was an accident, Dad. Honest.* The words seemed to have a hollow ring to them. His mind looped back to the present – Henry's sleeping face. How could he sleep after what had happened? Adam shoved the manuscript off the desk, scattering pages across the floor. It was one thing to wonder whether Henry had deliberately hurt a bird. But this... this made him nauseous with self-disgust.

He went after Ella. She was in the orangery, drinking wine and drunkenly stabbing a trowel at the soil. "You're wrong," he said forcefully. "I don't believe Henry would ever hurt anyone on purpose."

She gave a contemptuous laugh. "You sound like you're trying to convince yourself."

Adam dropped to his haunches, seeking Ella's eyes. "It's been a shitty enough day already. Let's not fall out on top of everything. It's just a book. If you don't like it, I'll tear it up and start again."

Ella looked at Adam narrowly for a moment, then her expression softened and she shook her head. "I overreacted. I'm just stressed."

Giving her a *Don't-worry-about-it* smile, Adam took her hand and led her to the sitting room. "Lie down," he instructed. "I'll make you that cup of tea."

While he waited for the kettle to boil, Adam checked on Henry. The sandwich was gone, but Henry still appeared to be asleep. A sharp sense of shame stealing over him, Adam retrieved the plate and returned downstairs. When he took Ella her cup of tea, he found that she too was asleep. He covered her with a blanket, went to the study, gathered up the scattered pages and took them to the kitchen. He opened the Rayburn and made as if to throw the manuscript onto the glowing embers, but hesitated, his features twitching with uncertainty. He shook his head. No. Burning the thing would be as good as admitting Ella was right. He would complete it and prove to her and himself that she was wrong.

CHAPTER 23

Determined not to stop until the manuscript was finished, Adam set to work more fervently than ever. He wrote in a white heat, pausing only to flex the stiffness from his fingers. Like someone sprinting towards a cliff edge in darkness, he could sense the end getting closer but couldn't see it. It was the dead of night when he stopped suddenly, feeling more like he'd hit a wall than fallen off a cliff. He stared in dismay at a page as blank as his mind. For long minutes his pen hovered over the paper, but nothing more would come. A finger of panic touched him. Had his block returned? *You've just burned yourself out,* he told himself. *Take a break.*

He rose and opened the door. The hallway was pitch dark. He flipped a light switch and went to the sitting room. Ella was snoring on the sofa. The grandfather clock ticked in its corner. Another sound caught his attention – the distant ringing of a bell. *Ding, ding, ding* it went as rapidly as an alarm.

The ringing seemed to be coming from somewhere inside the house. But where? Adam returned to the hallway. The sound was faintly louder there. It drew him towards the stairs and, with a creeping sense of inevitability, into The Lewarne Room. As if afraid something might be waiting to leap out at him, he warily opened the secret panel. The ringing jumped up a notch in volume. His heart following suit, he fetched matches and a candelabra.

He ducked into the passageway and, brushing cobwebs from his eyes, climbed the wooden stairs. The noise was louder on the first-floor. He carried on up the next flight of stairs. The tolling continued to rise in volume, jangling along the passageways like an old fire engine. *Ding, diNG, DING!*

Suddenly, like a throttled scream, the noise stopped.

He stood motionless, ears straining. Silence.

Who had been ringing the bell? He could think of one obvious candidate – Faith. But why would she want to alert them to her presence? It didn't make any sense. Maybe it was part of the ritual she and her friends had been enacting in the sitting room. Anxiety swelled his chest. *The sitting room. Ella!*

The candle flames guttered as Adam whirled on his heels and hastened back downstairs. He let out a breath of relief at the sight of Ella sleeping soundly. His eyes travelled the room, checking for anyone lurking in the shadows.

A faint sound, like a mouse scratching inside a wall, drew his gaze to the centaur painting. His forehead wrinkled. Was there something different about the centaur's eyes? As if he'd been shoved, he suddenly reeled backwards and landed heavily on his backside. The centaur had winked! Heart hammering, he scrambled to his feet and edged towards the painting. He ran his fingers over the eyes. They were remarkably lifelike, but they weren't real. Had it been a trick of his imagination or had someone been looking through the peephole?

"I know you're there," he said with a tremor in his voice.

Dead silence.

He flinched and span around as Ella said, "Who are you speaking to?"

Moving quickly to her side, he said, "Faith's boyfriend could have been right. I think she's still in the house."

Ella jolted upright. "What makes you say that?"

"I'll explain later. We need to check on Henry."

Hand in hand, they hurried upstairs. Henry lifted his head as they entered his room. "What's going on?" he asked sleepily.

Ella opened her mouth to reply, but Adam raised a silencing hand and jerked his chin towards the mirror. He scooped up Henry.

"Has someone else broken in?" asked Henry, wrapping his arms and legs around his dad.

Adam shushed him and they made their way down to the entrance hall, peering into every shadow. Adam put down Henry, picked up the phone and dialled 999. "I think there's an intruder in our house," he told the operator.

The operator took his address and instructed him to wait outside for constables to arrive.

"Put your shoes and coat on," Adam said to Henry.

As Henry turned to the coat-stand, Ella said to Adam in a sharp whisper, "Just what makes you think Faith's in the house?"

Adam glanced to make sure Henry wasn't listening. "The centaur's eyes moved."

Ella's mouth formed an O of understanding.

Both of them flinched as an unearthly scream ripped through the house. Ella reached out protectively for Henry. He hid behind her as a figure emerged from The Lewarne Room.

Faith's trembling arms were outstretched like a crucifixion. She was naked. Her slender body was criss-crossed by bloody scratches and mottled with ugly bruises. She was panting heavily and her pupils were glassy and unfocused. Like a sleepwalker, she shuffled towards Adam.

Ella caught hold of Adam's hand and tried to pull him towards the front door.

He prised her fingers away. "She needs help."

"Be careful," hissed Ella as, holding his hands up in a calming gesture, Adam approached Faith.

"I'm not going to hurt you," he said.

A glimmer of focus swirled into Faith's blue eyes. Like a puppet whose strings had been cut, her arms dropped limply to her sides.

"Get a blanket," Adam said to Ella. Towing Henry behind her, she hastened to the sitting room. Faith shied away as they passed her. They returned with a blanket. As Adam wrapped it around Faith, she trembled like grass in a breeze.

"Who did this to you?" he asked.

Faith's eyes flitted between Adam and Ella, full of desperate appeal. Her mouth opened and closed, but no words came. Tears spilled over her eyelids.

"We need to open the gates for the police," said Ella. Adam motioned for her to go. She left the house, once again pulling Henry along after her.

Adam eyed Faith worriedly. Her breathing was a dry rasp. Her lips were cracked as if she hadn't had a drink in days. He turned towards the kitchen. She let out a low moan and feebly grasped his hand. "It's OK," he soothed. "I'm just going to get you a drink of–"

He was interrupted by another ear-splitting scream tearing from Faith. Her eyes swelled like over-inflated balloons as if she'd seen something over Adam's shoulder that terrified her beyond words. He followed her line of sight and saw only an empty space. She broke away from him. The blanket fluttered to the floor as she ran out of the front door.

Adam gave chase, calling out. "Faith, stop. There's no need to be scared."

Faith showed no sign of having heard him. Heedless of the gravel biting into her bare feet, she streaked down the driveway. Ella and Henry were returning from the front gates. They shrank to one side at the sight of the wild-eyed girl. She passed them without a glance.

"What happened?" Ella asked Adam.

"I don't know," he replied, not slowing his pace.

Beyond the gates, Faith veered through a gap in the hedge. A grassy field sloped down towards the coastal path. The first blue-grey light of dawn was parting the curtains of night. Adam caught up with Faith near the far side of the field. He tried to catch hold of her, lost his balance and fell flat on his face. Winded, he struggled upright. Faith was scrambling over a dry-stone wall. He dove after her and grabbed a trailing foot. With a desperate strength, she wrenched herself free and hurtled across the path.

"No!" cried Adam as she disappeared over the rim of Satan's Saucepan.

He climbed over the wall and peered into the yawning void. The waves boiling on the boulders far below were still hidden in darkness. There was no sight of Faith either. He shouted her name. Only his voice echoed back at him. He stood rooted by shock until he heard Ella calling him. Tears glazed his eyes as he went to her.

CHAPTER 24

Day Seven

Ella was waiting by the gates with Henry shivering in his pyjamas at her side. "Where is she?" she asked anxiously.

"She's gone," said Adam.

"What do you mean?"

Adam darted a glance at Henry. "She's *gone* and she's not coming back."

Catching his meaning, Ella pressed a hand to her mouth. Adam started towards the house. Henry made to follow, but Ella caught hold of his hand and pulled him backwards. "I'm not going back in that house," she said.

Adam looked over his shoulder at her. "We can talk about this later, Ella. Right now I need to phone the coastguard." He motioned with his chin at Henry whose teeth were chattering like castanets. "And he needs to get warm."

Adam quickened his pace. Keeping tight hold of Henry's hand, Ella followed slowly. She paused on the porch, staring at the front doorway as if it was a mouth that wanted to swallow her whole. "I'm freezing," said Henry, dragging at her.

Footstep by footstep, Ella allowed herself to be drawn into the entrance hall. Adam was on the phone. "Yes, that's right, Satan's Saucepan," he was saying. "I don't know. I couldn't see her. OK. I will."

Adam put the phone down and turned to Ella. "A helicopter is on its way. I have to go back to the cliffs and show them where she fell."

"Is that woman going be OK, Dad?" asked Henry.

Adam shook his head sadly. "No, Henry. I'm afraid she's not."

"Wait," Ella said with a tremor in her voice as Adam turned towards the front door. "Do you have to go right now?"

"There's nothing to be scared of."

Ella's eyebrow pinched together. "So you keep saying, but that girl looked–" She broke off, glancing at Henry. "Go warm yourself up by the Rayburn. Shout if you need me." Her eyes uneasily followed Henry into the kitchen, then returned to Adam. "That girl looked as if she'd been attacked by a wild animal. What could have done that to her?"

"I don't know. Maybe she did it to herself."

"Why would she do that?"

"I don't know," repeated Adam, irritation sharpening his tone. "I do know this – she wasn't right in there." He tapped his temple.

"But what if–"

"What if what, Ella? What if she was attacked by a ghost or a demon? Are we really going to stand here talking bollocks when a woman's fallen from the cliffs?"

"Jumped," corrected Ella. "She didn't fall. Something in this house scared her so badly that she threw herself off those cliffs."

Adam shook his head. "You don't get it, do you? Nothing in this house scared her. She scared herself with a load of crap about rituals and demons." A hitch of pain came into his voice. "And do you know why? Because it's easier to believe in that stuff than to accept the truth that this–" he gestured at their surroundings, "what we can see and touch – this is all there is."

Adam and Ella stared at each other for a moment. Tears trembled on both their eyelids. Ella gestured towards the front door. "You'd better get going."

"I'll be back as soon as I can and we can talk about…" *Leaving.* Adam couldn't bring himself to say the word. The thought that by tonight they could be back in London lay like a lead weight in his stomach.

He headed down to the cliffs, this time going via the back gate whose frame was cracked and splintered from being jimmied open. He peered into the windswept chasm again. Pink fingers of dawn were creeping through the rock arch. His stomach clenched as he spotted a body spread-eagled across a boulder just beyond the reach of the waves. Faith's limbs were bent at unnatural angles with bones protruding through the skin like broken sticks. Her skull was split open like a smashed egg. Blood masked her face. He swallowed hard, holding back nausea.

So much blood…

A dot appeared in the sky to the north, rapidly growing into a fat-bellied red-and-white Coastguard helicopter. He waved to it and pointed out the body. As a coastguard was lowered into Satan's Saucepan on a winch cable, Adam turned away with relief and made his way towards the house.

One of the policemen who'd attended the break-in was coming the other way. "They'd better work fast," he commented, looking at the helicopter then out to sea. "Weather forecast says there's a fog bank moving in."

Several police cars were parked in the driveway. Constables were milling around as if awaiting instructions. Ella was giving yet another statement in the kitchen. Henry was on her lap, head resting against her shoulder, eyes shut.

"I found Faith," said Adam, dropping wearily onto a chair.

"Is she alive?" Ella asked without much hope.

"No."

She lowered her eyes. Adam laid his hand on hers.

A dark-haired, forty-something woman in a suit that matched her Celtic blue eyes entered the kitchen. She glanced at Henry and introduced herself in a hushed voice, "I'm Detective Sergeant Penny Holman."

"No need to whisper," said Ella. "He's spark out."

Penny showed them a mugshot of a grim-faced girl. "Is this the woman who broke into your house?"

"Yes," answered Ella.

Adam stared at the photo. When the sergeant repeated her question, he blinked and said, "That's her."

"Her name's Faith Gooden," said Penny. "She was twenty-one-years old and lived in Newquay."

"Twenty-one," Ella repeated with a shake of her head.

"I'd like your permission to do a forensic sweep of the property. I'd also like to take DNA swabs and scrapings from under your fingernails."

Adam frowned. "Are we under some kind of suspicion?"

"Absolutely not," said Penny. "It's just procedure. From what I've read about Miss Gooden, I'd say the injuries you described were in all likelihood self-inflicted. She was a very troubled young woman."

Adam threw Ella a *See, I told you so* look, before asking the sergeant, "Troubled how?"

"Her parents died in a car crash in..." Penny consulted a notebook, "2007. Faith was put into foster care. In 2013 she was arrested for using heroin. She spent a year in a juvenile detention centre, during which time she self-harmed and attempted suicide."

Adam and Ella exchanged a sad glance at this brief tragic life story.

"Could you show me where you first saw Faith," said Penny.

Adam took her to The Lewarne Room. Penny gave a little shudder at the cherubic baby being murdered in its mother's arms. "It sends a chill through you to look at it, doesn't it?"

"Yes," agreed Adam, staring at the painting, his overwrought eyes taking in every detail as if for the first time – the mother's knotted forehead, her helpless expression, the dagger piercing the child's throat, the murderer's grimly determined face. Perhaps as a small act of mercy, the murderer's hand was covering the baby's eyes. The knife wound was strangely bloodless. Adam knew only too well that in reality there would be streams of blood, spilling out faster than hands could stop it. His gaze moved to the words carved over the fireplace – 'THEY ARE NO MORE'. A small sob forced its way out of him.

"Are you OK?" asked Penny.

Adam nodded. "It's been a difficult night."

The sergeant looked at him intently. "When I showed you the photo of Faith you seemed thrown by it."

Something about the photo had bothered Adam, but he couldn't nail down what it was. "It took me a moment to recognise her, that's all."

Penny peered through the secret panel. "I understand my colleagues already searched these passageways."

"Twice."

"Then Faith must have been hiding somewhere else. I'm told you don't have access to the tower?"

"That's right. The door's locked. I don't have the key."

"Is there a basement?"

"No."

Penny cocked an ear towards the tiled floor. "Is that water I can hear?" She dropped to her haunches and pressed a hand to the floor. "These tiles are really cold. Are you certain there isn't a basement?"

Adam felt a sudden proprietorial protectiveness towards the house. Yes, a woman was dead, but that didn't give the police the right to pry into the old place's secrets. Next thing they would be pulling up floors and knocking holes in walls. Maybe they'd even force entry to the tower. Booted feet tramping up to the top of the tower could put the entire house at risk. "You should speak to Rozen Trehearne or her solicitor Niall Mabyn. They know a lot more about this house than I do."

They returned to the kitchen. "I'm afraid you'll have to stay in here until Forensics have completed their sweep," Penny informed them.

When the sergeant left the room, Ella asked Adam, "So what do you want to do?"

"What do you mean?"

"You know full well what I mean. Are we going back to London?"

Adam's gaze strayed out of the window to the garden and the sea. How could he leave all this behind? "The newspaper said this place was too good to be true. And it was right."

Ella released a relieved breath. "Thank god you've seen sense. As soon as the police are finished, we'll start packing."

Adam shook his head. "You misunderstand me, Ella. I'm not saying I want to leave. I'm saying that if you want something good you have to fight for it."

Ella frowned, but before she could make a reply a Forensic officer entered the kitchen. The officer ran a cotton-wool bud around the inside of Adam's mouth, sealed it in a plastic tube, then took some scrapings from under his nails. When it was Ella's turn, Henry stirred and let out a low moan. Ella shushed him.

"How much longer will you lot be here?" Adam asked the officer.

"We'll be a while yet."

"Can I take my son up to his bed?"

"I'll find out for you."

The officer left and Ella said, "I don't want Henry up there alone."

"He'll be fine. The police–"

Ella cut Adam off with a shake of her head. "There's nothing the police can do that will convince me we're safe in this house." Her voice took on an imploring tone. "There's something going on in this place... Something... I don't know what, but we'd be stupid to stay here. Surely you see that, Adam?"

"What I see is that we'd be giving up a chance at a real future because of a girl who was mentally ill long before she came here."

The Forensic officer poked his head back into the kitchen and told them it was OK to take Henry to his room. Adam made to lift Henry off Ella's lap.

She tightened her grip on him. They eyeballed each other over their son. With a little wrench, Adam prised Henry free.

"Adam," Ella hissed as he turned away.

Without looking at her, he headed for the stairs. He paused on the landing as a sound as deep as a whale's mating call resonated through the windows. Several miles out to sea the newborn sun was being extinguished by a bank of pea-soup fog. In the bedroom, as he tucked the duvet around Henry, the horn blared its doleful warning again. Henry opened his eyes. They looked almost black in the gloom. The realisation of what had bothered Adam about Faith's photo stiffened him like a cold wind. Her eyes were blue. The eyes in the painting had been dark brown. At least, that was how they'd appeared. It could have been a trick of the shadows.

Comforted by the sight of his dad, Henry slid back into sleep. Adam leaned in, studying every curve, crease and freckle of his son's face. So beautiful. If any harm came to him... He shook his head. *No harm will come to him because you won't let it. You're going to find out what's going on in this house and sort it out once and for all.* He kissed Henry's forehead and straightened to leave.

Catching sight of himself in the mirror, he huffed out an annoyed breath. Someone had moved the sodding wardrobe again. Had it been like that before the police came? As he pushed it back across the mirror, Rozen's voice seemed to echo in his ears – *When you get back to the house look in all the mirrors. Look as closely as you can.* He frowned in thought. The cryptic remark held some deeper meaning. He knew Rozen well enough by now to be sure of that. But he'd looked in every mirror in the house and seen nothing out of the ordinary. The lines on his forehead sharpened. No, he hadn't looked in every mirror.

Leaving the bedroom door ajar, he returned downstairs and entered The Lewarne Room. He scrutinised the photo of Walter, looking past the industrialist's disgusted face into the tall arched mirror. It reflected a wall of large stone blocks. His finger traced a thin, dark line down the wall. Was that a crack?

He glanced towards the spidery crack in the external wall. Was it a continuation of the one in the photo? He lit a candelabrum, ducked into the secret passageway and descended to the damp, mossy corridor that passed under the entrance hall. He examined the granite block wall. The blocks looked to be about the same dimensions as those in the photo. Was the arched mirror on the other side of them?

He went up to the entrance hall, rummaged through his coat pockets and found what he was looking for – a beermat with an address and telephone number written on it. He turned to the front door.

"Where are you going?" asked Ella, appearing from the direction of the kitchen.

"To speak to someone."

"Who? Rozen?"

"I won't be long," Adam replied evasively.

"What if Henry and I aren't here when you get back?"

He glanced at Ella, his eyes half-apologetic, half-imploring. "Just give me a couple of hours."

CHAPTER 25

Drizzle dampened Adam's face as he hurried to the car. He started the engine and manoeuvred past the police vehicles. The helicopter was gone. The fog bank was a mile or so out to sea, advancing steadily. It seemed that the coastguard had beaten the fog to Faith's body. Unease lined his forehead. What answers – if any – would the body give up?

Adam followed the winding lane down into Treworder. A fishing-boat was swaying shoreward over choppy waves. Heavy steel links clanked as a tractor hauled a boat up onto the shingles at the back of the beach. He pulled over outside a small bungalow perched on the valley side high above Rozen's cottage. A gusting wind ruffled his hair as he knocked on its door. It was opened by a bleary-eyed, unshaven figure in a tartan dressing gown and slippers. The sleepiness departed Doug Blackwood's eyes at the sight of Adam.

"Mr Piper. What can I do for you?"

"Sorry if I woke you," said Adam. "I'd like to speak with you about Fenton House."

"Oh." The surprise in Doug's voice was supplanted by an eager, "Come in, come in."

He ushered Adam to an armchair in a little living room. A coffee-table was cluttered with the familiar detritus of a writer's workplace – laptop, coffee-stained mugs, scribbled notes, an empty wine glass, an overflowing ashtray. Doug swished open the curtains, revealing the blue half-moon of Treworder cove and a view, partially obscured by bushes and trees, of Fenton House. Satan's Saucepan was disappearing into fog. "Tea? Coffee?"

"No thanks."

"It's no bother. I'm making coffee. I had a late session last night." Doug peered over his glasses at Adam. "Looks like you did too."

Adam confirmed the observation with a heavy sigh. "OK, I'll have a coffee."

Doug went back into the hallway. He returned with two mugs and handed one to Adam. He seated himself on a shabby sofa and lit a cigarette. Settling back, he puffed on his cigarette and waited for Adam to speak.

Now it came to it, Adam found once again that he was reluctant to talk about Fenton House. If Rozen or Mr Mabyn caught wind of him having spoken to Doug, it could render moot any decision about whether or not to remain living there. "You have to promise not to put what I tell you into your book."

"I'm not sure I can promise that."

"My family and I could get kicked out of our home."

"You said you're not permitted to allow anyone like me into Fenton House, not that you can't speak about it."

Adam gave a flick of his hand as if to say, *What's the difference?*

"If I'm reading this rightly, you're here because something out of the ordinary has happened and you want my advice," said Doug.

Adam nodded cagily.

"Well I'd have to be a real bastard to exploit a fellow writer in need," continued Doug. "So how about this? You can read my manuscript before I send it to my publisher, and if there's anything in there that could get you in trouble I'll remove it. Does that put your mind at rest?"

"Not entirely, but it doesn't make any difference," admitted Adam. "I need to find out what the deal is with that house and you're the only person I can think of who'll give me a straight answer."

"I'll do my best. I've dug up a lot about Fenton House, but obviously I'm limited by lack of access to the house itself."

Doug took a drag on his cigarette, looking expectantly at Adam. Adam puffed his cheeks as if unsure where to begin. He'd only intended to talk about Faith, but when he opened his mouth he found himself giving Doug a play-by-play account of everything unusual that had happened since moving into Fenton House. It felt good to get it all out, especially the shame he felt for suspecting Henry of killing the robin. The only thing he didn't mention was Jacob. His tongue diverted around his dead son as automatically as water flowing around a rock.

Doug broke in several times, digging for details – particularly about The Lewarne Room and the secret passageways.

When the story reached the present moment, Adam fell silent and waited half-expectantly, half-anxiously for Doug to speak.

Doug stubbed out his cigarette and lit another. "I was a psychologist for twenty-one-years before I..." he paused for the right phrase, "fell from the true faith. I'm going to speak to you as a psychologist first, then as a parapsychologist. You've told me a lot, but not everything. You and your son are clearly carrying a heavy burden."

Adam grimaced, his gaze falling away from Doug. "Henry had a twin brother – Jacob..." His voice faltered. He cleared his throat and, struggling to keep tears out of his eyes, he told Doug about the accident.

Doug nodded as if he'd expected to hear some such thing. "You blame yourself of course. But part of you also blames Henry."

"That's not true," Adam said vehemently.

"Yes it is." There was no judgement in Doug's tone. It was a simple statement of fact.

"I..." Adam trailed off, hanging his head as he recalled Ella's angry response to his manuscript – *The boy's the killer, isn't he? The boy who just happens to have curly hair and freckles like Henry.*

"What you're feeling is completely normal. Over the years, I saw numerous patients who were struggling with similar feelings."

Adam raised his eyes hopefully. "And how did they get past those feelings?"

"Some of them never did. Others came to an acceptance that sometimes terrible things happen that are no one's fault and there's nothing we can do about it except try to move on."

"That's why we came here. To move on."

"It's not a matter of geography. You can't run away from what's in here." Doug touched his temple.

"So what do I do?"

"You talk to your wife and son as openly as possible."

Deep furrows formed on Adam's forehead. "How do I tell my son that part of me blames him for his brother's death?"

"I know it's hard, Adam, but if you don't confront this it will eat away at you for the rest of your life. Neither you nor your family will ever find real happiness. Not here. Not in London. Not anywhere."

Both men were silent for an extended moment. Adam's face twitched with uncertainty, then he gave a sudden nod. "I'll do it." His voice was tense with resolve. "Even if it breaks apart my family, I've got to try."

"There's always that risk, but I don't think it'll happen. It's clear you love your family. And as my mum used to say, love finds a way of getting us through."

"Love finds a way," Adam repeated to himself.

"OK. I've spoken to you as a psychologist. Now comes the part where I speak to you as a parapsychologist." Doug leaned forwards. A sudden intensity came into his voice. "I advise you to go back to Fenton House, pack your belongings and leave there today."

His words set Adam's heart racing. "Are we in some sort of danger?"

"Let's just say I think someone's playing a game with you."

"Who? Rozen?"

"Whoever or whatever that 'someone' is, their intentions are certainly not benign."

"Why would anyone want to hurt me and my family?"

"You and I are writers. We're always searching for complex motivations, but the world is not complicated." Doug divided the air into two with his hand. "Good and evil. There are things whose sole purpose in this world is to cause suffering. Many people subscribe to the theory that all those 'things' are manifestations of the same one 'thing'."

Adam gave a low laugh of understanding. "You're talking about the Devil. Are you seriously suggesting the Devil is out to get me?"

Doug smiled at his scepticism. "Do you know what Fenton means? It's a variant of the Cornish word venton, which translates to spring or fountain. Fenton House is built on a natural spring."

"That makes sense. Like I said, there's running water beneath the house."

"Natural springs are powerful conductors of energy. They're notorious for high concentrations of paranormal activity. Why do you think Walter Lewarne built a house on that particular spot? Walter developed a keen interest in spiritualism after his parents died in a boating accident in 1908. He befriended many of the leading mediums of his day. They would hold séances at his house in Kensington. Then came the build up to the First World War. Rumblings of political discontent on the continent. Walter moved to Treworder. From here he ran his arms manufacturing business, amassing a vast fortune as war loomed on the horizon. Walter also had a taste for the risqué, which he was able to indulge in the privacy afforded by Fenton House."

"You mean the naked masquerade balls. Rozen told me about them. She said they caused a big scandal."

"Back then that type of behaviour was enough to get you ostracised by society, especially in a rural community like this. In an attempt to repair his reputation, Walter ploughed thousands of pounds into local good causes – schools, hospitals and the like. Then war broke out and his financial fortunes took a severe turn for the worse."

"Surely with a war on he should have made more money than ever."

"You'd have thought so, but at the end of 1914 Walter effectively committed career suicide by ceasing all arms production in his factories. He never publicly explained his decision, but the prevailing theory was that he'd had an attack of conscience. What you've told me seems to confirm that theory." Doug rose to pluck a Bible from a bookshelf. He flipped through it and read aloud, "A voice was heard in Ramah. Lamentation, weeping and great mourning. Rachel weeping for her children, refusing to be comforted because they are no more."

"They are no more," echoed Adam. "The inscription in The Lewarne Room."

"It's a quote from the Gospel of Matthew about the Massacre of the Innocents, when Herod attempted to kill Jesus by putting to death every child in Bethlehem under two-years-old. The phrase was also used to describe the fate of young German soldiers killed during the battle of Ypres in 1914. Twenty-odd thousand student soldiers are said to have been buried in a mass grave after the battle. The huge casualties opened the public's eyes to the reality of modern warfare. The effect on Walter was obviously profound. Despite mounting debts and being portrayed as an appeaser and a traitor by the press, he refused to resume arms production. In the end, it was all for nothing. The government commandeered his factories. That must have been a crushing blow because Walter was rarely seen in public again."

Doug turned to the bookshelf and withdrew three black and white photos from a pile of papers. "I found these in The British Library." He arranged the photos side-by-side on the coffee-table. Together they formed what appeared to be a triptych painting of the Last Supper. The long haired, bearded and serene figure of Jesus sat at the centre of a rectangular table covered with a white cloth set with a plate, a goblet and a loaf of bread. His twelve disciples were arrayed around the table to either side of him. Their sad faces were haloed by pale light – all except for one. At Jesus's left hand was a man clutching a bulging purse. The man was slim with short grey hair and vaguely familiar aquiline, high-cheek-boned features. It dawned on Adam where he'd seen the face before – the man was an older looking Walter Lewarne. Walter was drawing back from Jesus with an expression that suggested he'd seen or heard something deeply disturbing.

"Walter commissioned that painting in 1917," said Doug. "Is it hanging in the house?"

"Not that I'm aware of. Maybe it's in the room where Walter's photo was taken."

"Note that Walter is sitting at Jesus's left-hand side. That's where Judas usually sits clutching the bag of coins he received in payment for betraying his master."

"So Walter agreed with what the press were saying about him."

"It's not that simple. Judas's betrayal wasn't against one man or even one nation, it was against the whole of humanity. But in a strange way the newspapers may have been right about Walter being an appeaser. You mentioned hearing a bell ringing on several occasions. Well in Buddhism and Shamanism bells are used to summon the spirits of the dead to ritual meals. Food is laid out to honour the dead, but it can also be an act of contrition."

"You think Walter was pleading for the forgiveness of dead soldiers?"

Doug nodded. "I also think it's possible that his summons was answered by something else. Something seeking to exploit his emotional distress."

"By 'something' you mean the Devil." The scepticism was back in Adam's voice.

"Call it what you will. It all amounts to the same thing."

"OK, assuming for a moment that you're right and Walter accidentally summoned the Devil or some sort of demon or whatever. Then what? Did this thing force him to hang himself?"

"This thing – let's call it the Entity for simplicity's sake – doesn't force anyone to do anything. That's not its way. It finds a person's weakness – it could be something they lust after or suffer guilt, fear or grief over – and it uses that weakness to attack and seduce them. Faith Gooden wasn't thrown off the cliffs, she was merely led to their edge. Do you understand what I'm saying? The Entity is waiting for you to invite it in."

Adam smiled, although a cold sensation was prickling through him. "And how would I do that?"

"Isn't that obvious? By remaining at Fenton House."

Adam's smile vanished. "What if I say you're talking a load of bollocks?"

"Then I'd say that the Entity is halfway to achieving its goal."

"Which is?"

"The Entity's purpose is simple – it wants you and your family to die because it has never lived."

"And if we leave Fenton House will this thing leave us alone?"

"I wish I could say yes, but the Entity isn't attached to a particular place."

"Then there's really no point in leaving."

"Actually there's a lot of point to it," disagreed Doug. "Just because the Entity can follow you doesn't mean it will. If you make this decision together as a family, it may give up its attack. The Entity is fickle. That's *its* weakness."

Adam pressed his fingers to his temples as if to hold his head steady. "Explain something to me. If Fenton House really is evil, how did Rozen live there all those years and walk away none the worse for it?"

"I never said Fenton House is evil. I said the spring makes it a focal point for paranormal activity. But that isn't necessarily a bad thing. Some people live in such locations because they believe it will bring good fortune. It comes down to what you believe. Can a house be evil? Or does that evil only exist because we brought it there? As for Rozen... As far as anyone around here knows, she hasn't had a close relationship with anyone since her mother's death. She has no living relatives. For the past twenty-nine-years she's been utterly alone, and sometime soon she'll die alone. I don't call that walking away none the worse for it. Let me ask you something, Adam. What did you think about Rozen when you found out why she was giving up Fenton House?"

"I thought she was eccentric. Possibly mad."

"And you chose to exploit her madness. I'd say that's as good a reason as any to leave Fenton House."

Adam felt a bite of anger. Not at Rozen, but at himself. This time he knew Doug was right. They were silent for another while. Doug lit a third cigarette. Adam looked out of the window, his eyebrows knitted together as if he was wrestling with a difficult choice. The fog was pressing against the glass. He felt like he was staring into the inside of his own head. As if he'd reached a decision, he stood up suddenly and said, "Thank you, Doug."

"I hope I've been of some help," said Doug, rising to shake Adam's hand.

He showed Adam to the front door. The wind had dropped to a dead calm, amplifying the mournful blare of the foghorn. Fog as thick as porridge concealed everything beyond the reach of a hand.

"One more thing," said Doug. "This'll make me sound like an old hippy, but whatever decision you make do it with love. Love is the most powerful defence you have, be it against psychological or supernatural attack."

Adam smiled again, this time without scepticism, then he groped through the fog to his car.

CHAPTER 26

The fog parted reluctantly in front of the bumper as Adam edged down into the valley. He pulled over at Boscarne Cottage, got out and knocked on its door. A minute passed. He wondered whether Rozen was in. The faint light seeping out of the windows suggested she was. Another thought occurred to him. What if for some reason she couldn't answer the door? What if she'd fallen ill? As he peered through a window, the door opened.

"Good morning, Adam," said Rozen.

She was attired as ever in her turquoise dress. Her ruby red smile was also in attendance. But Adam was struck by how grey and frail she looked. The spark had deserted her eyes. She was slightly stooped as if in pain.

"Are you OK, Rozen?"

"I'm fine, thank you, Adam. A tad under the weather. Please do come in." With arthritic slowness, Rozen led him to the cosy living room. The fat pug glanced at him despondently from the hearth rug.

"Edgar's looking a bit under the weather too," observed Adam.

"He's very sensitive to how I'm feeling. I'm making breakfast if you're hungry."

"Thanks, but I can't stay long." Adam's voice softened apologetically. "I just came to say that we're leaving Treworder."

Rozen's smile faltered for a second. A disappointed frown added to her wrinkles. "I assume from your tone that you're leaving for good." When Adam nodded, she continued, "May I ask why?"

For her own sake as much as for his, Adam wasn't sure it would be wise to tell her the truth – whatever that might be. "We realised we made a mistake coming here. I'm sorry for all the bother we've put you to."

Rozen wafted away his apology. "Let's be honest, Adam, I didn't do this out of the kindness of my heart. I did it for Mother."

A cold finger of unease touched Adam at the mention of Winifred. "I have to get back. We're leaving today. I'll drop the keys off with Mr Mabyn."

"You looked in the mirrors, didn't you?" Rozen said as Adam turned away. "What did you see?"

"I saw my face."

"But that wasn't all, was it? You saw Mother, didn't you?"

There was such a painfully hopeful note in Rozen's voice that Adam couldn't bring himself to say no. She'd never known the love of anyone but her mother. She had nothing to hold on to but her belief that Winifred was waiting for her beyond the grave. Hoping that he was atoning somewhat for taking advantage of that vulnerability, he said, "Yes."

Rozen took a quivering breath. "How did she seem?"

Adam thought about Winfred's portrait. One word stood out in his mind. "Sad."

"Yes, that's Mother. Sad in life. Sad in death. Apparently Father was the exact opposite. He never stopped smiling." Rozen pointed to her own smile. "That's where I inherited this from. Mother couldn't look at me without thinking of Father, which only made her all the more sad. Did she say anything?"

"She told me to leave Fenton House."

"Ah." Rozen nodded as if she finally understood. "Then of course you must do so at once. Mother knows best."

Adam started to head for the door, but Rozen spoke again. "I have one last question, Adam. Well, it's more of a request actually. May I have a kiss goodbye?"

Doug's words echoed in Adam's mind – *For the past twenty-nine-years she's been utterly alone.* How could he say no? He bent to give Rozen a quick kiss. She clasped her hands to his face. With a strength her birdlike frame didn't appear to possess, she held his lips to hers. Her lips were hard and hungry. With a muffled grunt, he prised her hands away and drew back. The kiss had ignited a feverish light in her eyes. He stared at her speechlessly for a second before hurrying from the cottage. A salty trace of the kiss lingered on his lips as he drove away. He wiped his mouth, but the taste stayed with him.

Fenton House loomed through the fog like a shadow made solid. Adam was relieved to see that the police were gone. He hurried inside, calling for Ella. No reply. The silence sketched lines on his forehead. He looked in the sitting room. She wasn't there. His feet echoed rapidly on the stairs. "Ella," he shouted again.

She emerged from Henry's bedroom, pulling the door to behind herself. "Keep your voice down. You'll wake him up."

Adam threw his arms around her and hugged her tight. "I'm sorry," he breathed in her ear. "I lost sight of what's most important. This place blinded me, but I see now that I was wrong."

Ella pulled back to look in his eyes. "Does that mean we're leaving?"

He nodded. "We should never have come here in the first place."

She smiled, stroking her hands down his face. "I love you."

"I love you too."

"And what about Henry? Do you love him?"

It made Adam wince that Ella would even need to ask such a question. "Of course I do."

"Then we'll find a way through all this."

"That's what Doug said."

"Who?"

"Doug Blackwood. I went to speak to him about Fenton House. He said love finds a way of getting us through."

"What else did he have to say?"

"A lot that made no sense and some that made a lot of sense. The gist of it was that we should pack up and leave here as soon as possible."

"So what are we waiting for? Let's start–"

Ella broke off as Henry's bedroom door swung open. Henry's cheeks were mottled with angry red splotches. He glared at his parents, his fists clenched at his sides as if for a fight. "I heard what you said. I don't want to leave."

"I know you like it here, Henry," Adam said softly. "I do too."

"Then why do you want to leave?" he demanded to know.

"Because this house... Well, it's just not safe. We've already had one break-in. What's to stop other people from doing the same?"

"We're getting new locks."

"If people want to get in here, they'll find a way." Adam summoned up a somewhat strained smile, reaching to rest a hand on Henry's shoulder. "It's not all bad. You'll be able to see your old friends."

Henry shrugged him off. "I don't have any friends in London."

"You don't have any friends here either," pointed out Ella. "You don't even have a school to go to."

"I don't care. I'm not going back to London. You can't make me!"

"Yes we can, Henry. We're your parents and you'll do as we say."

Adam could tell from the tremor in Ella's voice that she was on the verge of losing her patience. He made a calming motion. Henry's eyes began to overflow with tears. His voice rose shrilly. "You always ruin everything. I fucking hate you both!"

"How dare you speak to us like that," retorted Ella.

Doug's parting advice came vividly to Adam's mind – *whatever decision you make, do it with love.* "Please let's not fall out about this."

His plea fell on deaf ears. Pushing past him, Henry made to run off towards the stairs. Ella caught hold of his wrist. "Where do you think you're going?"

"Let go!" Henry tried to twist free. "You're hurting me."

"Then stop struggling."

Henry lashed out at Ella, his fingers hooked into claws. His nails drew four bloody lines on her cheek. She let go of him with a gasp. He sprinted away and disappeared down the stairs.

After a few seconds of stunned silence, Ella yelled, "Henry, get back here!"

She went after him. Adam was only a few paces behind her. Fingers of fog were curling around the open front door. Ella shouted for Henry from the doorstep. The fog swallowed her voice. She pointed left. "I'll go that way. You go the other. We'll meet at the backdoor."

The fog beaded on Adam's forehead, trickling into his eyes as he searched the tangle of reeds that fringed the pond. He groped his way past the robin's unmarked grave to the outhouses. The gloomy, cluttered buildings had an abundance of hiding places. It took a while to search them all. When he eventually arrived at the backdoor, Ella was already there. "We'll never find him in this," she said with a frustrated swipe at the fog.

"Have you been down to the back gate?"

"No."

"Let's try there."

Adam took Ella's hand and they hurried along the garden path. Panic touched him when he saw that the gate was open.

Ella voiced his fear. "Oh god, what if he falls?"

They passed through the arch of hedge. The coastal path seemed to have shrunk to a tightrope in the fog. Waves whooshed against rocks far below, as invisible as the sound they perpetually generated. Ella tightened her grip on Adam's hand. "I feel dizzy."

"I'll go on by myself. You wait here in case Henry comes back."

She drew a steadying breath. "No. We'll cover more ground if we split up."

"Then you head towards the village," suggested Adam. There was only a few hundred metres of cliff top path for Ella to negotiate in that direction.

"He can't have gone far without his shoes and coat on." It was a statement that sounded more like a question. Ella's wide brown eyes looked to Adam for reassurance.

Trying his best to sound as if he believed it, he replied, "He'll be fine." He felt a strong reluctance to let go of Ella's hand. "Be careful."

She managed a small smile. "You too."

Ella edged away, her arms outstretched like a blind person feeling for obstacles. Adam watched the fog envelop her before he set off more quickly in the opposite direction. On and on he advanced through the dreamlike whiteness, encountering no one, pausing every so often to futilely peer around and call for Henry. The nearer he drew to Lizard Point, the louder the eerie voice of the foghorn became. He too started to feel dizzy. Not with fear, but with tiredness. He hadn't slept in over twenty-four-hours. He stumbled several times and almost lost his footing. The fog distorted his sense of distance, but upon reaching the lifeboat station he knew he'd come roughly two miles. Fingers of cold air penetrated his jacket. He thought of Henry barefooted and in only his pyjamas. Surely he wouldn't have made it this far.

He turned back the way he'd come. His body seemed to grow heavier with every step. By the time he arrived at Fenton House, he felt dead on his feet. Entering by the backdoor, he called for Ella and got no reply. He'd been searching for almost two hours. Surely she should be back by now? But then again, she could have carried on past the village. He nodded to himself. That's what she'd do. And at the speed she'd been going, it would take her a lot longer to cover anything like the same amount of ground as he had done. It made him nervous to think about her teetering along the fog-bound path. One misstep and she might follow Faith off the cliffs. He looked at the grandfather clock. He'd give it ten minutes to get his legs back, then he'd go in search of both her and Henry.

He slumped onto the sofa. God, he was so tired. His eyelids felt as if dumbbells were dragging them down. Yawning, he rested his head against a cushion. Sleep pulled at his weary limbs. He tried to shrug it off, but its grip was too strong. A sound pierced his weariness – footsteps. His eyelids parted. Ella was standing in the doorway. She had her back to him. He sat up, blinking the blur of sleep from his vision.

"Ella."

She showed no sign of having heard. He noticed something strange – her hair was wet. It clung to her, smooth and glistening. So did her knee-length summer dress. Her skin was visible through the white cotton.

"Ella," he said again. "Did you find him?"

She moved silently into the hallway. Adam's eyebrows knotted. What was the matter with her? Why didn't she answer? He rose and went into the hallway. There was no one there. He looked in the kitchen. Empty. His heart speeding up with each step, he stuck his head into the orangery and dining room. No Ella. His gaze moved to The Lewarne Room. Its door was ajar. He took several hesitant steps towards it.

"Dad."

Adam jerked around at the sound of his son's voice. Henry was standing by the front door, arms hugged across his pyjama top, teeth chattering uncontrollably.

"Where the hell have you been?" Adam's tone seesawed between anger and concern.

"I was in the treehouse."

"You're in big trouble. How could you have hit your mum?"

"I'm really sorry, Dad." Tears trembled in Henry's big brown eyes. "I just can't stand the thought of going back to *that* house."

Adam sighed. He knew exactly how Henry felt. An image flashed through his mind of Jacob sprawled out in a puddle of blood on the porch floor. The thought of seeing that place again was like a hand twisting at his insides. Putting an arm around Henry, he ushered him into the warmth of the kitchen.

As Adam put fresh wood into the Rayburn, he asked, "Did you see your mum leaving the house just now?"

"No."

"Stay here. I'm going to look for her."

"Will you tell her how sorry I am?"

"You can tell her yourself."

Adam hastened from the kitchen. He looked in The Lewarne Room. It was empty. His eyes lingered on the secret panel. She wouldn't have gone into the passageways, would she? He shook his head. More likely she'd gone back out in search of Henry. He hurried to the garden.

"Ella! I've found Henry!"

Silence was his only reply. He made his way down to the cliffs again. As fast as he dared, he headed along the coastal path towards Treworder. He couldn't see Satan's Saucepan, but he could feel its huge, empty presence. A clamminess that had nothing to do with the fog swept over him as he neared the spot where Faith had plummeted from the cliffs. He pulled up abruptly as his right foot met with thin air. His hands darted out, desperately seeking something to stop him from overbalancing. He winced as his fingers closed around a spiky gorse branch. He steadied himself, then crouched down to inspect the path. His stomach gave a lurch. A section of the path was missing. A small landslip of earth and pebbles trailed down the cliff. The gap it had left behind was only an arm's length across, but that was enough for someone to fall through. A wooden handrail had been erected to protect walkers at the spot. The rail was broken at its centre and hung down in a V.

"No, no, no…" gasped Adam, dropping on to his belly to get a better look through the gap. There was nothing to see but a shifting white wall. "Ella!" he shouted, almost hoarse with fear. "Ella! Ella!"

Nothing. Not a sound besides his own rapid breathing and the hiss of the sea.

He shook his head, murmuring, "This isn't happening. This isn't happening." The pain where the gorse spines had pierced his palm suggested otherwise.

Sobs shook his body. Oh god, first Jacob, now Ella. It was too much to bear. He gave another shake of his head. *You don't know she's down there. And even if she is, she could still be alive.*

"Ella, if you can hear me, hold on," he called into the void. "I'm going for help."

Heedless of the danger now, Adam ran along the path. He stumbled to his knees and scrambled upright, then he was in the garden and the house was gradually taking shape, its outline shifting like a living thing in the fog. He burst into the entrance hall, snatched up the phone, dialled 999 and breathlessly told the operator what had happened.

"Dad, what's going on?" asked a tremulous voice from behind him.

Adam turned to Henry. Rage surged up his throat at the sight of his son's butter-wouldn't-melt face.

"What are you looking at me like that for?" Henry asked nervously.

First Jacob, now Ella. Two events separated by hundreds of miles, but connected by one common factor. Adam took a step towards Henry, his whole body quivering with barely contained fury.

Henry retreated towards the stairs. "You're scaring me."

"It's your fault." Adam's words came in a raw hiss. "It's all your fault."

They held each other's gaze for a breathless moment, then Henry turned and fled up the stairs. Adam gave chase. Henry sprinted along the landing to his bedroom and thrust the door shut. There was the click of a key turning in the lock. Adam hammered on the door, shouting, "Open this door you little bastard!"

"No," Henry yelled back. "Stop it! Go away!"

But Adam couldn't stop. He pounded on the door hard enough to make the walls tremble and the skin peel off his knuckles. Henry screamed and cried. Still, Adam didn't stop. It felt like all the emotion that had been pent up over the past ten months was exploding from him. He continued until sweat was running down his face and his lungs burned for oxygen. Finally, he collapsed to his knees, head in hands, sobbing.

CHAPTER 27

Adam stayed on his knees until he heard approaching sirens. Sucking the blood from his knuckles, he rose and went down to the front door. Flashing lights penetrated the fog. A trio of police cars and a Coastguard 'Search & Rescue' Landrover materialised. Detective Sergeant Penny Holman got out of the lead car.

"I think Ella's fallen into Satan's Saucepan," Adam told her.

"You think?"

"I didn't see it happen, but part of the path has... has... Oh Christ..." Adam hauled in a ragged breath, fighting to keep from breaking down.

Penny relayed instructions to her colleagues. Two constables moved off towards the cliffs. The coastguards set about kitting themselves out with harnesses, ropes, slings and other climbing gear.

"Let's go inside," said Penny, motioning for the remaining constables to accompany her and Adam into the entrance hall. "Now just try to stay calm, Mr Piper, and tell me exactly what happened."

"Ella was searching for Henry. He ran off when we told him we're moving back to London."

The sergeant's eyebrow lifted. "You're moving out of Fenton House?"

"Yes... No... I err..." stammered Adam. Were they still moving out?

"Where's your son?"

"He's in his–"

Adam fell silent as Henry appeared at the top of the stairs. Henry's eyes were puffy from crying. He descended the stairs, refusing to meet Adam's gaze.

Penny gave Henry an up and down look as if searching for signs of injury. "Your dad tells me you ran off."

"I was hiding because I don't want to go back to London."

"Did you see your mum go down to the cliffs?"

"Is my mum dead?" Henry asked with the glassy, blank stare of someone in shock.

"We don't know. We'll do our best to find her. I need you to be really strong, Henry. Can you do that for me?"

He nodded.

"Good boy. Let's sit down and see if we can get to the bottom of all this."

They went into the sitting room. Adam and Henry sat side by side on the sofa. Adam instinctively went to put an arm around his son's shoulders, but Henry shifted away from him. Sergeant Holman seated herself in an armchair.

"I'm not sure what else we can tell you," said Adam. "I was asleep on the sofa when I was woken by... Ella."

Picking up on Adam's hesitancy, Penny said, "You don't sound entirely sure that it was Ella."

"No, no, it was her. It's just that I didn't see her face." Adam pointed to the doorway. "She was over there. She went into the hallway. I went after her, but she'd gone back outside. Then Henry showed up."

Penny made a rewind motion. "Let's go back to earlier this morning. What happened before the argument?

"I'd been into Treworder to speak to Doug Blackwood. He's a parapsychologist writing a book about Fenton House. I wanted to ask him whether he thought it was safe for us to stay here."

"And what did he say?"

"He advised us to leave and I decided to take his advice."

"So you believe this house is haunted?"

"I..." Adam faded off, thinking about Ella's wet hair and dress. She'd looked as if she'd just been for a swim fully clothed.

"After speaking to Mr Blackwood did you come straight back here?"

"No. I stopped by Boscarne Cottage to tell Miss Trehearne that we were leaving."

"At roughly what time was this?"

"About eight o'clock. I was only there for ten minutes. Then I came back here. Ella and I argued with Henry and he ran off." Adam left out the part where Henry hit Ella. He didn't want the police getting any funny ideas about what might have happened. *Funny ideas?* piped up a sardonic voice in his head. *You mean like you thinking Henry is somehow responsible for the deaths of his brother and mum?* He dropped his gaze away from Penny as if fearing she might read his thoughts.

"How did you hurt your hands?" she asked, pointing to Adam's skinned knuckles.

"I..." Adam stumbled ashamedly over his reply. "I hit a door after losing my temper with Henry."

Penny looked at Henry. "Is that what happened?"

He nodded.

"Can you show me your hands, Henry?"

"What for?" asked Adam.

Without replying, Penny rose and moved to inspect Henry's outstretched hands. She nodded as if they confirmed something she'd expected to find. "There's blood under your fingernails, Henry. Can you tell me how it got there?"

"He scratched his mum's face when she tried to stop him from running away," said Adam.

"Please let Henry answer for himself," said Penny. She looked intently at Henry. "Did you scratch your mum?"

He gave another nod.

Penny's gaze moved to Adam, then back to the silent boy. "Would you prefer to talk to me alone, Henry?"

Adam shot her a frown. "Why would he want to talk to you alone?"

"Please, Mr Piper, I'm just trying to work out what's going on here."

"I've told you what's going on," snapped Adam. "We're not hiding anything from you."

"I never said you were. I'm just wondering why your son's so scared."

Another jolt of shame went through Adam as he looked at Henry and saw that Penny was right. Henry's head was sunk down between his shoulders. His hands were clasped white-knuckled on his lap. There was a tremor to his bottom lip. Adam's gaze returned to the policewoman. "I don't know what you're trying to imply, but I've told you everything there is to tell."

"I'd like your permission to take fingernail scrapings from Henry."

"No chance."

"I can get a court order. It'll take longer, but the end result will be the same. This way we'll be out of your hair that much quicker."

Adam heaved a sigh. His head was pounding. The sergeant's questions were like fingernails being raked down a chalkboard. And after all, what harm was there in the police taking scrapings? "OK."

Penny fetched a Forensic officer. Henry let out a low whimper at the sight of the pointed plastic fingernail scraper. "There's nothing to worry about, Henry. It's completely painless," Penny assured him.

Henry held still as the scrapings were taken and sealed in envelopes.

"Well done, Henry," said Penny. "One last thing, I need you to show me where the argument took place."

They went upstairs. There were thin smears of blood on Henry's bedroom door. Adam spread his hands as if to say, *See.* The Forensic officer remained upstairs while Adam, Henry and Penny returned to the sitting room.

"I assume you're going to hang around here until we find your wife?" Penny said to Adam.

As he nodded, the thought went through his head, *What if Ella's been swept out to sea? What if her body is never found?*

Penny left the room again. Adam turned to Henry with contrite eyes. "I'm sorry, Henry," he said. "I shouldn't have shouted at you like that or said what I did. This isn't your fault. You didn't make us come to this house. I did. If it's anyone's fault, it's mine."

Warily, Henry looked at his dad from under his eyelashes. "Is that what you really think?"

Now it was Adam's turn to look away. "Yes."

"Liar," muttered Henry.

They sat in heavy silence, listening to police moving about the house. Penny poked her head back into the room and beckoned Adam into the hallway. "The coastguards have reached the base of the cliff, but they haven't found anything yet," she informed him.

The words held both hope and fear. Either Ella hadn't fallen after all or she was somewhere at the bottom of the English Channel.

"I didn't want to ask you this in front of Henry," said Penny. "But is there any possibility that Ella could have decided to leave Treworder without you?"

"You suggesting she might have walked out on us?"

"It happens."

Adam shook his head hard. "Ella wouldn't do that."

"What about her mental health? Has she ever shown suicidal–"

"No," broke in Adam, his voice cracking again. He couldn't bear any more questions. He jerked around and headed for the sofa.

Henry was sitting with his knees drawn up to his chest, staring blankly at the floor. He looked as if all the expression had been slapped from his face. Adam wanted to put his arms around him and hold him tight, but he couldn't bring himself to. *First Jacob, now Ella.* The thought was like acid burning its way to the centre of his brain.

After what felt like hours, Penny came into the room again. "We're all done here for now," she said. "Are you sure you want to be alone?" The question was directed at Henry. "I can leave a constable behind if you like."

His voice tightly controlled, Adam said, "We'll be…" He trailed off. He'd been about to say *fine*, but he realised that was about as far from the truth as east was from west.

"One last thing, Mr Piper. Could you write down the names and contact numbers of Ella's parents and any siblings and friends?"

Adam winced as he thought about Ella's parents. Sooner or later he would have to speak to Richard and Linda. But not now. He couldn't face that now.

"Someone will be in touch as soon as there are any developments," Penny said as Adam handed her the list of names. "And, of course, you'll let us know if Ella shows up."

Adam nodded.

Penny gave Henry a lingering look as if waiting for him to say something. When he didn't, she turned to head for the front door.

CHAPTER 28

As the police vehicles disappeared into the fog, Adam closed the front door and returned to the sitting room. Henry was gone. Hearing footfalls on the landing, Adam went upstairs. He caught a whiff of Ella's perfume. It drew him to her dressing gown hanging on the back of their bedroom door. He clutched it to his face, filling his lungs with her sweet, musky scent. The material muffled his agonised moans. Oh Christ, there was nothing he wouldn't have given not only to smell her, but to touch her and hold her. Reluctantly releasing the dressing gown, he continued along the landing.

Henry's bedroom door was locked again. Adam tapped on it, saying softly, "I really am sorry, Henry. I was confused. I still am."

Silence. Then his ears caught a sound that set his heart beating fast – a faint click, like someone pressing a spring-loaded button.

"Henry," he said more loudly. "What are you doing in there?"

No reply.

"Answer me or I'll force my way in!"

Adam waited a few seconds before thrusting his shoulder against the door. It shuddered but held firm. He stood back and slammed a foot into the sturdy wooden panels with the same result. There was no way he was getting through the door without a crowbar. It occurred to him that there was more than one way into Henry's bedroom. He darted into the opposite room, pressed the two-way mirror's release mechanism and ducked into the passageways. He felt his way forwards until he saw light seeping through Henry's bedroom mirror. The wardrobe had been moved aside yet again. The room was empty.

"Henry!" he shouted. His voice reverberated along the passageways and found only silence. On the verge of tears, he pleaded, "Please, Henry! I'm sorry. I'm so sorry."

More silence. So loud it almost pummelled him to his knees. Propelled by panic, he stumbled through the darkness of the passageways. No Henry. Only dust, cobwebs and fear. After some time – he didn't know how long – he emerged into The Lewarne Room. The room was spinning like a fairground ride. He fell to his knees, clutching his head as if to stop it from splitting apart.

A faint gurgling found its way through his anguish. Something about the sound made him spring to his feet and run to the phone in the entrance hall. He started to dial 999, but hesitated. Twice the police had searched the house for Faith and twice they'd failed to find her. Why should it be any different with Henry? He dialled Doug instead.

When Doug picked up, Adam blurted out. "Ella and Henry are missing. Ella fell... At least I think she fell. I don't know... I–"

"Slow down, Adam," said Doug. "Take a breath and tell me what's happened."

Adam drew in a shuddering breath and resumed more slowly, "Ella might have fallen into Satan's Saucepan. The Coastguard are searching for her. And now I can't find Henry. He went into the secret passageways." By way of explanation, Adam added in a voice heavy with shame, "I tried to do things the way you said – with love – but it all went wrong. I don't know what to do, Doug. I feel like I'm losing my fucking mind."

"Listen to me, Adam." Doug's voice was calm but insistent. "Here's what I want you to do. Keep looking for Henry. Call his name. Tell him how much you love him. I'll be there as soon as I can."

"You're coming over? If word gets back to Rozen..." Adam trailed off meaningfully.

"You want to leave Fenton House anyway, don't you?"

"Yes, but not without Henry and–" *Ella.* Adam's voice snagged on the name. It seemed almost certain that he would be leaving without her no matter what.

"I'm the best chance you've got of finding your wife and son."

"Are… are you saying Ella might be alive?" asked Adam, stammering at the possibility.

"I don't know if she's alive. I don't want to give you false hope, but besides Rozen no one knows more about Fenton House than I do. If anyone can get to the bottom of what's going on there, it's me."

Adam was silent for a moment, racked with uncertainty. Then he said, "OK," and hung up quickly as if afraid he would change his mind.

He went outside and found his way through the fog to the half-finished treehouse. No Henry. He returned to the house. His voice echoed along its hallways. "Henry, can you hear me? There's no need to hide. I love you!"

He'd almost shouted himself hoarse by the time the hollow thunk of the front door knocker resonated throughout the house. He ran to answer the door. Doug had shaved since Adam last saw him. A leather satchel was slung over his shoulder. His eyes were bright with anticipation and something else – not fear but something akin to it. Adam glanced uneasily into the fog beyond Doug's shoulder.

"Don't worry," said Doug. "No one saw me coming here."

Adam motioned for him to come inside. Doug stepped forwards, but hesitated on the threshold like someone testing cold waters and deciding if they wanted to take the plunge. His eyes lit up as he caught sight of Winifred's portrait. He moved in for a closer look. "I see what you mean," he said, studying Winifred's pale, delicate face. "So sad and beautiful." He took a camera out of his satchel and photographed the portrait.

"I thought you were here to help me find my son, not gather material for your book," said Adam.

"Sorry. Force of habit." Doug returned the camera to his satchel. "Did you do as I said?"

Adam nodded. "I've searched everywhere except the tower."

"Take me to its door." Adam led Doug up to the attic. Doug ran his fingers over the ivory stars and ebony planets inlaid into the door, murmuring, "Absolutely exquisite workmanship." He examined the lock. "There's no way we're opening this without a key."

"What if there's another way into the tower?"

"There might well be, but how would we find it?"

"How would Henry have found it?"

"Perhaps someone showed him." Doug's gaze moved along the walls and ceiling as if he expected to see some spectral figure floating nearby.

"Please," Adam's voice was a quivering bundle of barely restrained nerves, "no more supernatural bullshit. Just help me find Henry. After that you can take all the photos you want."

Doug gave him a sympathetic smile. "To hell with the photos. We're going to find your son even if it means taking this place apart brick by brick." He placed a steadying hand on Adam's shoulder. "OK?"

Dredging up a faint smile of his own, Adam nodded.

"Show me where you last saw Henry," said Doug.

They went to Henry's bedroom. Doug looked under the bed and in the wardrobe, saying, "The most obvious places are often the last places we think to look."

When his search turned up nothing, Doug took out a torch and headed into the passageways. He made his way through them with eyes as wide as a child in their favourite toy store, occasionally pausing to listen and tap at a wall. He lingered beneath the entrance hall for several minutes, examining the mossy flagstones and rust-streaked stone blocks.

A dull red glow trickled through The Lewarne Room's secret panel. Doug approached the room as if he was walking on ice. He took in the paintings, the words carved above the fireplace, the glittering serpentine pedestals.

He picked up the photo of Walter. "Any idea where this was taken?"

"No, but the blocks in it are about the same dimensions as those under the entrance hall."

Doug nodded to indicate that he'd made the same observation. Dropping to his hands and knees, he pressed his ear to the tiles. He moved around the floor, feathering his fingers over the embossed fleur de lis pattern. He stopped on a line of black grouting. "There's a gap here."

Adam ran a fingertip along the grouting. There was a crack as thin as his fingernail. He traced out a square four tiles by four tiles. "It could be a trapdoor."

"My thoughts exactly."

Doug took out a penknife. He slid the tip of its blade along the gap. "I can't feel anything that could be a release lever." His brow puckering in thought, he looked at the words over the fireplace. "They are no more," he murmured. He approached the fireplace and reached up to feel the letters. They were smoothly varnished with no visible joins between them and the wooden backplate. He tried pressing and twisting them. Nothing seemed to move, but suddenly there was a sound like a spring being released.

"Look," exclaimed Adam. One side of the four by four square had risen a centimetre or so. Adam tried to lift it further, but it was stuck fast. "Give me your knife."

Adam pushed the blade between the tiles and levered its handle downwards. The blade bent and snapped with a ping. "Wait here. I'll be back in a minute," he said, springing up and running to the front door. He plunged into the fog again, found his way to the outhouses, then returned to The Lewarne Room with a hammer and chisel. He hammered the chisel into the gap, cracking the surrounding tiles.

"It's moving," he said, wrenching at the chisel.

Millimetre by millimetre the trapdoor grated upwards, until it popped jack-in-the-box style into an upright position. Its wooden underside was etched with a crucifix and criss-crossed with what appeared to be scratch marks.

The subterranean room exhaled a breath as cold as a winter morning and as fusty as a long-sealed crypt. A steep flight of stone steps led down into darkness. A figure clothed in tatters of greyish material was huddled up at the top of them. The figure's eye sockets were empty. Their mouth appeared to be fixed into brown-toothed smile. There was no flesh left on their bones, but a few wisps of dark hair still clung to their skull.

Adam and Doug exchanged a wide-eyed glance. Doug shone his torch into the aperture. The orange light played on a glassy surface. "Water. Looks like it's two or three feet deep."

More bones wrapped in floating tendrils of decayed clothing trailed across a flagstone floor. The torch's beam lingered on a second skull whose jaw hung open as if emitting a silent scream, before moving on to a collapsed section of exterior wall. Clear water trickled into the room through a hole as smooth and round as a throat. Had the room's prisoners tried to tunnel their way out? Or had the underground spring forced its way through the foundations?

"George, Sofia and Heloise," Adam said quietly, as if afraid of disturbing the Trehearne family's eternal rest.

"I only see two skulls."

"The other could be underneath the rubble."

"I think we may have just solved a twenty-two-year-old mystery," agreed Doug. He traced his fingers along the scratches on the underside of the trapdoor. "They must have got trapped down there somehow."

Doing his best to avoid the skeleton, Adam lowered himself through the trapdoor. His foot nudged a bone. The material overlaying it crumbled like ancient parchment and the bone rattled down the steps and hit the shimmering surface with a splash. Adam dipped a finger into the water. It was so cold it burned. "Are you coming down?" he asked.

Doug shook his head, glancing uneasily at the skeletons. "We don't want the same thing that happened to them to happen to us."

Adam reached up to take the torch from him and swept its beam over the room. The light landed on a pair of frayed black velvet curtains dangling down into the water – surely the same curtains Walter had photographed himself in front of. The curtains swayed slowly. Was the current moving them or was it something else – something hiding behind them? Adam's heart skipped in protest as he lowered himself into the icy water. It came up to his waist. His feet stirred up swirls of silt as he waded towards the curtains.

He drew the sodden material apart. A face haggard with anxiety and exhaustion stared back at him from beyond the curtains – his own face reflected in a tall arched mirror.

"Saint Michael the Archangel, defend us in battle. Be our protection against the wickedness and snares of the Devil. May God rebuke him–"

Adam turned to Doug, frowning. "What's that you're saying?"

Doug nodded at the skeletons. "I was saying a prayer for them and for us."

"I told you, I don't want to hear any of that crap," snapped Adam, making his way back to the steps and clambering up them. He slumped shivering onto the red sofa. "Where the hell is Henry?"

"The only place left to look is the tower."

Adam shook his head. "There's about as much chance of him being in the tower as there was of him being in there." He jabbed a finger towards the trapdoor. "It's like you said, he's probably somewhere so obvious we haven't–" He broke off suddenly, springing to his feet. "I think I know where he is."

"Where?"

Without replying, Adam ran from the room and headed for the backdoor. The fog was as thick as ever. It clung to him like candyfloss as he descended to the cliffs and advanced recklessly along the tightrope of a path. A strip of yellow plastic tape with 'CAUTION DANGER' on it cordoned off the spot where the path had collapsed. A small figure was sitting on the wrong side of the tape, staring into Satan's Saucepan.

"Henry!" gasped Adam. He threw his arms around his son and drew him back from the cliff edge.

"I can't find her," Henry said through chattering teeth, his voice hollowed out by anguish. "Are you still angry with me?"

Adam hugged him tight. "No." He pulled away to look in Henry's eyes. "Honestly." There was no lie in his voice. He felt nothing but relief. "Just don't do that to me again. If I lose you too I... I don't know what I'd do." That part *was* a lie. If he lost Henry too, Adam had a pretty good idea what he'd do. What would he have left to live for if his entire family was gone? "Come on, you're freezing. Let's get you back to the house."

As they inched along the path, they met Doug coming the other way. Doug smiled at Henry. "Your dad's been worried sick about you."

"He was looking for his mum," explained Adam.

Doug nodded as if to say, *Yes, I'd guessed that.* "Well now we can all look for her together."

CHAPTER 29

Back at the house, Adam changed into dry clothes while Doug heated a pan of soup. Henry swallowed his soup mechanically, not seeming to taste it. Adam was too chewed up with worry to eat. Afterwards, he wrapped Henry in a blanket on the sofa and set about lighting a fire. Doug headed off, camera in hand, to make another sweep of the house for Ella.

By the time flames were crackling in the hearth, Henry had dozed off. Adam perched at his side, staring at him as if afraid he might disappear again.

After a while, Doug came into the room and gave an apologetic shake of his head.

A grimace of disappointment passed over Adam's face. "Thanks for trying."

"Listen, there's a spare bed at my cottage. Why don't you and Henry come and stay with me?"

Adam shook his head. "How can we leave here? What if Ella didn't fall? What if she's just lost in the fog?"

"Then the police will find her or she'll find her way to help once the fog clears. Either way, you don't need to be here. Unless, that is, you're starting to wonder whether my bullshit's true."

Adam's gaze drifted towards the doorway where he'd last seen Ella. There had been something off about her, something more than simply her wet hair and dress. "Honestly, I don't know what to think any more."

"I realise you don't want to hear this, but everything I've seen here has left me more convinced than ever that Walter Lewarne brought something into this house–"

"You're right, I don't want to hear it," cut in Adam.

Doug held his camera out to Adam. "Take it. Delete the photos. I don't care about them. I just want you to listen to what I've got to say."

Sighing, Adam motioned for him to put the camera away. "I suppose that's the least I can do after everything you've done."

"You believe there's only one reality, but you're wrong. There are alternate realities, places neither here nor there but somewhere in-between."

"You mean the afterlife?"

"That word is just another label. I'm talking about other dimensions that exist parallel to our world. Dimensions where there are *things* that are constantly looking for a way into this world. Just as there are people in this world who are searching for a way into those other worlds."

"People like Walter Lewarne."

"Walter had an overwhelming desire to speak to the dead. That's dangerous enough in itself. When spirits don't pass on, it's always for a reason. And that reason usually isn't good. Such spirits are angry, lost and confused. They often don't realise they're dead. All they know is they feel wronged and hunger for some sort of resolution. Speaking to them can provide that resolution, but I think Walter tried to go a step further. I think he was searching for a way to allow spirits to enter the physical plane. For that he would have needed a portal."

Adam's eyebrows lifted in realisation. "The mirror."

Doug nodded. "It's a commonly held superstition that mirrors are doorways to the spirit world. Covering a mirror would usually be enough to prevent spirits from travelling freely between this world and the next, but it might not stop something as powerful as the Entity from doing so. Not in a place like this where the energies are multiplied a hundredfold by local geology."

Adam's forehead wrinkled in thought. "How would someone open such a doorway?"

"Some would say you need to have psychic abilities. I believe that all you need is the will, the desire, the love."

"The love," Adam repeated, a heart-crushing image of Ella rising into his mind. "So if Ella was..." Glancing at Henry, he lowered his voice to a whisper. "If Ella was dead I could use that mirror to contact her?"

Doug frowned. "Theoretically, but like I said it would be extremely dangerous to try."

"Would I need to perform some kind of ritual?"

"We're getting off track. The point I was–"

"You're the one who started this conversation, Doug," interrupted Adam. "So come on, tell me how it's done."

"You don't need any ritual. All you need to do is look in the mirror and call to your loved one."

"And what if that doesn't work?"

"You remember what I said about Shamans preparing meals to honour the dead? You could try cooking something Ella loves to eat."

"Beans on toast. That's Mum and Jacob's favourite," said a child's voice.

Adam and Doug turned to Henry.

"How long have you been awake?" asked Adam.

Henry shrugged, but the strange light in his eyes suggested he'd been listening long enough.

"I was just saying to your dad that the two of you are welcome to stay at my cottage," said Doug. "How would you like that, Henry?"

"Are my mum and brother inside a mirror?"

Doug smiled as if the idea was absurd. "Of course not."

"So where are they?"

"I don't know."

"Then how do you know they're not in a mirror?"

There was no debating with a child's logic. Doug looked to Adam for back-up. "Doug's right," said Adam. "Jacob and your mum aren't inside a mirror."

"So where are they?" repeated Henry, his voice a flat challenge.

"They're… They're somewhere else," Adam answered unconvincingly. As Henry opened his mouth to respond, Adam added, "No more arguing, Henry." He folded his arms to show the conversation was over.

Henry and he stared at each other, competing in a silent battle of wills. After a moment, Henry snapped his mouth shut. Adam turned to Doug. "Thanks again for your offer, but we're staying here for now."

Doug sighed resignedly. "Promise me one thing, Adam. If you try to contact Ella, don't do it here."

"I won't do it here or anywhere else," said Adam, rising to show Doug to the front door. "Why would I? It's all bollocks, isn't it?"

Doug threw him a wry look. "The dead are dead. Leave them be." He glanced towards the sitting room. "For his sake."

"He's all I've got left. I'll jump off those cliffs myself before I let any harm come to him."

Doug grimaced. "Don't talk like that. Remember. Faith wasn't thrown off the cliffs, she was merely led to their edge." His gaze moved to The Lewarne Room. "What are you going to do about *them*?"

"I'll call the police tomorrow. I've had all I can stand of them in the house today. The Trehearnes have been missing twenty-odd-years. One more night won't make any difference."

Doug pushed his lips out as if he wasn't sure that was true. They shook hands and Doug headed for his car. The fog closed around him like curtains. Adam locked the front door. He went to the backdoor and locked that too. No one else was getting in or out of the house today.

CHAPTER 30

When Adam returned to the sitting room, Henry said, "We could try speaking to Mum in a mirror. She might be able to tell us where she is."

"No."

"Why not?"

"Because it's dangerous."

"Why is it dangerous if you don't even believe in it?" persisted Henry.

"Listen, things are bad enough already. I don't want to do anything that might make them worse. That includes scaring the crap out of ourselves by doing something stupid like that."

A frown gathered on Henry's forehead. "I don't think it's stupid. We could try to talk to Jacob as well." There were suddenly tears in his eyes. "I want to talk to Jacob. I want to say sorry to him."

Tears threatened to find their way into Adam's eyes too. "You've got nothing to say sorry for, Henry."

Henry narrowed his eyes as if trying to work out whether that was what Adam really believed. "I don't see how anything could make things worse," he muttered, lying back down with his face to the cushions.

Adam laid a hand on his son's back. "We've still got each other."

Henry sobbed into the cushions. Adam kept his hand where it was until Henry's tears subsided into sleep. His own eyes rolled with exhaustion. He rose to chuck a couple of logs on the fire. He needed to stay awake in case the police called. He made himself a coffee and sat in the armchair, listening for the phone, wanting and not wanting it to ring. He kept glancing at the grandfather clock. Minutes crept by like hours. Hours passed like days. His head felt as heavy as a breeze-block. It lolled back against the cushions. His eyelids drifted shut.

"Ella." The name passed his lips in an agonised murmur. "Ella…"

"I'm here, Adam. Don't leave. Please stay with me."

The words seemed to come from behind him. The sweet scent of Ella's perfume filled his nostrils. Eyes snapping open, he jerked around. There was no one there.

Blinking dazedly, he told himself, *You were dreaming.*

And yet it had seemed so real. Ella's voice, the smell of her perfume. So real...

Hauling in a shuddering breath, he rose to his feet. Henry was still asleep. Adam padded into the hallway. He stopped outside The Lewarne Room, his face a mask of pained uncertainty. Slowly, like a fish being reeled in, he approached The Lewarne Room and reached for the door handle. He snatched his hand back like a child caught in some mischief as a shrill *brrrinnng, brrrinnng* split the silence. He spun around to snatch up the phone's receiver.

He could barely find the breath to speak. "Yes?"

"Adam?"

The voice made his stomach plummet. "Linda." Ella's mother was the last person he wanted to talk to right now.

"A policewoman phoned. She asked all sorts of questions about Ella and you. She..." Linda stumbled over her words, struggling to keep control of her emotions. "She said Ella is missing."

From somewhere Adam summoned up the strength to reply, "She may have fallen from the cliffs."

There was a sudden clunk as if Linda had dropped the phone. The sound of her sobbing seemed to reach Adam from a great distance.

Richard came on the line. "Just what the hell's going on?" he demanded to know. "Where's my daughter?"

"I..." Adam's eyes returned to The Lewarne Room's door. "I can't stay on the phone. The police might try to contact me."

"Don't you dare hang up. Put Henry on the phone. I want to talk–"

"I'm sorry, Richard," interrupted Adam.

He put the receiver down. Almost immediately the phone rang again. He picked it up and Richard barked at him, "I'm warning you—"

Adam hung up again. He waited a moment. When the phone remained silent, he turned to approach The Lewarne Room. Moving faster now, he opened the door and entered the room. He shuddered. The flooded basement seemed to have sucked all the warmth out of the air. He peered through the trapdoor. The skull grinned up at him. Picking his way through the bones, he descended the steps and lowered himself into the water. This time he was ready for the numbing cold. Instead of fighting it, he used it to give him strength.

He sloshed to the mirror. The top half of it was above the water. He took hold of its silver frame and attempted to lift it. It came away from the wall and sank against the flagstones with a dull clunk. He dragged it across the floor and up the steps, causing a minor landslide of bones. He lifted it through the trapdoor and balanced it against the wall adjacent to the shuttered window. Its surface was smeared with translucent slime. He cleaned it with his sleeve. The hollow-eyed face that looked back at him from the glass was almost like a stranger. *What the fuck are you doing?* The thought came and went in a breath, displaced by an image of Ella in her wet dress.

"Who phoned?"

Adam flinched around at Henry's voice. Henry was staring at him from the doorway with a knowing gleam in his eyes. "No one. Go back to the sitting room."

"No. I want to help."

"Do as I say, Henry."

Henry shook his head. "I'm going to help and you can't stop me." He pointed to the mirror. "I'm not scared of that."

Adam almost smiled. Jacob had always been the brave one of the twins. He'd teased Henry for his timidity. But it seemed Fenton House had forced

Henry to finally find his courage. Adam left the room. Henry followed him into the kitchen.

"I'll make toast," said Henry as Adam opened a tin of beans.

They took the beans on toast to The Lewarne Room, set it down on the floor and stood side by side staring into the mirror.

"What now?" asked Henry.

"I don't know. I suppose we speak to your mum."

"And Jacob."

"And Jacob," Adam agreed somewhat reticently.

"What should I say?"

"Just tell them how you feel."

Henry leaned forwards as if trying to see into the deepest recesses of the mirror. "I'm sorry for hurting you Jacob. I... I didn't mean to," he began in a faltering voice. He took a deep breath as if to steady himself, but then his words came in a pleading rush. "I'm sorry for hurting you too Mum. Please don't leave me like Jacob did. Please come back. I promise I won't ever hurt you again."

Henry lapsed into sniffling silence. Adam gently brushed his son's tears away before turning his own gaze to the mirror. At first he looked at the reflection of the room. Then he stared into his own eyes. An itch grew between them. Reaching for the right words, he began, "I'll never forgive myself for what happened to you, Jacob. I'd give my life to be able to tell you how sorry I am. I want to say sorry to you too, Ella." His voice dropped to an almost inaudible murmur. Tears of shame filled his eyes. "What you said about my book. You were right. That's why I made us move to this house. To try to escape those thoughts, but they followed me here. I hate myself for them. Sometimes I feel as if I never deserved the family you gave me. But I want you to know that from now on things will be different. If you come back to me I'll never let you down again. Just come back. Come back. Come back..."

Adam trailed off into silence. Several seconds passed.

"Nothing's hap–" Henry started to say. He broke off as the phone rang again.

"Jesus Christ," said Adam, pressing a hand to his hammering heart. "Who's that now?"

He hurried to pick up the phone, ready to slam it back down at the sound of Richard's voice.

"Mr Piper?"

His heart accelerated even faster. It was Detective Sergeant Holman! "Have you found her?" Everything inside him clenched painfully tight in readiness for Penny's reply.

"I'm afraid not."

A strange mixture of relief and disappointment swirled through Adam. "So why are you calling?"

"We've reluctantly decided to postpone the search until the fog lifts. The forecast says it should clear by tomorrow morning."

"Tomorrow morning," Adam echoed hollowly. If by some miracle Ella hadn't been killed by the fall or swept out to sea, she would surely succumb to exposure long before then.

"I'm sorry but we've done all we can for now."

"Thanks for letting me know."

"There's something else, Mr Piper. We've had a call from Ella's father. He expressed concern about Henry's welfare. Would it be possible for me to speak to Henry?"

Adam scowled inwardly. Bloody Richard. Did the meddling old sod really think he'd hurt his own son? Adam called Henry to the phone.

"How are you holding up, Henry?" asked Penny.

"I'm OK."

"I can come over to the house if you like."

"No thanks. Bye."

With this curt response, Henry handed the phone back to Adam. "Satisfied?" asked Adam.

"I'm sorry," Penny apologised again. "You understand we have to follow through on every call where a child's welfare is concerned. I'll let you know when the search resumes."

Adam hung up, then took the phone off the hook. There would obviously be no more news tonight. He remained motionless for a moment, his eyes swimming with pain. Drawing in a deep breath, he returned to The Lewarne Room. Henry had resumed staring into the mirror. Adam shook his head at himself, feeling like a fool for calling to Ella and Jacob in the mirror. Next thing he'd be scrawling hocus pocus on the floor like Faith and her friends.

"Enough of that, Henry," said Adam. "This isn't—"

He broke off as Henry whirled around with eyes as big as saucers. "I saw Mum," breathed Henry.

Adam's eyes raced around the room. They were the only ones in it. "Where?"

Henry pointed towards the secret panel. "She was over there, but when I turned round she was gone."

Adam opened the panel. The passageway was empty. "Are you sure it was her?"

Henry nodded. "She was wearing the same dress as earlier."

"Was..." A hesitancy came into Adam's voice, as if he wasn't sure he wanted to know the answer to the question in his mind. "Was her dress wet?"

"I don't think so, but I only saw her for a second. You believe me, don't you Dad?"

Adam's gaze returned to the mirror, fraught with uncertainty. He had a sudden strong urge to pinch himself and see if he woke up.

"You believe me, don't—" Henry started to repeat.

Adam shushed him sharply, cocking his head, "Do you hear that?"

"It's the bell," exclaimed Henry.

The ringing was rapid and continuous. It seemed to be coming from a long way off. Adam ran into the hallway. "It's louder here."

Henry lifted his eyes towards the ceiling. "It's coming from upstairs."

They climbed to the landing, Henry a couple of steps behind Adam. The ringing drew them to the attic door. When they opened it, the volume jumped higher. They continued up to the attic. Adam pressed his ear to the tower door. The ringing reverberated through it as clear and high as birdsong. "Someone's in the tower."

"It's Mum," Henry said with desperate certainty. He clenched his fist and pounded on the door, yelling, "Mum! Mum!"

Adam caught his wrist. "You'll hurt yourself. We need tools." He pulled Henry away from the door and downstairs to The Lewarne Room. He grabbed the hammer and chisel and raced back to the tower door. The ringing continued relentlessly as he hammered the chisel between the door and frame above the lock. There was a splintering sound as he levered the chisel back and forth. He yanked it loose and repeated the process below the lock. A gradually widening gap appeared. Sweat dribbled down Adam's face as he thrust his weight against the door again and again. Suddenly it burst inwards, taking him with it.

CHAPTER 31

Adam fell to his hands and knees in front of an ornate cast-iron spiral staircase. Pale light filtered into the stairwell from overhead. The ringing of the bell cascaded down to greet him. Henry rushed to help his dad back to his feet. The staircase rattled ominously as Adam started up it. Crumbling mortar trickled from finger-width cracks that zig-zagged their way up the bare stone wall. Rozen hadn't been lying about the tower's structural damage.

Adam softened his footfalls, motioning for Henry to do the same. The stairs wound up to a small landing where the ringing was as loud as a fire alarm. Stepping cautiously on warped floorboards, Adam moved through a stone archway. It led to a circular room five or six metres in diameter furnished with a round table and thirteen chairs. In front of each chair, the table was set with silver plates, cutlery and wine glasses. At its centre was a serving platter, a cut-glass decanter and an ornate candelabra draped with melted wax. The remnants of what looked to be a recently eaten meal were scattered across its dark wood surface – half-eaten biscuits and slices of bread, crisp packets and chocolate bar wrappers, open tins of soup and beans. More wrappers and tins were scattered across the floor.

A book lay open on the table. Heloise's book! A drawing of a robin had been scribbled out so furiously that the paper was torn. 'TRAITOR' was scrawled across the page.

The triptych oil painting of the Last Supper hung on the wall, divided up by four arched windows. The cardinal points of the compass were engraved into stone lintels above the windows. The panes had been painted black, blocking out all but a faint glow of daylight.

To the right of the table was a mattress strewn with grubby blankets. A faded and frayed red satin dress was crumpled up at the bottom end of the mattress. Adam's breath stopped in his throat. A woman was sprawled amidst the blankets, naked except for the ropes that bound her hands and feet and what appeared to be a cloth gag hanging loose around her neck. Blood trickled down one of her wrists that she'd managed to work free. There was blood on her face too. She was maniacally swinging a silver hand bell. She stopped at the sight of Adam and Henry, a sob of relief escaping her.

"Ella!" cried Adam, rushing to her side and clutching her to him. "How... What..."

"She attacked me," said Ella, her voice a dry croak.

"Who did?"

"Heloise."

"Heloise?" Adam shook his head. "That's not possible, we found–"

"It *was* her," Ella cut in sharply enough to discourage any further debate. "Untie me."

As Adam set to work on the knots, Ella found a weak smile for Henry. "Hello my darling."

"Are you OK, Mum?" asked Henry, his voice a tiny tremor.

"I'll be fine. We just need to get out of here as fast as possible."

"These knots are too tight to untie," said Adam. He turned to grab a carving knife from the table. "Stay still," he warned as he sawed at the rope.

"Hurry," urged Ella. "That woman is insane. She killed her parents because they tried to leave this house. She'll do the same to us if we try to leave."

"Why?"

"Because she's lonely and bored. At least that's the impression I got."

The serrated blade found its way through the rope encircling Ella's ankles. Adam turned his attention to a knot tethering her to an iron ring on the wall.

"Dad!" gasped Henry.

"What is it?"

"Something's moving on the stairs."

Adam and Ella exchanged a wide-eyed look as the spiral staircase clanked. Someone was coming up it! Clump... clump... clump... The footsteps were as steady as the tick of a clock. With each one, Adam felt as if more of the air was being sucked out of his lungs. He resumed sawing frantically at the rope. Ella winced as the blade nicked her skin.

"Don't slow down," she hissed.

The rope was halfway cut through. Ella attempted to squirm her hand free. Slickened by blood, it slipped through the loop. A figure stepped into view, faceless in the shadows of the archway. Manoeuvring Henry and Ella behind him, Adam thrust out the knife in warning.

The figure advanced from the shadows, revealing thin white hair combed over a liver-spotted scalp. Sharp blue eyes stared from a long, narrow face.

"Mr Mabyn," exclaimed Adam, his voice caught between relief and caution. Did the taciturn old solicitor know about Heloise? "What are you doing here?"

"I received a phone call from Miss Trehearne informing me that you intend to move out of Fenton House." Despite the bizarre scene, Mr Mabyn's tone was as dry as ever. "I have some documents for you to sign, but I see that this is not the time." A flicker of something – possibly concern or perhaps merely curiosity – showed in his eyes as he looked at Ella. "Do you require an ambulance, Mrs Piper?"

"The only thing we require is to get the fuck out of this house," she retorted. "Now move out of our way."

Mr Mabyn stepped aside. "Why would I stop you from leaving? Indeed, you can no longer remain here even if you wanted to. The conditions of your tenancy have been breached."

Ella's eyes flashed with accusation. "You know about her, don't you? That's why we weren't allowed up here."

"I assure you, Mrs Piper, I have no idea what you're talking about."

Ella scowled doubtfully. "I'm going to tell the police everything."

"You must do as you see fit."

"Stay where you are," Adam warned, edging towards the archway.

The solicitor spread his hands. Adam stopped suddenly. With a sharp intake of breath, Ella dragged him and Henry behind the table as another figure emerged from the archway. Heloise was the same height and build as Ella. She had the same shoulder-length, thick brown hair too. Ella's pink lipstick glistened on her lips, offset by skin as pale as a prisoner after months in solitary. Ella's white cotton dress clung to her damply. The upper half of her face was concealed behind a glittering silver-filigree masquerade eye-mask. She moved with a catlike slow-grace, her soft brown eyes flitting between the room's occupants.

For a moment, there was silence as if no one knew how to react. Then, with only the slightest tremor betraying his apprehension, Mr Mabyn said, "This is private property."

In reply, Heloise whipped a knife out from behind her back.

"Don't!" cried Adam as she thrust it at the solicitor.

Ella screamed and made to cover Henry's eyes, but he batted her hand away.

Mr Mabyn grunted and doubled over as the blade pierced his shirt and slid into his belly. For a second there was no blood, but as Heloise pulled the knife free a crimson stain bloomed like… *Like a rose*, thought Adam.

The solicitor's knees went from under him as Heloise plunged the blade into his back. He hit the floor face first and rolled over. A strand of rusty spittle stretched from the corner of his mouth as he rasped, "Please, please…"

Heloise stooped to slash at his throat. Frothy arterial blood spurted into her face. Mr Mabyn trembled as if an electric current was being passed through him. Eyes bulging, he let out a gurgle like an emptying sink. Then the silence returned, more deafening than any bell.

Heloise straightened, her gaze coming to land on Adam. The sadness in her eyes pierced him as deeply as a knife. Her gaze pleaded with him. He could almost hear the words in her mind – *Don't leave. Please stay with me.*

Ella snatched the carving knife from Adam. She whirled to hack at a section of the painting, revealing a cavity. A ladder bolted to the wall went down into darkness. Ella tore at the canvas until she'd created a hole big enough to clamber through. She thrust Henry towards the ladder. "Climb down!"

Henry descended from view. Ella followed him, pausing to look anxiously at Adam. "Come on."

"Go," he hissed, keeping his gaze fixed on Heloise. "I'll be right behind you."

As Adam retreated towards the ladder, Heloise took a step towards him. "Don't come any closer," he warned, jabbing the knife in her direction.

Stay, pleaded her eyes. *Stay here with me.*

"No," he said, his voice shaky but resolute.

Heloise opened her mouth wide and screamed – the angry scream of a child who couldn't get what they wanted.

Adam dove for the ladder. He fell half-a-metre before catching hold of a rung. Without looking to see if Heloise was pursuing him, he scuttled down the ladder. At the bottom was a small space hemmed in by crumbling lathes and plaster walls. One of the wall panels stood open, barely visible in the gloom. Beyond it was blackness.

Hands grabbed at Adam from above. Long fingernails raked at his face. He struck out blindly with the knife and another ear-piercing scream rang out. He threw himself into the blackness and thrust the wall panel shut. It trembled as Heloise pounded wildly against its other side. He rammed the knife into the floorboards at the base of the wall, wedging it shut. He jerked around as more hands caught hold of him.

"It's me," hissed Ella.

Adam groped for her hands. "Where are we?"

"I think we're in the passageways. She's been coming and going this way all day."

"Where's Henry?"

A frightened little voice piped up from behind Ella. "I'm here, Dad."

Another childishly enraged scream spurred Adam into motion. Ushering Ella in front of him, he hastened away from the sound. "If we're on the second-floor, there should be a left turn just up ahead."

"Here it is," said Henry.

They groped their way down a flight of stairs. A pinprick of light lanced into the passageway through a peephole. Adam felt about until he found a concave section of wall. It slid outwards at a push, revealing Walter's bedroom. He closed the moveable, cherub-wreathed pillar and shoved a dressing-table in front of it.

They made a dash for the stairs. At any second Adam expected Heloise to spring from some other secret panel, knife in hand. As they passed The Lewarne Room, he glimpsed the open trapdoor. An image flashed through his mind – George and Sofia trapped in darkness, clawing at the trapdoor until their fingernails were broken and bleeding. How long would it have taken them to die? Days? Weeks? Had Heloise stood overhead, waiting for their screams to stop?

Ella grabbed a coat and shoes on her way out of the front door. Shaking himself free from the horrific questions, Adam snatched up the car keys from the sideboard and followed her and Henry outside. Winifred's portrait looked on sadly as they fled the house.

The weather forecast had got it wrong. The setting sun was burning its way through the fog, gradually unveiling the garden. The sea was still hidden from sight.

They piled into their car. As Adam started the engine, Henry pointed skywards and cried out, "Look!"

Adam followed the line of Henry's finger towards the top of the tower. Heloise was standing on one of the windowsills. She was naked except for the masquerade mask. Her skin shone paler than the fog. A noose was looped around her neck. Like a bird taking flight, she spread her arms and stepped off the windowsill. She plummeted several metres before the rope snapped taut and the noose tightened. For several long seconds, she jerked about like a crazed puppet, kicking her legs and clawing at the air. Then she was still.

Adam and Henry gawped up at Heloise as if transfixed. Ella broke the spell. "Can we please leave now?"

Wrenching his gaze back down to earth, Adam accelerated around Mr Mabyn's Mercedes towards the gates.

CHAPTER 32

"You're bleeding," Ella said to Adam.

He glanced at his reflection in the rearview mirror. A pair of gouges glistened on his forehead. "Heloise scratched me."

"She could have done a lot worse."

"I don't think she wanted to kill us."

"No, she wanted to *be* me. She kept asking about you. What's his favourite this and what's his favourite that."

"Like the questionnaire."

The fields were materialising from the fog. Cows were grazing peacefully. Here and there, in the valley below, glimpses of thatched roofs were visible. The normality of the scene seemed strangely unreal to Adam.

"Do you think Rozen knows about Heloise?" he asked.

"Of course she does. Otherwise how else could Heloise have survived all these years? Do you remember when we first went to the house there were no dust sheets in Walter's bedroom? I bet Heloise slept in there."

Adam braked at the end of the lane, his brow furrowed.

"Why have you stopped?" asked Ella.

"The other day Rozen asked me to look in all the mirrors in the house. That's how I found the basement where Heloise trapped her parents."

"Perhaps that's what Rozen wanted."

"Why would she want that?"

"How should I know? Maybe the secret got too much for her. Does it really matter?"

"Yes, it matters." Adam turned the car onto the lane that sloped down into Treworder.

"Why?" Ella said in a voice that was equal parts annoyance and apprehension. "Let the police deal with Rozen."

Adam shook his head. "She owes us some answers."

"I don't want to see that old lady again," Henry put in from the backseat.

"You don't have to," said Adam. "You and your mum can stay in the car. Don't worry, Henry, Rozen can't do anything to hurt us."

"Can't she?" Ella asked doubtfully. "For all we know Rozen helped Heloise murder her parents."

"You didn't see her this morning. She could barely walk to the front door. I'm sorry, Ella, but I have to do this. I need to look her in the eyes and find out if she knowingly put us in danger."

"What will that achieve?" Ella jerked her thumb towards Fenton House. "She's as crazy as her niece."

And you chose to exploit her madness. A grimace passed over Adam's face as Doug's words came back to him. "Perhaps I feel as if we owe her something too. Her last living relative is dead. I think it would be best if she heard it from me, not some stranger."

Ella's silence suggested she reluctantly agreed with that last part. She stared out of the window as the road wound down past the whitewashed cottages and along the front of the cove. The streets were empty. Two ranks of fishing boats blocked off the rear of the shingle beach. Waves curled into the seaweed-strewn shore. The air smelled of brine and dead fish. The little village had a deserted, desolate feel.

Adam pulled over next to a phone box. "You call the police while I'm speaking to Rozen."

Ella caught hold of his arm as he made to leave the car, her eyes wide with worry. He gave her what he hoped was a reassuring smile. "I won't be long." A curious light came into his eyes. "Earlier today I thought I saw you by the sitting room door. Your hair and dress were wet."

"It wasn't me."

Adam nodded as if that was what he'd expected to hear. He made his way past The Smuggler's Inn to Boscarne Cottage. There were no lights on in the front windows. The curtains were closed. He approached the front door decisively, but his fist hovered hesitantly over it. He thought about Rozen's parting kiss, the strange strength he'd felt in her frail hands as she held him to her lips. Perhaps he should leave it to the police to tell her about Heloise? He recalled something Rozen had said about her niece – *She was the sweetest little girl you could ever hope to meet.* That hardly tallied with the wild-eyed creature that had tried to stop them from leaving Fenton House. Heloise had almost tricked him into believing Ella's ghost walked the hallways of the house. Perhaps she'd used Rozen's beliefs to similarly manipulate her.

He knocked on the door. A moment passed. He knocked again and waited another half a minute before bending to call through the letterbox, "Rozen, it's Adam."

No reply.

He tried the handle. The door was locked. He glanced around as if uncertain what to do, his gaze coming to land on the alley that led around the back of the cottage. He headed for the back gate. It swung inwards at a push. The living room curtains were open. The hearth emitted a soft, reddish glow. Rozen was sitting in her armchair, her face lost in shadow. Edgar lay at her feet.

Adam knocked on the glass. Rozen didn't move. The pug lifted his head. Looking mournfully at Adam, he gave out a high-pitched whimper. A cold hand closed around Adam's heart at the sound. He knocked louder. Rozen remained motionless. Edgar rested his chin back on her slippered feet, closing his eyes.

Adam looked at the French door's lock. The key was in the other side. He picked up a pebble from a rockery and hit the pane of glass adjacent to the lock. It cracked, then shattered at a second blow. He reached through, turned the key and opened the door.

"Rozen," he said again, his voice hushed with apprehension.

He didn't expect a reply. Even the deepest sleeper would have been woken by the breaking glass. Edgar lifted his head again, growling as Adam entered the room. "It's OK boy," said Adam, holding out his hand.

His growl softening back to a whimper, Edgar clambered to his feet and waddled across to nose at Adam's hand.

A strong smell of faeces hit Adam as he moved around the armchair to get a better look at Rozen. Her bony fingers were folded together as if in prayer in the lap of her turquoise dress. Her bifocals were perched on her nose, but her eyes were closed and deeply sunken into their sockets. Her skin hung in slack grey folds around her face and neck. Bright red lipstick couldn't conceal the bluish tinge of her lips. She wasn't smiling anymore. Her mouth hung open, the tongue protruding as if she was blowing a raspberry at Adam.

He touched her throat. No pulse. A faint warmth suggested she'd only been dead a short time. His forehead twitched with the struggle to know what to feel. Sadness? Relief?

He stared at Rozen for a moment as if awaiting an answer to an unasked question, then turned and left the room. Edgar followed him into the garden and along the alley to the car. Adam opened the backdoor, scooped the dog up and passed him to Henry. A smile of delight lit up Henry's face. "Hi Edgar," he said, laughing as the pug licked his face.

Adam's heavy heart lifted like the fog as he watched them.

"What about Rozen?" Ella asked.

The heaviness returning, Adam looked at her and gave a grim shake of his head.

"You mean..." Ella trailed off into shocked silence as Adam nodded. She heaved a sigh, her gaze drifting towards the sea. The sun had fully broken through. It looked like it was going to be another beautiful day.

CHAPTER 33

One year later...

Dozens of copies of the same book were displayed on the bookcase. The cover depicted an ornate silver-framed mirror with 'Between Worlds' scrawled across it in what might have been lipstick or blood. Adam was sitting at a desk in front of the bookcase. A long queue of people stretched away from the desk.

With a somewhat fixed grin, Adam chatted and answered questions. The questions almost invariably followed the same pattern – *Do you think Rozen knew about Heloise? Don't you think it's strange that she died at the same time as Heloise? How do you think Rozen died? Do you really believe Fenton House isn't haunted?*

Adam's answers were always the same – *I don't know. Rozen was an old woman who passed away in her sleep. There's nothing strange about that. Fenton House was never haunted, at least not by ghosts*

The people queuing for Adam to sign their copy of his book rarely looked convinced by his reasoning, especially not when it came to that last question. In fact, the more he denied Fenton House was haunted, the more eager most people seemed to believe the opposite was true.

The questions made Adam all the more glad that he'd expunged certain elements from the story – most importantly, the mutilated toy bunny and any suggestion that Henry might have deliberately hurt his brother.

Adam's smile failed him as a woman slapped a dog-eared copy of his book down on the desk. His pen hovered over the cover. "Aren't you going to sign it?" asked the woman. "I've come a long way for this."

Adam signed inside the cover 'To Detective Sergeant Penny Holman. I hope you enjoyed the book.'

"I'm not sure if enjoyed is the right word," said Penny. "It's certainly an interesting read."

Adam handed back the book. When Penny didn't move away from the desk, he reluctantly asked, "Is there something else I can do for you?"

She unfolded a sheet of paper and placed it on the desk. It was headed by 'Forensic Biology Laboratory Report. Confidential. Samples submitted. Trace DNA from fingernails.'

Adam frowned at it, then at Penny. "What is this?"

"Those are the lab results from your son's fingernail scrapings. In all the commotion after your short stay at Fenton House they were somehow misplaced. They only came to my attention a few days ago. You needn't read the rest. It's very technical, but the upshot is that both your wife and Faith Gooden's blood was found under Henry's fingernails."

A sudden queasiness lurched up Adam's throat. He pushed back his chair and moved from behind the desk.

"How do you think Faith's blood came to be under Henry's nails?" asked Penny, pursuing him to the bookshop's entrance.

The sun was shining from a clear sky. Shoppers, workers and tourists streamed along Oxford Street, each lost in their own world.

Adam tried to settle his churning stomach with a deep breath of exhaust-fume scented air. Penny repeated her question, looking at him so intently that it was all he could do not to squirm like a worm on a hook. His mind was looping back over the night of Faith's death. He recalled the way she'd shied away from Ella and Henry as they fetched her a blanket. Had Henry accidentally touched her? Yes, that must have been what happened.

Who did this to you? he heard himself asking Faith. He saw her looking pleadingly at Ella. Or was she looking at Henry? Why would she have been looking at Henry like that?

232

Adam swallowed hard. Oh Christ, he felt ready to vomit all over Penny.

"Henry helped me wrap a blanket around Faith," he suddenly found himself saying. "That must be how he got her blood on him."

Penny's eyes narrowed. "Why didn't you tell me that at the time?"

"I don't know. I suppose it didn't seem important. There was so much else going on." Dragging a smile back onto his lips, Adam asked, "Is that all or can I help you with something else?"

Penny continued to stare at him like a cat studying its prey. He fought to keep his smile in place. His mind was painfully full of Faith shuffling from The Lewarne Room, her body a bloody latticework of scratches. His throat bobbed again. He wasn't sure how much longer he could hold back the queasiness.

"I was surprised to find out you haven't put Fenton House up for sale," said Penny. "Do you plan on moving back down there at some point?"

"No." This time Adam's answer had the ring of absolute truth.

Penny nodded approvingly. "No offence intended, but I'm glad to hear it." She extended her hand. "Thanks for signing my book."

Adam shook her warm, dry hand with his cold, clammy one.

He remained where he was as Penny moved off into the crowded street. As soon as she was out of sight, he ran to the nearest bin and retched into it. When the queasiness finally subsided, he headed for Oxford Circus Underground Station without bothering to rinse the taste of vomit from his mouth. It was preferable to the taste of the lie.

The Tube and bus journey was a blur until he passed Whipps Cross Hospital. His troubled eyes lingered on the redbrick building where Jacob had died. *I didn't mean to hurt him, Dad... It was an accident... Honest.* It had been a long time since Adam had thought about what Henry said in the emergency room, but now the words rang out like a bell in his head.

He got off the bus and entered a warren of terraced streets. He stood outside his house for several long minutes, his eyebrows knotted. Passing a hand over his face, he erased all the lines except the faint scars inflicted by Heloise.

A yapping started up as he opened the front door. Edgar ran to greet him, wagging his stubby tail. Ella wasn't far behind. "How did it go?" she asked.

A weary smile returned to Adam's face. "It went well."

"Was there a good turn out?"

"Yes, all five of my fans showed up."

Ella smiled at the dry remark. "You've got a lot more fans than that these days."

Adam's gaze fell to the porch floor – Jacob, the shattered glass, the blood. So much blood... *It was an accident... Honest...*

A frown touched Ella's forehead. "What's wrong, Adam? Has something happened?"

He looked at her uncertainly. He knew he had to tell her about the lie, make sure she was on the same page as him. But he just couldn't bring himself to say the words. Jacob's death had added years to her face. Since returning from Cornwall, those years had gradually dropped away. The old sparkle was back in her eyes – the sparkle of mischief and joy that had first attracted him to her. "I'm tired, that's all. It's been a long day."

Ella took his hand and gave it a gentle squeeze. "You know I'm proud of you."

"I'm not so sure that book's anything to be proud of."

"Well Henry and I disagree. You took something horrible and turned it into something good."

Adam turned away to hide the troubled look that passed over his face at his son's name. He hung up his jacket and headed for the sofa. Edgar settled down in his favourite spot in front of the hearth.

"We had a call from the solicitors," Ella told him as she fetched them both a glass of wine. "There's been another offer on the house."

Adam shook his head in bewilderment. "Another one? Don't these people care about what happened there?"

"Apparently three murders and the same number of suicides aren't enough to put them off. Or maybe that's why they're so interested in buying the place."

"Hmph, it wouldn't surprise me," Adam agreed sardonically. "How much are they offering?"

"*A lot.*" Ella's voice was heavy with emphasis. She showed Adam a figure scribbled on a piece of paper.

His eyes widened as if he was considering the offer, but then he shook his head. "I don't care how many zeros they add, we're not selling. That house can stand empty until it rots to the ground for all I care."

Smiling as if that was what she'd hoped he would say, Ella leaned in to kiss him. He inhaled her perfume as if it would clean the taste of the lie out of his mouth.

They drew apart as Henry charged into the room. In the past year Henry's limbs had grown gawkily long and a light fuzz had sprouted above his upper lip. His voice seesawed between high-pitched and gruff as he exclaimed, "Dad, you're back. Yay."

He enveloped Adam in something halfway between a hug and a wrestling hold.

"OK, OK, I'm happy to see you too," said Adam, disentangling himself. He gave Henry a searching look. "What have you been up to?"

Henry shrugged. "Will you wrestle with me?"

"Your dad's too tired to–" Ella started to say.

"No I'm not," interrupted Adam. Henry squealed with delight as Adam scooped him up and whirled him around before collapsing in a heap with him on the rug.

Henry pinned Adam's arms. "Do you give in?"

Pretending to writhe in pain, Adam tapped the floor in submission. Henry jumped up, raising his hands in triumph.

Adam reached to pull Ella down onto him. She resisted, smiling and shaking her head. Laughing, Henry grabbed her too and helped drag her to the rug. Adam and he tickled her until she was tearful and breathless with laughter. Then Adam enfolded both of them in an embrace and held on as if he was scared to let go.

ABOUT THE AUTHOR

Ben is an award-winning writer and Pushcart Prize nominee with a passion for gritty crime fiction. His short stories have been widely published in the UK, US and Australia. In 2011 he self-published *Blood Guilt*. The novel went on to reach no.2 in the national e-book download chart, selling well over 150000 copies. In 2012 it was picked up for publication by Head of Zeus. Since then, Head of Zeus has published three more of Ben's novels – *Angel of Death, Justice for the Damned and Spider's Web*. In 2016 his novel *The Lost Ones* was published by Thomas & Mercer.

Ben lives in Sheffield, England, where – when he's not chasing around after his son, Alex – he spends most of his time shut away in his study racking his brain for the next paragraph, the next sentence, the next word...

If you'd like to learn more about Ben or get in touch, you can do so at www.bencheetham.com

OTHER BOOKS BY THE AUTHOR

House Of Mirrors

(Fenton House Book 2)

What will you see?

Two years ago the Piper family fled Fenton House after their dream of a new life turned into an unspeakable nightmare. The house has stood empty ever since, given a wide berth by everyone except ghost hunters and occult fanatics.

Now something is trying to lure the Pipers back to Fenton House. But is that 'something' a malevolent supernatural entity? Or is there a more earthly explanation? Whatever the truth, Adam and Ella Piper are about to discover that their family's future is inextricably bound up with the last place they ever wanted to see again.

The Pipers aren't the only ones whose fate is tied to Fenton House. Three thieves seeking their fortune and a mysterious redheaded woman are also converging on the remote Cornish mansion.

Over the course of a single stormy night, each of them will be forced to confront their true self. How far are they willing to go in pursuit of their deepest, darkest desires? How much are they prepared to give in order to simply survive till dawn?

Mr Moonlight

Close your eyes. He's waiting for you.

There's a darkness lurking under the surface of Julian Harris. Every night in his dreams he becomes a different person, a monster capable of evil beyond comprehension. Sometimes he feels like *something* is trying to get inside him. Or maybe it's already in him, just waiting for the chance to escape into the waking world.

There's a darkness lurking under the surface of Julian's picture-postcard hometown too. Fifteen years ago, five girls disappeared from the streets of Godthorne. Now it's happening again. A schoolgirl has gone missing, stirring up memories of that terrible time. But the man who abducted those other girls is long dead. Is there a copycat at work? Or is something much, much stranger going on?

Drawn by the same sinister force that haunts his dreams, Julian returns to Godthorne for the first time in years. Finding himself mixed up in the mystery of the missing girl, he realises that to unearth the truth about the present he must confront the ghosts of his past.

Somewhere amidst the sprawling tangle of trees that surrounds Godthorne are the answers he so desperately seeks. But the forest does not relinquish its secrets easily.

Now She's Dead

(Jack Anderson Book 1)

What happens when the watcher becomes the watched?

Jack has it all – a beautiful wife and daughter, a home, a career. Then his wife, Rebecca, plunges to her death from the Sussex coast cliffs. Was it an accident or did she jump? He moves to Manchester with his daughter, Naomi, to start afresh, but things don't go as planned. He didn't think life could get any worse...

Jack sees a woman in a window who is the image of Rebecca. Attraction turns into obsession as he returns to the window night after night. But he isn't the only one watching her...

Jack is about to be drawn into a deadly game. The woman lies dead. The latest victim in a series of savage murders. Someone is going to go down for the crimes. If Jack doesn't find out who the killer is, that 'someone' may well be him.

Who Is She?

(Jack Anderson Book 2)

A woman with no memory.

A question no one seems able to answer.

Her eyes pop open like someone surfacing from a nightmare. Shreds of moonlight glimmer through a woodland canopy. How did she get here? A thousand bells seem to be clanging in her ears. There is a strange, terrible smell. Both sweet and bitter. Like burnt meat. Her senses scream that something is very, very wrong. Then she sees it. A hole in the ground. Deep and rectangular. Like a grave...

After the death of his wife, Jack is starting to get his life back on track. But things are about to get complicated.

A woman lies in a hospital bed, clinging to life after being shot in the head. She remembers nothing, not even her own name. Who is she? That is the question Jack must answer. All he has to go on is a mysterious facial tattoo.

Damaged kindred spirits, Jack and the nameless woman quickly form a bond. But he can't afford to fall for someone who might put his family at risk. People are dying. Their deaths appear to be connected to the woman. What if she isn't really the victim? What if she's just as bad as the 'Unspeakable Monsters' who put her in hospital?

She Is Gone

(Jack Anderson Book 3)

**First she lost her family. Then she lost her memory.
Now she wants justice.**

On a summer's day in 1998, a savage crime at an isolated Lakeland beauty spot leaves three dead. The case has gone unsolved ever since. The only witness is an amnesiac with a bullet lodged in her brain.

The bullet is a ticking time bomb that could kill Butterfly at any moment. Jack is afraid for her. But should he be afraid *of* her? She's been suffering from violent mood swings. Sometimes she acts like a completely different person.

Butterfly is obsessed with the case. But how can she hope to succeed where the police have failed? The answer might be locked within the darkest recesses of her damaged mind. Or maybe the driver of the car that's been following her holds the key to the mystery.

Either way, the truth may well cost Butterfly her family, her sanity and her life.

The Lost Ones

The truth can be more dangerous than lies.

July 1972

The Ingham household. Upstairs, sisters Rachel and Mary are sleeping peacefully. Downstairs, blood is pooling around the shattered skull of their mother, Joanna, and a figure is creeping up behind their father, Elijah. A hammer comes crashing down again and again...

July 2016

The Jackson household. This is going to be the day when Tom Jackson's hard work finally pays off. He kisses his wife Amanda and their children, Jake and Erin, goodbye and heads out dreaming of a better life for them all. But just hours later he finds himself plunged into a nightmare...

Erin is missing. She was hiking with her mum in Harwood Forest. Amanda turned her back for a moment. That was all it took for Erin to vanish. Has she simply wandered off? Or does the blood-stained rock found where she was last seen point to something sinister? The police and volunteers who set out to search the sprawling forest are determined to find out. Meanwhile, Jake launches an investigation of his own – one that will expose past secrets and present betrayals.

Is Erin's disappearance somehow connected to the unsolved murders of Elijah and Joanna Ingham? Does it have something to do with the ragtag army of eco-warriors besieging Tom's controversial quarry development? Or is it related to the fraught phone call that distracted Amanda at the time of Erin's disappearance?

So many questions. No one seems to have the answers and time is running out. Tom, Amanda and Jake must get to the truth to save Erin, though in doing so they may well end up destroying themselves.

Blood Guilt

(Steel City Thrillers Book 1)

Can you ever really atone for killing someone?

After the death of his son in a freak accident, DI Harlan Miller's life is spiralling out of control. He's drinking too much. His marriage and career are on the rocks. But things are about to get even worse. A booze-soaked night out and a single wild punch leave a man dead and Harlan facing a manslaughter charge.

Fast-forward four years. Harlan's prison term is up, but life on the outside holds little promise. Divorced, alone, consumed by guilt, he thinks of nothing beyond atoning for the death he caused. But how do you make up for depriving a wife of her husband and two young boys of their father? Then something happens, something terrible, yet something that holds out a twisted kind of hope for Harlan – the dead man's youngest son is abducted.

From that moment Harlan's life has only one purpose – finding the boy. So begins a frantic race against time that leads him to a place darker than anything he experienced as a policeman and a stark moral choice that compels him to question the law he once enforced.

Angel Of Death

(Steel City Thrillers Book 2)

They thought she was dead. They were wrong.

Fifteen-year-old Grace Kirby kisses her mum and heads off to school. It's a day like any other day, except that Grace will never return home.

Fifteen years have passed since Grace went missing. In that time, Stephen Baxley has made millions. And now he's lost millions. Suicide seems like the only option. But Stephen has no intention of leaving behind his wife, son and daughter. He wants them all to be together forever, in this world or the next.

Angel is on the brink of suicide too. Then she hears a name on the news that transports her back to a windowless basement. Something terrible happened in that basement. Something Angel has been running from most of her life. But the time for running is over. Now is the time to start fighting back.

At the scene of a fatal shooting, DI Jim Monahan finds evidence of a sickening crime linked to a missing girl. Then more people start turning up dead. Who is the killer? Are the victims also linked to the girl? Who will be next to die? The answers will test to breaking-point Jim's faith in the law he's spent his life upholding.

Justice For The Damned

(Steel City Thrillers Book 3)

They said there was no serial killer. They lied.

Melinda has been missing for weeks. The police would normally be all over it, but Melinda is a prostitute. Women in that line of work change addresses like they change lipstick. She probably just moved on.

Staci is determined not to let Melinda become just another statistic added to the long list of girls who've gone missing over the years. Staci is also a prostitute – although not for much longer if DI Reece Geary has anything to do with it. Reece will do anything to win Staci's love. If that means putting his job on the line by launching an unofficial investigation, then so be it.

DI Jim Monahan is driven by his own dangerous obsession. He's on the trail of a psychopath hiding behind a facade of respectability. Jim's investigation has already taken him down a rabbit hole of corruption and depravity. He's about to discover that the hole goes deeper still. Much, much deeper...

Spider's Web

(Steel City Thrillers Book 4)

It's all connected.

A trip to the cinema turns into a nightmare for Anna and her little sister Jessica, when two men throw thirteen-year-old Jessica into the back of a van and speed away.

The years tick by... Tick, tick... The police fail to find Jessica and her name fades from the public consciousness... Tick, tick... But every time Anna closes her eyes she's back in that terrible moment, lurching towards Jessica, grabbing for her. So close. So agonisingly close... Tick, tick... Now in her thirties, Anna has no career, no relationship, no children. She's consumed by one purpose – finding Jessica, dead or alive.

DI Jim Monahan has a little black book with forty-two names in it. Jim's determined to put every one of those names behind bars, but his investigation is going nowhere fast. Then a twenty-year-old clue brings Jim and Anna together in search of a shadowy figure known as Spider. Who is Spider? Where is Spider? Does Spider have the answers they want? The only thing Jim and Anna know is that the victims Spider entices into his web have a habit of ending up missing or dead.

Made in United States
Troutdale, OR
06/22/2023